THE HARVEST

ALEX HUNTER

Black Rose Writing | Texas

ISBN: 978-1-68513-539-3
LIBRARY OF CONGRESS CONTROL NUMBER: 2024946556
PUBLISHED BY BLACK ROSE WRITING
www.blackrosewriting.com

Printed in the United States of America
Suggested Retail Price (SRP) $21.95

The Harvest is printed in Minion Pro

PRAISE FOR
THE HARVEST

"Hunter weaves a tale that has the "modern horror fairytale" feel of books like *Coraline* or *IT*, while weaving in mature topics that add weight to the narrative. His exploration of grief, found family, and the search for purpose create some truly hard-hitting moments. I was thoroughly rapt by this novel."

–Carlos E. Rivera, author of *The Local Truth, Blackout,* and *A Hole in the World*

"This is a book for those who enjoy King, Lovecraft, and Poe. It is a fresh and original, chill-inducing journey to be taken at night, when embers flicker low, and moon shadows paint the walls with spectral dreamscapes. Be very afraid."

–Bill Schweitzer, author of *Doves in a Tempest*

"*The Harvest* is delicious, slow-burning horror with genuinely disturbing moments, made memorable by the author's imagery and willingness to understate. Chilling."

–Brian Kaufman, author of Mary King's *Plague and Other Tales of Woe*

"Hunter masterfully transforms a quaint, close-knit street into a microcosm of evil. Demons and memories are palpable here—real forces to be feared and fought by an unlikely group of heroes. Despite the darkness and grief permeating every page, *The Harvest* is a kaleidoscopic reflection on friendship reminiscent of Stephen King's *IT*."

–Stephenie Sanders Jacob, author of *Pyramidia*

To Ben, for everything.

ACKNOWLEDGEMENTS

To you, the person who chose to read this book instead of something else - you're amazing.

To the first-eyes club: Anita Sharry, Paula Bateman and Jacqui Court-Walker. Sorry I gave you nightmares, let's have lunch.

Thank you Claire Hughes and Sarah King for making this a better story, and Bob Fear for invaluable feedback.

To the supportive online community at The Novelry, thanks for all the advice. You made me a writer.

Thank you

THE
HARVEST

CHAPTER ONE

The orphanage was like a bruise as you turned onto the street.

A Victorian building, plain, with a single storey made of red brick that years of pollution had blackened. Its façade had a series of small sash windows, most of which were broken and covered by dark metal grilles, placed high.

People walking by would sense the place was staring down upon them, many quickening their pace without thinking. The building gave the impression of melancholy and neglect.

There wasn't any graffiti on the orphanage's walls, unusual in this part of town. The place remained unsullied by the army of local taggers.

Standing outside in the drizzle, surrounded by a small collection of cardboard moving boxes, Tim Waverly considered the peculiarity of calling such a place home. At twenty-eight and single, it seemed like the best solution for him, if he wanted to remain in London. He couldn't bring himself to contemplate a house share.

He waved at a child who stared at him through the window of a flat on the other side of the street, smiling when they ducked out of sight.

In the trees above him, magpies chittered, a sharp, angry sound like a rebuke.

Tim knew little about the place, but had been told that years of confusion about the building's ownership, along with various legal disputes, stalled plans to develop 'luxury apartments' on the site.

The representative from Guardian Angels, Xander, who met him at the orphanage earlier that morning for orientation, was the type of upper-middle-class Londoner who attended the minor co-ed independent school Tim taught at. In a tight-fitting suit paired with shiny brown brogues without socks, Xander looked like someone who shared too many selfies on social media.

Checklist pinned to a plastic clipboard, Xander had rattled through a series of guardianship rules which were basic enough. Formalities done, he'd looked up from the clipboard and asked, "So, what's your story then, dude?"

Tim, teeth on edge from being addressed as dude, explained his position. Given teachers weren't highly paid, even in the private sector, he wanted to save for a mortgage, but had no way to do so. He didn't tell the man that finding rent for the last place was a struggle, and that the Angels' flyer pushed through his letterbox had seemed some kind of sign:

We'll help you fly!

Are you a YOUNG PROFESSIONAL struggling with your rent every month and tired of paying someone else's mortgage?

Is the high cost of living making it IMPOSSIBLE to save towards a deposit for your own home?

If that's you, become a GUARDIAN ANGEL!

For a LOW monthly fee, you can live as a property guardian while saving £££££££ towards a PLACE OF YOUR OWN!

Enjoy a sense of FREEDOM without the worry of greedy landlords! Don't delay, call us TODAY...

"Couldn't the old Bank of Mum and Dad step in?" Xander asked, emphasising his words with air-quotes.

"They would have if they weren't dead - there wasn't much to inherit." This last, from Tim, had the desired effect and killed the conversation. Xander had handed him a large bunch of keys, run a hand through over-waxed hair, and said his goodbyes.

The low fee for this place (Xander insisted it wasn't rent) was key to Tim's decision to take it on. His housing costs were reducing by almost seventy percent, so he'd have some spare money to pop into his savings account for the first time since...well, ever.

Given the orphanage's age and level of disrepair, his living quarters for the next six months weren't much better than a hostel. The Guardians had cobbled together an apartment with plain stud walls and squeezed it into a small, dark corner of the building (Tim had been instructed not to place anything on the walls, as it was one of the rules). A flimsy, lockless, PVC 'front door' added little security, while sparse furnishings were provided. The initial impression was of a large prison cell.

The apartment had a tiny, windowless bathroom (shower, no bath) which stood to one side of a combined living/kitchen/bedroom studio, with barred windows set higher on the external wall than might be expected. *Perhaps they were worried about the orphans trying to escape,* he thought.

Tim was just thankful that the apartment had services attached to it. There was a small boiler for hot water and electric heaters. Most other parts of the building remained without power.

Outside the apartment, the orphanage was a dark warren of corridors lined with small rooms. The place smelled sour. Years of emptiness and the spread of damp, he supposed. Many spiderwebs, dotted with the desiccated remains of flying insects, were epic, and he vowed to tackle these as a priority, not keen to meet their architects.

When he'd first been to look at the place, he had been led into what had once been a large industrial kitchen. Apart from a few cabinets, doors hanging off, and steel worktops, there were few clues as to the room's previous use. Someone had stripped out all the appliances.

As he unpacked his few personal possessions, Tim's thoughts turned back to the day the Guardian Angels had accepted his application. He'd been on an overheated bus, staring out at the rain through fogged windows, on the way back to his rented flat after giving blood. Donating was something he'd done since he was a late teen, every twelve weeks like clockwork. One legacy, perhaps, of having lost his mother to aggressive leukaemia when he was just a boy. The other legacy, less welcome, was a tendency to melancholy which he'd been medicated for, having balked at the idea of talking therapy. That he'd not needed the medication for several years pleased him.

Sitting towards the rear of the top deck, avoiding eye contact with other passengers, he had taken the Guardians' call. The excitement of the news, combined with the loss of a pint of blood and the vehicle's heat, had made him rather unwell.

He remembered feeling outside of himself for a short time, black spots crowding in on his vision like small insects and having to take several careful breaths in order to avoid the embarrassment of being taken ill and the attendant inconvenience to other travellers.

Tim, rocking with the motion of the bus, had noticed a noise drilling into his brain. A baby on the lower deck having a screaming fit.

•   •   •

He saw the writing during a recce of the orphanage.

He had to use a flashlight; there was no power in this part of the building, and little light from the darkening sky outside made its way through the windows. Turning the corner into yet another corridor, Tim came to a stop as the torchlight picked out letters scrawled deep into the faded plaster. He ran the dim light across the words which ran the full length of the space from floor to ceiling:

"Suffer The Children."

Placing the torch on the stone floor, Tim found himself compelled to touch the biblical quote, the nail on his index finger picking at the edge of the huge S, causing dust from the old plaster to rain down to the floor, flickering in the torchlight like tiny sparks. He winced as a sharp piece of masonry lodged under his fingernail. Looking down, he saw a bead of blood, black in the light from his torch, oozing from beneath the nail, and sucked the end of his finger, tasting copper.

Moving his hand across the uneven wall, he heard an echoing bark of laughter. A man, he supposed, passing by in the street outside.

BANG! BANG!

The sudden noise made Tim flinch, wrenching his attention from the writing on the wall as the sound reverberated around the building. It took a few moments for him to realise where it was coming from. The heavy brass knocker struck the orphanage's sturdy main door for a third time, emphatic. BANG!

He groaned. Meeting new people wasn't his favourite thing. He considered ignoring it, but the knocking came again, insistent. *Perhaps Xander forgot to tell me another rule*, he thought.

Retrieving the torch and taking one last look at the words defacing the wall, he headed toward the large front door. When he hauled the door open, he was greeted by a frizzy-haired woman swathed in what appeared to be a random collection of clothing. Patterned materials cascaded over her in a clashing multitude of coloured layers. At first glance, she could have been anywhere from thirty to fifty-five.

The woman beamed and thrust a sad bunch of flowers at him. "I knew it! You're actually going to live here!" she said.

She held out the hand which wasn't holding any flowers, and he shook it. "Louise Sanglin, fifty-four Oldfield Street, I spotted you emptying your little car earlier."

"And you brought flowers," Tim said. While he enjoyed addressing a class of teenagers, he liked his own company. Despite this, he gestured behind him, knowing that she was expecting to be invited in and feeling anxious about being considered impolite by any of his new neighbours.

"I've never been inside this old place," she said as he walked her to his apartment. "I've always thought it was creepy standing empty at the end of the road."

He looked at her. "I hope you've had a tetanus booster. I think the plan is to pull it down, build luxury flats, but I'm probably going to be here for at least six months, as property guardian. Caretaking the building, essentially." Reaching the threshold of the apartment, he gave a small shrug. "This is me."

"Interesting. Having this place to yourself I mean," she said, sitting on the sofa while he made coffee. "You're braver than I am. It's got a funny atmosphere, hasn't it? But here you are, actually living in the strangest building on the street!"

Tim, thinking back to the words scratched into the wall, began saying that, strictly speaking, his address was on the A-road which ran along the bottom of Oldfield and realised she wasn't listening.

Louise Sanglin was a talker, and Tim was content to say little. He sometimes wondered if standing up all day in front of his students had made him less inclined to speak to people outside of school, the quiet man grown from the bookish child.

"So, here's the thing," she was saying about the orphanage, "I've lived here for a decade, but I've rarely seen anyone walk into this old place. People say there was a campaign to get it closed down, and it's remained abandoned ever since." She glanced around at their surroundings and Tim caught a momentary expression pass across her eyes, as if she had sensed something distasteful.

Mrs Sanglin said that she was married to Stephan, who spent much of his time working overseas. "Dubai, so loads of tax-free money, the downside being that we spend less time together than we'd like." Tim assumed they were childless, as she didn't mention any.

He pegged the woman as an inveterate gossip and avoided sharing any personal information, certain she would broadcast it to the rest of the neighbourhood.

Despite his reluctance to share his own history, Louise delighted in taking Tim through a verbal snapshot of Oldfield Street, or at least those inhabitants who made themselves known to their little community. This being London, it amounted to about twenty percent of them.

She told him about Sean and Andrew, a young gay couple who ironically referred to themselves as 'Shandrew' and lived with their dog, Molly. "Cute little thing, a bit of an intimate sniffer, if you know what I mean."

Louise thought the "old dears" in the street loved having a gay couple as neighbours, while parents of teenage boys were suspicious. Tim took this speculation with a pinch of salt.

She had apparently been to their house on various occasions. "You'd never know it, but that place used to be a real mess, honestly awful. When we came here, it was a jumble of flats, bedsit central, God knows who was living in there. Those boys have done a huge amount of work. Everything, top to bottom. It belongs in a magazine!"

Tim grew irritated as she shared her opinion about the residents of Oldfield Court. The affordable housing across from the orphanage resembled his childhood home. She described its residents as "in the street, but not part of our community," and he resisted the temptation to ask her how a property guardian who couldn't afford normal rent might fit into her community. He was certain his arrival was catnip to the local gossip network.

When she got to the Warwicks, Tim stopped her. "Lucy Warwick? Bit of an emo?"

"That's her, wears black. I imagine she doesn't make it easy for her parents. They're churchgoers, I believe."

Tim grimaced, unhappy about living in such proximity to a student, but kept his counsel.

Keen to be alone, he stood and was thankful that his unwanted visitor took the hint. As she gathered her things, she warned him that one of the flats in Oldfield Court was "known to the police as a drug-den."

When Mrs Sanglin had said her goodbyes, with an open invitation for "dinner or brunch sometime" (which Tim made a mental note to avoid), he called it a night.

Wrapped in the duvet, itself piled with coats, and still wearing socks in the cold bed, he spent several minutes engaged in a fruitless attempt to focus on his paperback but gave up after trying to read the same page three times.

The impact of moving had caught up with him. He gave an extravagant yawn, then another, before settling down for his first night in his new home.

In the dark, something stirred. Right at the edge of his awareness, just as sleep took him, Tim could hear a baby's cries.

•   •   •

Wanting to get things looking as homely as possible, Tim attacked his living quarters with gusto. He wiped and bleached surfaces and vacuumed the floors. Afterwards, he changed the placement of the sparse furnishings and set out his small but treasured collection of books in a way he found pleasing to the eye.

He had spent the morning further exploring the building beyond the walls of his living space. It was bleak. There were few adornments, its warren of narrow, damp-smelling, corridors almost identical. Some of these led to dead-ends, making the place confusing to navigate. From time to time, he found signs of habitation in the building's darkest corners–in one he spotted an ancient game of hangman etched above the skirting board, faint letters spelling out SCR-AM, and could imagine whispering children playing their game while lying on the floor.

He hadn't counted the bedrooms leading off these corridors, but there were about fifty or sixty. These were cramped cells with breezeblock walls and sturdy doors fashioned from thin metal bars. Most were without windows. Quite a few of the bedrooms still had small, iron-framed beds on which thin, damp mattresses lay. Dark stains covering the mattresses caught Tim's attention, and he didn't want to think about them.

Under one bed, he'd spotted a shoe which was missing its pair. Age had softened the old, black leather, which was mottled with musty white mould. This discovery caused Tim a surprising and intense wave of sadness. Having lost his own mother when he was little, he thought he understood something of the children who had inhabited these mean rooms, their loneliness and isolation. Turning the small shoe around in his hands, he had a rare and vivid memory of his mother smiling down at him, as he got fitted for a similar pair, for primary school, he assumed.

He wondered what his students, in their comfortable homes with modern conveniences, would think of the place. No doubt, these poor, parentless children had been forced into lives that would horrify and confuse his students. They were comfortable in their own homes and surrounded by the conveniences of modern life.

Besides its many bedrooms, the orphanage had two dismal, grey bathroom blocks. These housed rows of basins, twelve in all, open showers and toilet cubicles without doors. This was both sad and disturbing. Along with the barred bedroom doors, it gave the impression that the staff didn't grant the children who had lived here any privacy from each other or from their warders.

The institutional atmosphere of the place was depressing and claustrophobic, despite the large footprint of the building.

As guardian, Tim was required to undertake certain tasks which he needed to fit around his full-time teaching job. The Guardian Angels expected him to check the building each morning and before he turned in for the night. Failure to do so would cause the termination of his contract, as set out in Xander's list of rules.

As well as keeping an eye on things, he had to attend to minor repairs, ironic, he thought, in a building earmarked for demolition. Given the sheer scale of the orphanage, and the filth and detritus present everywhere outside the confines of his small living quarters, Tim wasn't sure what repairs would be considered important. The

Angels had left him a haphazard pile of tools in the cavernous old kitchen.

That evening, he sat behind the closed plastic door of the apartment, thinking about his tour of the orphanage. He wondered if he should set up a spreadsheet to organise any tasks. It seemed a sensible idea, and he'd already decided to start with the cobwebs, which hung from the ceilings and covered surfaces like ancient shrouds.

Thumbing through his phone, pondering a takeaway, he glanced up. His stomach lurched as if from a sudden alteration in the room's air pressure.

An unusual stain was visible on the solid outside wall, next to the television. It appeared to be the type of mark that, perhaps, one could see better by not looking straight at it. He moved closer, and the effect reduced, so he resumed his seat.

Sitting back, chewing at the edge of his thumbnail, Tim couldn't determine what it was about the stain (*it's a handprint*, popped into his head) that seemed so uncanny. He stared at it, unblinking, for a few moments before realisation dawned.

He could see the fingerprints and palm lines. A rush of cold air sliced through the space, accompanied by a further twist of nausea deep in his bowel.

The handprint didn't look like someone leaning against the wall had left it. It looked like someone's hand pressing *through*, as if seeking to escape from inside the wall. He felt a sudden, urgent need to rub it away.

CHAPTER TWO

As Tim first spotted the strange mark, and just a hundred yards along Oldfield Street, Mary MacDonald took a sip from her last cup of tea of the day (she'd given up her bedtime drink some months ago, to avoid waking in the night).

Mary enjoyed relaxing in the space she'd created. Although she had been born in a room upstairs, she'd recently transformed the house from a standard, cramped Victorian terrace into what she'd always wanted. Like many of the neighbouring houses, she'd had hers knocked through and extended, and it now reflected her taste for modern comfort. She thought her transformation project had built a great oak from a small, unimpressive acorn.

She had taken full advantage of her late husband's life insurance pay-out, combined with the sale of their other property, to open the space, extend the kitchen and have a luxury bathroom plumbed in on the upper floor. Mary then filled her home with soft fabrics and tactile surfaces, not for her the chintz and trappings of which many older people seemed fond.

Like her house, the rest of Oldfield Street might appear unchanged, but she knew the street scene was little more than a series of façades. Straggle-toothed survivors of an earlier age. Buildings which had remained standing through wars, economic disasters, and smaller, more personal tragedies. These old places hid cavernous spaces, countless extensions and, sometimes, myriad tiny flats–many of which were dismal, little more than a single room.

Mary gazed down at her Kindle, *A Spool of Blue Thread* by Anne Tyler, classical music burbling from the high-end sound system, and considered, as she often did, the other significant change in her life. The death of her husband, Iain.

A heart attack had taken him at seventy. A banal death for an ordinary man. She hadn't been unhappy in her marriage, but she hadn't been *happy* either. With the benefit of her advancing years, she recognised it had been more a state of enforced togetherness, in common with many couplings of their generation. She had spent years playing a role to which she was unsuited, that of dutiful housewife and surrogate mother to her husband. There had been no malice in Iain's expectations, but he simply hadn't shared Mary's sense of adventure and longing for experience.

As for many women of her age, marriage had served as an escape. Mary had been travelling *from* her upbringing as opposed to travelling *to* something. Her mother, a devout Irish Catholic, for whom Mary felt little affection, had had many siblings and three children of her own before the early death of her own husband.

As well as being named after the Virgin, Mary and her siblings, twins five years her senior, grew up with what she'd termed their mother's 'scripture strictures'.

Among the strictures, a series of randomly enforced rules based, Mary assumed, on some biblical grounding, were clear boundaries as to interactions with the opposite sex. Making eye contact with a man was beyond the pale. Holding hands with a man was considered sinful, as was going out without a covered head on Sundays. Her mother's religiosity became more pronounced after everything that happened with Mary's brother, Lionel.

In Iain, she'd found someone thrillingly *ordinary*. At first, Mary loved his agnosticism, and the escape he provided from her mother, whom she'd ignored, mostly, from the point of their marriage.

The MacDonalds hadn't been blessed, or cursed, with children and for that, she was grateful. Oh, she liked children well enough, but she wasn't sure she'd have known what to do with one. Iain, an underwriter, had drifted through life with a dazed expression, as if dropped into position from a great height.

Sex between the couple had been as perfunctory as it was rare–she chuckled and sipped her tea. Ian had never been keen, and her attempts to increase his interest doomed to failure.

Mary took pride in her honesty, not least to herself. She was well aware her life had, in many ways, begun after Iain's death when she'd been able to throw off the suffocating persona of a devoted housewife. Though she missed his company, she finally had the freedom to make the house her own and travel abroad.

Oh, how she loved to travel! Since widowhood she'd decided no more summers in damp, grey English seaside towns, instead spending time in France and Greece and a memorable adventure on the QE2.

Unlike some of her peers, Mary's mind at seventy-three remained pin sharp. She had no patience for what she considered foggy thinking and despised being treated like an old person. Life, in her opinion, was for living.

When her mother passed away in an assisted living facility, her mind and memories long gone, Mary and her sister Cecily found themselves the owners of this house, but they had no interest in it. Mary and Iain rented out their own home, a small flat nearby, bought out Cecily's share for less than it was worth, and moved in. While Mary had been resistant to moving back, Iain dismissed her concerns about the past and everything that had taken place with impatience, speaking instead of the "financial prudence" of making the investment.

That Lionel, Cecily's twin, was disinherited, was hardly a surprise given everything he'd put their family through.

The last of her tea done, her thoughts turned to the message circulated to the street WhatsApp group by Louise Sanglin. With indiscriminate emojis, she alerted recipients about the "attractive" young man who was acting as some sort of caretaker at the eyesore, which sat like an unwanted guest at the bottom of the street.

Mary hated that place.

She wasn't surprised the silly gossip had rushed down there with unseemly haste to quiz the man. Mrs Sanglin would have been desperate to share her opinion with the street. Mary supposed he couldn't be aware of the strange history of the place. If he was, he'd be a fool to spend even a night there. She wondered if the bones of the building held terrible memories, and hoped he'd be safe on his own.

With a deft flick of her wrist, she killed Classic FM and pulled up the on-screen programme guide on her cable service. Her hope was to find a relaxed programme to occupy the rest of her night. After getting comfortable in bed, she intended to catch up with her social media feeds and then resume reading Anne Tyler.

A sudden noise made her turn her head. Music of some kind drifted through the night, discordant pipes and, carried along with it, the cries of a baby.

Oh, Lionel, she thought, *how did you get caught up in it all?*

CHAPTER THREE

Tim Waverly had woken, gritty-eyed, from a restless night.

The things he'd seen at the orphanage had fastened themselves to his dreams like leeches. He'd dreamed of old shoes falling from cobwebbed rafters, and hands reaching out to snatch at him as they clawed through crumbling plaster. A man's deep voice echoed through his sleeping mind, intoning "suffer the children" over and over, before giving way to dark, humourless laughter.

He imagined that a combination of losing his dad just a few months before, his unusual new living circumstances, and the end of the half-term holiday had affected him.

For the first time in months, he craved the tablets which dulled his mind and lifted his mood.

Tim pushed his head deeper into the pillow and groaned. On Mondays, tracking student absenteeism was a nightmare. Was it due to sickness or playing hooky? Mondays following holidays were the worst, with parents having taken their children overseas for an extended break without warning. Against the rules, but St. Isaacs' parents paid fees and felt entitled.

The kids would be a nightmare today, his colleagues even worse. He resolved to keep away from the staffroom.

•   •   •

Tim's second-period lesson was a slog. He'd been taking his class through Roman Catholic attitudes towards marriage and family, a subject about which they had zero interest, committed Catholics making up a tiny number of the student body. The kids inevitably discussed celibacy before marriage, triggering a series of mocking questions.

Invariably, his class asked him for his own view on such matters, knowing he was unmarried, while suppressed laughter filled the room. Face reddening, he'd spent several minutes bringing order back to the class.

Tim enjoyed teaching - most of the time. In contrast to his old state school, St. I's gave teachers an easy ride. That said, the attitudes of kids whose parents were paying for the privilege of a private education tested his patience on the best of days.

•   •   •

That lunchtime, as Tim walked to the shop for a sandwich and a bag of crisps, and the florid head of Phys Ed, Sam Gladding, jogged to the pub for his customary pint of stout, a number of students sat on the ground behind the gym. The latest addition to campus had become a favoured hangout for St. Isaacs' various tribes, offering refuge from staff scrutiny.

The gym's single-storey, pebble-dashed, utilitarian lines stood in stark contrast to the wedding cake Edwardian excesses of the main building.

Lucy Warwick, fifteen and staring down the barrel of impending GSCEs, had reached a strange point of deep-seated concern about what the future might hold, combined with boredom about the present.

The bright spot of Lucy's days was spending time with Korrey Amari, her closest friend since they'd met at primary school, and the person who kept her sane. She was pleased to spend her lunch breaks with him, as the alternative was to spend it alone. Lucy disapproved of many of her classmates. She thought they wasted time staring like zombies into their phones or trying to hook up, sometimes simultaneously. It was tragic.

Not tragic was having a fellow traveller into the realms of the unusual and unexplained, an enthusiasm that had grown stronger since Korrey's sister had left for university, and Lucy revelled in his increasing interest. The yin to her yang, he was enthusiastic about *everything*, bouncing around like Tigger, and quick to laugh. In contrast, Lucy tended towards the dark in humour, fashion, and general approach to life.

Korrey, known to all (including his mother) as Pig, for being both the skinniest boy in their year and having the largest appetite, sat with his long legs folded beneath him as he tucked into a sub, crisp and full-Coke combo.

Lucy pondered his metabolism with envy as he told her, in great detail, around mouthfuls, about a podcast he'd listened to at the weekend. The subject, the Langham - a luxury hotel in London's West End, just a few miles and far removed from the cold concrete on which they sat. The programme focussed on the less luxurious elements of the hotel.

"Makes the Overlook look like a kids' playground!" Pig said, arms lifted and eyes wide. "One of the most haunted places in the whole of London, so they say. So anyway, witnesses have confirmed sightings of at least five spirits at this hotel. Five! How cool is that? A BBC journalist saw one, so that makes it totally real from where I'm standing.

"He was staying at the hotel. The room number's easy to remember because it was 333, and he saw a ghost right in front of him, clear as you are now. The ghost didn't seem to have legs, just floated there, actually in the room!"

"Oh right," Lucy said, playing it cool. "So, what happened next? Did he take a photograph or film it?"

"You won't believe it Lucy," Pig rolled his eyes, "he ran off, shit scared! Seriously, it was literally his job to get the proof. It would've changed everything, making him the most famous journalist in the country, maybe even the world!

"Other people have seen it too, though. Not to mention other manifestations in different parts of the hotel."

Despite maintaining an air of nonchalance, Lucy's interest was, of course, well and truly piqued, and she resolved to both download the podcast and see if she could persuade her parents to take her and Pig to dinner at the Langham. She'd have to box clever, though, and present it as an idea for a special occasion.

Her mum, being a God-botherer, would go grey if she knew the real reason for the teens' interest.

Lucy, scratching at her thigh through the polyester skirt of her hated uniform and glancing over at a huddle of illicit vapers, was thinking for the millionth time how illogical her mother could be, believing as she did in the 'holy' spirit but refusing to consider any other kind.

That thought led her to the news she had been burning to discuss - the arrival of Mr Waverly in her street.

She and Pig had shared some breathless and hyperbolic WhatsApp messages during the half-term break, but they hadn't discussed it face to face because of Pig being away visiting his grandparents somewhere outside London.

They spent the rest of the break sharing a dusty bag of Haribo that Pig liberated, triumphant, from the deepest recesses of his rucksack, while engaged in a serious debate about the merits of a teacher living a few doors down from your home. Consensus: no merits, only nightmare.

Lucy liked Mr Waverly well enough, or at least she didn't *dislike* him, but she had zero interest in bumping into him outside of school. It would feel weird.

They were tidying up after themselves when the bell rang for afternoon lessons (Lucy, English Lit, Pig, Maths).

While en route to the main building, and dizzy with thoughts about the Langham Hotel, they agreed Lucy would order a ouija board using her dad's Amazon account.

•   •   •

That afternoon, Sanjay Mistry stared out of the window in the front room of his home in Oldfield Court, a ground-floor flat which Sanjay thought horrid.

He and his parents had moved there several months before. His dad said that the owner of their old home had sold it, although Sanjay didn't understand why this meant they had to leave. His view was of the abandoned building, which sometimes wormed its way into Sanjay's dreams.

He was thinking about the tofu curry Mummy served for dinner every Monday. Anita, Sanjay's mother, ran her household like his headteacher, ensuring that dust had no chance to settle as she wiped away at floors and surfaces, and served meals in rotation.

A blackboard hung in the kitchen, setting out the daily meal schedule, with tofu curry next to the legend: MONDAY. Sanjay would never dare say it, but he thought tofu curry tasted like poo. What he wanted was fish fingers with chips and baked beans, his favourite dinner in the whole wide world, and one which he'd happily eat for every meal. It annoyed him it wasn't next to MONDAY on the blackboard. Instead, it was next to FRIDAY, which seemed forever-away.

Tofu was one of many things Sanjay disliked. Others included bedtime, porridge, lace-up shoes, and most of the girls in his class.

At eight, influenced by his Mum, he'd developed a strong internal sense of 'Good' and 'Bad', a subject about which he would prattle on about at length, given half a chance.

He knew, for example, that his form tutor Miss Bateman counted as Good because she was kind and gave him extra special help with his sums.

Sanjay knew Ms Fletcher, the classroom assistant, was Bad because he'd seen her outside the mini mart, smoking a cigarette. Smoking was very Bad (perhaps the worst thing of all) and he'd been so shocked he had told his parents.

Sanjay's best friend, Jacquie, was very Good, compared to Peter Eames. Peter, in his last year at primary school, was Bad because he picked his nose in the playground, swore and flicked bogies at the girls. Sometimes he upset Sanjay by calling him racist names.

On this particular Monday, Sanjay stared outside with a pensive expression etched across his still babyish features.

He'd decided that autumn was Bad because everything died. His Dad had countered that it was Good because things were just sleeping and getting ready to awaken. Now, he knew, autumn was almost here. A cold, watery light had replaced the summer sun, and leaves were drifting from the trees.

The little boy focused his attention across the street. He pressed a little closer to the window, breath fogging the glass.

Sanjay had complex feelings about the empty building, not least because he didn't understand why he thought about it at all.

Even though he disliked the flat, having his parents there made it less horrid. He hated being woken up at night by the couple next door playing (Bad) but thought nothing about the other buildings in the street.

Except that one. He was afraid of it.

Bad, he thought to himself while staring unblinkingly across the street.

Very Bad.

And yet, it wasn't. Not exactly. In some corner of his mind, Sanjay understood it wasn't Bad any more than it was Good - it was simply an old, abandoned building, a bit scuzzy looking and sad.

He was captivated by an atmosphere emanating from the place. It was like it was built of autumn.

It would be a while before Sanjay could articulate such feelings, however. He was only eight.

•   •   •

Lucy had left Pig at school, where he'd taken himself off to the library for what he referred to as "panic study," having spent too much of his time in The Conjuring Universe in recent weeks.

Pig, in a state of anxiety about GCSEs, had expressed concern that he might lose his appetite from worry. Given her experience of her friend's eating habits, Lucy thought this unlikely.

Oldfield Street emerged around the corner, dank and dismal in the half-light of late afternoon, and Lucy couldn't help but sigh.

Her friend Amanda had left St. I's the previous year when her newly single mum had taken the plunge and used her divorce settlement to escape to the country. Amanda had taken to sending regular messages on WhatsApp detailing how dull life in the country was compared to London.

Gazing at the street, the countryside seemed like it might be a better place to live.

As she walked past the old orphanage, she thought again of Mr W. In her opinion, he was one of the better teachers at St. I's, and, though she would never share this, not ugly looking either.

All things considered, the thought of him living nearby gave her the ick.

Although she had nothing to hide, she worried that the teacher might focus on her conduct outside school or try to befriend her parents - which was horrific.

Pig was going to enjoy taking the piss, and she suspected he'd try to corral her into spying on the man's comings and goings.

She knew that inside knowledge-however vague-about a member of staff, and a teacher no less, would be strong currency among some cohorts of her fellow students. However, she liked to imagine herself beyond such gossip.

Lucy didn't think of herself as part of any tribe at school and had rejected the advances of other emo or goth kids, preferring to keep her friendships tight and anchored by emotional connection rather than shared interests. It was this that made the bond with Pig so special and why she'd always enjoyed Amanda's sarcastic company.

Glancing at the grim building her teacher now called home, Lucy had a disconcerting feeling, like a strange *pull*.

It was how she imagined a fish might feel as it bit down onto the hook.

It struck her how rundown it was. She had never considered it before - her typical walk home consisted of staring at cracked pavements, lost in music.

Stains ran down the walls like tears shed from the small, high windows. These had formed a crust of white against blood-red brick, and under the darkening sky, the building seemed more like an absence of a building than a building itself, more darkness than light. There was something rotten about it, as if it were home to depthless sadness and grief.

In some ways, Lucy's thoughts mirrored those of the little boy in the flat opposite - that the *space* was wrong, sour somehow, rather than the physical building itself.

Sad that her teacher had needed to move into such a place.

As she stared, Lucy lost track of everything else. At that moment, nothing mattered to her more than the orphanage. At the edge of her perception, she dimly registered a baby's cries and, behind that, something that sounded like the catchy music from a TV advert.

"Earth calling Lucy Warwick!"

Snatched from her focus, she was grateful that Pig wasn't here to see her jump out of her skin. He would *never* stop going on about it. Turning around, Mr Waverly greeted her, his face jaundiced in the streetlights which had just clicked on.

Hoping the conditions meant he couldn't discern her own colour, which she imagined as bloodless with fright, Lucy took a step back, uttered a garbled hello and smiled in what felt in the moment, a really unconvincing manner.

Before her teacher could attempt to engage her in conversation, Lucy stuffed her hands into the pockets of her coat and moved at a brisk pace towards the comforts of home.

•   •   •

A few houses along the street, Michael Slade looked at the personal files on his laptop.

He did this several times a week and thought of it as others might think of an amuse-bouche.

A palette-cleanser before a rich meal.

He came across one of his favourite recent snaps, and his hand paused, hovering over the mouse. It was the boy who'd moved into a flat down the street. Sanjay, Slade thought the child was called.

In the photograph, Sanjay had just walked into his bedroom, wrapped in a towel. The boy's attention was drawn to Slade standing outside, causing him to fumble with the towel at the right moment as he waved through the window.

Slade's breaths became shallow and fast. The child's skin was dark, and wet hair dripped onto beautiful, narrow shoulders.

You need to take that boy.

Michael Slade shook his head to dislodge the thought. He had a rule-look, don't touch.

CHAPTER FOUR

Later that evening, an icy hand brushed the collective necks of those who called Oldfield Street home.

7:00 p.m.

Sanjay Mistry sensed the wrongness first. It was like the times he lay frightened in bed - certain a Bad thing was hiding unseen in the darkness, waiting to gobble him up.

He stood on a small stool in front of the bathroom basin (to see into the mirror) while Mum supervised his tooth-brushing routine.

Brushing his teeth ranked as just about the most boring task of the day, although his mother had made him well aware of the dangers of tooth decay - Bad. He'd heeded Anita's suggestion to look at Granny Kalpna ("but don't say anything") as a good example of what happens when you don't brush twice a day.

Sanjay, squeezing toothpaste onto the brush, thought *Crest.* Staring, entranced by the brand name on the tube, he found himself mesmerised. *Crest, Crest, Crest.* Suddenly, his mind and body slipped *sideways.*

The next thing he knew, he was lying on his bed, his Mum sitting next to him.

"Hey lovely, you gave me a shock, Sanjay," she said. "Bit of a moment back there, hmm?" She placed a hand on his forehead and smiled. "Probably best if we get the doctor to look at you."

Sanjay's Mummy explained that he'd fainted, but she'd managed to catch him before he fell onto the hard floor. He was surprised, as he didn't feel sick at all.

As she left the room to call the doctor, Sanjay called her back. "Can we change toothpaste from now on, please?" he asked.

7:30 p.m.

Tim Waverly had been feeling out of sorts all evening.

He'd spent his day chiding himself about his overreaction to the mysterious 'handprint' on the wall. Back at work, surrounded by his colleagues and students, he'd wondered at his behaviour, trying to scrub it away, of all things! He reasoned that a handprint was inconsequential - perhaps someone, even himself, had simply been careless with dirty hands. It may be a trick of the light, his perception trying to fill some kind of blank. This was only a temporary place; he didn't need to worry about aesthetics.

It was clearer.

As soon as he arrived back in his apartment, seconds after inadvertently scaring poor Lucy Warwick half to death, he couldn't help but feel compelled to look. He had fought the compulsion for several minutes as he brewed a cup of tea and responded to a couple of emails. But now, here he was.

It *had* got clearer. The handprint appeared to *push* through the wall. It was threatening.

It had to be an illusion, his mind creating an image of something based on a passing resemblance and illuminated by dim electric light. He had read about people who saw the face of the Devil in the bark of a tree, or Jesus while spreading jam on their morning toast.

He'd tried various cleaning materials from a pile in the old kitchen the previous evening, scrubbing away at the plaster with no discernible difference. Whatever had caused the mark, it looked engrained in the paintwork, almost burned in.

While he taught religious studies, Tim was agnostic (so much so that he was closer to atheism) and wasn't prone to flights of fancy.

He presumed that his cleaning efforts had removed a top layer of dirt, hence the mark becoming more noticeable. Still, the mysterious image gave him a profound sense of dread.

There was a wrongness about it that caused him to fixate. It was like a cancer symptom a person is determined to ignore.

7:40 p.m.

Michael Slade's home, number fourteen, was owned by his great-aunt. She'd been placed in a nursing home some years before, enabling him, as her only surviving relative, to live there rent-free, something he considered akin to winning the national lottery.

If an icy hand, emanating from the abandoned building Tim Waverly now called home, tickled at the necks of other inhabitants of the street, Slade's was in a vice.

He sat back in his armchair, the living room lit only by the flickering light of his laptop. His needs were sated for now.

He didn't consider himself a wicked man, but rather a good man with bad appetites.

Slade grew up as the child of a feeder. While had never known his father, his late mother, Diane-herself thin as a whip-had been overwhelmed with love for her only child. She'd shown this in several ways, chief among which was food.

By secondary school, he had been moving beyond podgy to fat. This being an era long before body positivity, the young Michael Slade hadn't been encouraged to love himself as he was, but had endured his classmates' taunts, presenting a larger-than-life target for their physical and verbal aggression. Throughout all of this, and failing to recognise how miserable her son was, Diane continued to stuff him like a goose being fattened for its liver.

As an older teenager, he had become drawn towards the younger children. He hadn't understood, at first, but his instincts had told him to beware.

Now forty-two, he had built an unusual life. He'd made an effort with his appearance and, whilst he remained heavyset, he was in the best shape of his life. He'd also built the perfect circumstances with which to indulge his need to *see*.

Slade's personal life was a wasteland, which suited him just fine. He had no friends, and this didn't bother him. Colleagues from his old desk job were long gone, despite empty promises to stay in touch, and he had no cause or opportunity to meet anyone outside of the online world where he lived his happiest moments.

He had never experienced love - never felt the touch of another person, nor had he touched anyone himself. He thought of himself as living dead, sparking to life only when touring the blackest corners of the Dark Web. These regular visits were the times he found something close to happiness.

He gazed at his laptop. The screen displayed an image that stimulated him but would have disgusted most people.

The voice hadn't disappeared since he examined the Mistry boy's photo earlier.

It persisted, at times loud, at times faint, but always present. The voice kept repeating its instruction, as if on a loop - to take Sanjay from the flat at the end of the street.

He would never do that. His rule was clear: look, never touch. Even if tempted, he couldn't take a child from so close to his own home.

Could he?

Slade poured himself a large glass of whisky and then added to it. He needed these intrusive thoughts to stop.

10:42 p.m.

Lucy sat at the laptop in her room while her parents thought she was revising for her upcoming exams. They were delighted with this development, having worried that she was being too laid back about her studies, not least as the fees at St. Isaac's were crippling them.

In reality, she'd been engaged in a lengthy discussion with Pig via instant messenger. Pig, for his part, had been learning more about the Langham Hotel, sending Lucy a number of documents he said gave further credence to the various hauntings documented in the place. Lucy had encouraged him to pitch a feature to Fortean Times.

LW: Could be great. U so need to do it. Tell them you're a teen ghostbuster. Who u gonna call?! :)

PIG: I so AM gonna do it. But prob need to concentrate on exams 1st??

LW: FML when did u get so uptight??!!

Logging off after saying their goodbyes (To be continued tomorrow @ St I x), Lucy smiled to herself. Pig wasn't just her best friend; he was the kindest and most interesting person she knew outside of her own family. Her feelings for him were both warm and complex. She was jolted from her thoughts by a soft knock at her door, and her mum's voice through the wood.

"Lucy, revision's important I know, but so is *sleep*! It's a school night."

"Yes, mum. Night, love you!" Lucy called back, rolling her eyes. She experienced momentary guilt as she readied herself for bed, having done no studying at all. Oh well, there's always tomorrow.

A little later she was in bed, her father also having reminded her about needing to be refreshed for school. She was drifting to sleep when a man's voice said her name, wrenching her awake.

Lucy started, dazed. Must've been dreaming. Silence, apart from the background 24/7 hum of traffic on the A-road. She realised she wouldn't sleep anytime soon after staring at the ceiling for a long while.

She sat up and flicked on the lamp by her bedside.

The light it gave off was dim. Enough to read by, but not to illuminate the room. Lucy could just make out the chair where she always threw her clothes, despite her mum's incessant nagging about it.

She could see the sleeve of her school uniform blazer, hanging towards the floor, and what might be the pair of jeans she'd worn this evening.

The pile of discarded clothes shifted on the chair and the air bled from the girl's lungs.

It leaned forward towards where Lucy was sitting up in bed. Beady eyes glinted in the darkness. There was someone in the room.

Squinting and feeling her heart yammer like a cornered animal, Lucy tried to make out the figure. She rubbed her eyes; sure her mind was trying to make her discarded clothing into something human. Almost human.

It was a man, thin, but in the blink of an eye, it seemed to be someone else. Some*thing* else. Something ill-defined and *wrong*.

He/it (her mind would no longer accept it was just a pile of clothes) was staring at her.

It raised a hand. "Hello Lucy Warwick. I thought I could make use of you." Lucy shrank back in her pillows, terrified, and pulled the duvet towards her chin.

"Regrettably, I was wrong," the man/thing went on, "your usefulness has passed." The figure tutted as it shook its head. "What a waste. You were a special child once and I would have enjoyed you. But there's someone else, someone *extra*-special."

She gasped and, without thinking, leaped from under the covers. She ran to the door, which seemed a hundred miles away, and hit the light switch. A warm glow flooded the room.

The chair held a crumpled school uniform, a pair of jeans, and nothing else.

01:30 a.m.

Mary MacDonald woke from a fitful sleep. She felt sure she needed to speak to her new neighbour with urgency. While she had slept, her mind had been mulling over how to approach things, options twisting through her dreams like entwined snakes.

Sitting up, she gave a faint cry. Her dead brother, Lionel, stood framed in the doorway.

Despite the darkness, enough artificial light from the street came through the curtain to illuminate the swollen outline of Lionel's engorged penis, twitching like a giant insect against the drooping flesh of his old-man belly.

"Hello sister," the apparition said with a leer, "fancy a bunk-up?"

Mary shoved a corner of the duvet into her mouth to stifle her screams.

04:00 a.m.

Sanjay Mistry gave up trying to sleep.

He usually winked out, content with the certainty of his life, and enjoyed the happiest dreams, but tonight he hadn't been able to. He had lain in bed, tossing, turning, and getting annoyed about being hot and then cold while experiencing a sensation he didn't understand - dread. Something Bad was coming. He could feel it. The Bad Thing might already be here!

Sanjay ran his tongue around the ridges of his small teeth. *Crest,* he thought.

04:10 a.m.

At number twenty-one Oldfield Street, Molly, the spaniel, woke and howled as she'd never howled before.

CHAPTER FIVE

A weak sun had risen, veiled behind thick clouds, thirty minutes before Lucy and Pig held their crisis summit, their faces bathed in its sickly grey light, once again behind the gym at St. Isaac's.

They'd agreed to meet early in the morning, early for teenagers that is, after a series of urgent WhatsApp messages. Pig skipped breakfast, an unusual occurrence that highlighted the seriousness of the situation.

Given their interests, and symptomatic of the credulity of youth, the friends had quickly decided the most likely cause of Lucy's night-time visitation was a supernatural one. Pig expressed frustration that Lucy failed even to photograph the apparition.

"It wasn't my imagination," Lucy insisted for what seemed like the hundredth time. "It was there, in the corner of my room. Photograph or otherwise."

"And you've never seen him anywhere before?" Pig asked, a bit jealous that he'd experienced nothing ghostly the previous night. Or ever when he thought about it.

"No, I don't think so. The whole thing was weird, fuzzy, and kind of, well, *dim*. It's hard to explain. Beyond creepy, though."

Tearing into an emergency Curly Wurly he'd thrown into his rucksack on the way out of the house, Pig considered the implications, his heart racing. "I found loads of reports on the Web about horny ghosts and stuff," he said around a mouthful of caramel. "People have even reported sexual assaults and the words he used sound, well, along those lines, maybe?"

"Ew!" Lucy stared from under her dark fringe and gave an involuntary shudder.

"Of course," he went on, "lots of spirits are in the business of mischief. It's not like he, or it, did anything beyond creeping you out. It might not be capable of doing any actual harm."

"Why doesn't that little piece of mansplaining make me feel any better?" Lucy asked with a tight smile. "I'm certain this, whatever it was–*thing*–was targeting me. It actually said my name."

As is often the way with summits, there was much discussion and little decision. In the end, they agreed Lucy would keep a 'lookout' and spend the following night alert, in case of another manifestation.

For his part, Pig would dive into the internet to search for anything at all about such apparitions, assuming it had indeed been one.

Initial plans made; the pair went their separate ways to do some learning.

• • •

Michael Slade found himself unable to work.

The voice, which he now thought of as The Voice, had become his constant companion. It had even woken him from a drunken sleep, shouting Sanjay's name into his ear. It was as if the speaker was lying in the bed next to him.

As he'd stood brushing his teeth in the morning, exercises done through the sickly fog of hangover, The Voice had come to him over the buzz of the toothbrush.

"Bring me Sanjay Mistry. You need to *take* him."

The Voice remained with him through getting dressed, Alka Seltzer, and the news headlines.

Resolving to tidy his van, he left the house and walked to the end of the street where he'd parked up.

"MISTRY!"

The Voice erupted, triumphant and so loud that Slade felt almost physical pain. Slamming the van's rear doors (emblazoned with the legend: 'Pain-Free Panes, Window Cleaners'), he came face to face with *the* boy and his mother.

"Good morning," the woman said, flashing a bright smile.

He nodded and mumbled a hello, avoiding eye contact with mother or child, and the pair walked off down the street. He glanced back at the van and then at his watch.

He needed a drink.

•   •   •

In the waning light, Pig walked with Lucy to her house after school. The friends were buzzing because of the prospect of the ouija board having arrived and, most importantly, Lucy had dangled the possibility of dinner in front of him.

Not for the first time he wondered, as they ambled into her road, quite what made him find Oldfield Street so grim.

On the face of it, the streetscape was much the same as his own road - pretty terraced homes (apart from the plain social housing block and the orphanage), all smart front doors and Victorian mouldings like icing on a cake.

Perhaps it was the narrowness of the street which, combined with the leaf fall, gave a sense of dank and decay? Even in summer, the sunlight didn't penetrate the strip of pavement.

A plane roared overhead, close to landing at Heathrow, when Lucy gave him a nudge in the ribs. "Don't look!" she said, "Mr W's lodgings."

Pig looked as any person would when admonished to do the opposite.

He'd lived so long in the area that he always walked past the abandoned building without a second glance. It stood beyond repair in the dusk. The windows that weren't covered reflected the streetlights and gazed balefully upon passers-by. The tiled roof sagged as if under a great weight, and a gnarled tree was attempting to grow from between its cracked tiles.

Lucy's home, as ever, did its best against the road's gloomy atmosphere and Pig found his spirits lifted as they made their way to the jolly pink front door (and how Lucy had ranted about that home 'improvement').

Heading into the warm interior, they were greeted by her mum, Ellie, who seemed tense, which wasn't like her. Lucy appeared oblivious to her mum's mood.

"Hi Mum!" she greeted Ellie by launching in for a hug while grabbing an Amazon package from the hall table.

Ellie, whom Pig thought had already enjoyed her customary G&T, wrinkled her nose. "Did you spot the front wall when you left this morning? It might've been there then. Hello Pig, by the way, am I feeding you, dare I ask?"

Lucy shrugged, confused, while her mum rooted around in a cabinet before emerging with a torch.

"I'll show you - honestly, this street, whatever next?"

They trooped out of the front door into the autumnal gloom. When Ellie turned on the torch by accident, she shone it directly into Pig's face, blinding him. "Sorry darling Pig," she said, "look at this."

Ellie shined the torch onto the low front wall, revealing a bright yellow graffiti tag:

K is Risen!

"That's kind of odd. I wonder what it means?" asked Pig, folding himself over for a closer examination and running his long fingers over the paint.

"Frankly, Pig, I don't care," Ellie said. "I can't work out what paint was used. I've been scrubbing at the bloody thing for hours," she complained. "It's as if someone burnt it into the wall!"

Turning to her mother, Lucy forced a smile. "Don't worry Mum, I can help paint over it if you like."

"Good girl," Ellie smiled at her. "It's no use dwelling on it, I suppose. Nobody cares about private property these days. Why don't you guys head in and talk about whatever it is teenagers talk about while I shove something in the oven? Pig, decide - are you eating here besides having dinner at home?"

Pig considered this. "Nah," he drawled, "I'll let my mum know I'll sort myself a snack when I get home as I'm eating here, thanks Ellie."

He didn't clock Lucy rolling her eyes at her mother.

• • •

Away from prying parental eyes, Lucy tore open the Amazon package. "Yes!" she said, excited. She held out the box for Pig to see.

"So," he asked, "where and when?"

"I have an idea about that, but I'm not sure you're going to like it." Lucy flashed a smile at her friend.

"Go on."

"The ouija needs the right atmosphere to be effective, right? I read all about it."

Pig stared at their surroundings. Prints of skulls and strange figures adorned Lucy's walls, candles flickered on the flat surfaces, and she'd also lit an incense stick that filled her bedroom with wisps of smoke and a potent scent of patchouli. Silken purple, red and black scarves were hanging in ribbons from the ceiling.

"This has an atmosphere, I reckon," he pointed out.

"Not enough. I think we should do it at the orphanage if you-"

Pig held up a hand, cutting her off. "You mean the orphanage where Mr W is living? You know, our teacher, the one who could get us excluded from school, *that* orphanage?!"

Lucy raised her eyebrows and gave him a knowing smile. She rummaged in her school bag and found a crumpled piece of paper, which she waved at him.

"Ta-daaaa," she used her least excited voice for this, "year five parent-teacher evening. Friday seven 'til nine. The place will be empty. I doubt he'll get back before ten. You know how these things go on, because they serve drinks for the parents."

Pig realised, with a sinking feeling, that Lucy was going to get her way, as always. "Okayyyyy," he drawled, "so how do you propose to get in, ask to borrow his keys?"

"Don't you worry about how we're going to get in. Just make sure you're there, Piglet," Lucy smiled and blew her friend a kiss.

•   •   •

Mary MacDonald had spent the day brooding, afraid she was losing her mind as her mother had many years before, when dementia had claimed her.

The visitation, or whatever it had been, by her late brother in the night left her sleepless and haunted. She rarely had nightmares, and it seemed so real, but when she'd felt able to open her eyes, there'd been nobody there.

Maybe her night terror, which it must have been, was linked to the news about the young teacher moving to that dreadful place.

A building she'd fought alongside others to get shut down. His arrival had triggered memories which were locked away in the furthest corner of her mind.

That the unused building remained standing was a rare source of anger to Mary, who was not prone to powerful emotions. Now this young man was actually living there, the first inhabitant since it had ceased to house those poor children. It should have been demolished and forgotten decades ago.

His presence posed a risk. Nothing could be allowed to start things happening again. Afraid it might be too late, Mary resolved to face her fears. She needed to get into the building and meet the man. She had to warn him.

Placing her Kindle on the table, she took a sip of tea. She needed a plan.

CHAPTER SIX

The Voice, weakened by whisky and willpower, became a mere whisper, like smoke. Michael Slade decided to go to work.

Due to his disinterest in full-time employment, he had never considered working with children, despite it being the obvious career choice for someone with his specific interests.

Window cleaning had proven to be an inspired choice. It had taken a while to perfect his round, but after about eighteen months, he'd cracked it. A search on the local authority website had given him the catchment area for the local primary school. Bingo.

Because of this misplaced bureaucratic transparency, Slade found himself able to develop the perfect route. His round began on the roads closest to the school, as those children would be home earliest in the afternoons, before working its way out in concentric circles.

The results were beyond his expectations - people had innate trust in their window cleaner. Some young mums enjoyed visits from the large, muscular man who raced up his ladder with surprising, nimble grace and who always had a smile and a wave. Others acted like he wasn't there, which he preferred.

As summer drained away, Slade only had a few more weeks of prime hunting season - people would soon close their shutters and curtains against the darkening evenings. He would be forced to move to daytime weekend shifts, when he found the children were less likely to be at home and, also; he wasn't keen on being seen by the fathers.

In recent times, he'd upgraded his personal protection equipment, and added a camera to his hardhat. The camera meant it was easier to capture images of the children, and he'd given himself a fright when he'd almost come off a ladder on a windy day when attempting to snap a little one on his phone. When one mother had asked him about the camera, he'd rolled his eyes and said something about "insurance requirements."

It was from the hat-cam that he'd been able to capture his most treasured image, that of Sanjay Mistry in Oldfield Court, just a few yards away from his own home. He'd enjoyed many hours fantasising over the photo and had, after pixelating the face, shared it on the Dark Web. He delighted in receiving positive comments from like-minded individuals who appreciated the natural framing and fallen towel.

Determined to ignore The Voice whispering in the back of his head, he whistled a jaunty tune as he placed his hard hat on the passenger seat. Pain-Free Panes was ready to roll.

• • •

Tim Waverly turned onto Oldfield Street at dusk, feeling as if detention duty punished both the teachers and students.

When he left early that morning, a floral notecard had been pushed through the letterbox. Louise Sanglin, with instructions on how to join the street WhatsApp group. He'd placed this in the recycling bin, instincts telling him she needed to be avoided.

Tim nodded vaguely at an elderly woman walking towards him carrying groceries. He forgot her as soon as she'd passed by, when his attention was dragged backwards by a faint exclamation.

The woman had dropped one of her bags. An apple was rolling into the gutter and, reluctantly, he went back to help.

"You are most kind," she said, looking up as Tim picked groceries off the pavement and placed them into her bag. The elderly woman, resplendent in a smart tweed suit and felt hat, put him in mind of old films, her small, neat frame illuminated by the artificial light spilling from overhead.

Groceries secured, the woman stood and thrust out a gloved hand, which he shook. "Mary MacDonald," she announced.

He introduced himself, and she arched an eyebrow. "I heard someone had moved into that old place. We *all* heard from Mrs Sanglin," Tim detected the hint of a smile. "I've never been inside. Would it be too much if I popped in to have a look?"

Making conversation was the last thing he wanted, but his own politeness trapped him. Unbeknownst to him, this was what Mary had been banking on as she'd waited (for longer than she'd expected) for him to arrive.

"Now?"

She smiled, "No time like the present and," she made a show of glancing at her watch, "it's hardly the witching hour Mr Waverly. I take it you have teabags. And a kettle. I'll just pop the shopping into my hallway, and we can go straight down."

Tim knew he'd been backed into a corner and had no choice. So much for keeping himself to himself.

•   •   •

After dark, perched on his knees on the sofa in the front room of his home, Sanjay Mistry stared, once again, from the living room window. Sanjay was disappointed about not being allowed to skip school, but the doctor was kind.

Although the grown-ups had been speaking in low voices, Sanjay heard enough of the conversation between mother and doctor to suggest his funny turn was just that. "Not unusual," the doctor had said. He'd certainly been feeling quite well, although he'd used the opportunity provided by the funny turn to beg for extra custard creams.

As always, he fixed his gaze on the abandoned building opposite. "Bad," Sanjay said in a quiet voice.

• • •

As he walked across the living area, carrying a tray and wondering how soon he could rid himself of the second unwanted visitor to his new lodgings, Tim noticed that the old woman was staring, unblinking, at the mark on the wall.

"There are others," she said.

"I'm sorry?"

"These images. Oh, yes. There are others, I'm certain of it. Perhaps not now, but in the near future."

Mrs MacDonald looked up at Tim's quizzical stare. "Do sit down, Mr Waverly. If you can bear to listen to a pensioner's rambling, it would help if she didn't get a crick in her neck.

"I'm going to give you a history lesson."

Tim sat on the sofa as requested (ordered) and couldn't help feeling like one of his own students settling in for a class they were dreading. He worried that the woman might speak for some time.

Mary MacDonald took a sip of tea and closed her eyes with momentary pleasure.

"Lionel Bracken, my older brother, was haunted by images such as this. They destroyed his life or, at the very least, were one element which pushed him over the edge.

"Lionel and his twin, Cecily, came along five years before me. I always suspected I was an accident. The twins were a tight unit. I imagined that, to them, I was little more than an annoyance. Like a wasp buzzing around the place.

"Some of what I'm going to tell you is based on memory. The rest, I pieced together later.

"Lionel got on well with our mother. I always found her difficult. She was rather devout in her Catholicism, but he was a quiet, good boy and good boys love their mothers, don't they? Busy at work, Father was a distant presence at home, typical of the era.

"As Lionel reached his teens, mysterious marks - like this one," she gestured at the handprint, "appeared around the house, the same house I live in today, in fact. Initially, only a few, inconspicuous to anyone except a curious boy. Naturally, they caught his attention.

"One by one, the rest of us spotted them, of course. Our parents assumed Lionel was daubing them on the walls. At one point, Father gave him a hiding. Don't look shocked, Mr Waverly. Lots of children nowadays could do with it, in my opinion, although I suppose you'd know better than me."

Mrs. MacDonald sipped tea, closing her eyes, transported to the past. "Things went from bad to worse. Marks could appear anywhere and everywhere - a hand, a face, eyes. Our parents took to locking certain rooms, convinced Lionel was responsible, but still they appeared. He would deny any direct involvement in the mystery until his dying days."

Mary took another sip from her cup. "I'm sure you think all this sounds unlikely?"

Tim, determined to remain polite, responded. "It's probably water damage or something seeping through the paintwork. These buildings are old, and this place has been unoccupied for years."

"Well, that's as maybe, Mr Waverly," she said briskly. "I'm just telling you what I know, and I want to tell it correctly."

Settling himself into a more comfortable position, Tim motioned for her to continue, sensing her determination to complete her tale, and wondering how it related to what he was experiencing.

"Thank you. Where was I? Oh yes, Lionel had endured a beating, and the doors were being kept locked. And still, the marks appeared.

"So, the police were called because Mother was finding it hard to believe her beloved son had turned overnight into such a destructive boy. She wondered if, somehow, people were getting into the house from outside. Of course, they could find no evidence and, anyway, it was only on Sunday mornings that the house was sure to be unoccupied. We attended church.

"The police drew a blank. Time passed, and the images multiplied. Terrible nightmares plagued Mother, as well as my sister, Cecily, and myself. A doctor was called to assess Lionel for hysteria, of all things. Again, no sign of anything at all.

"In desperation, our parents invited the local priest to come and reason with my brother. The priest found it all very surprising and, according to Lionel years later, performed some kind of blessing. Nothing changed.

"In the end, our parents took drastic action. They sent Lionel away to a boarding school for 'troubled boys' where it seems he endured bullying by the other youngsters and was brutalised by the staff for a number of years.

"By the time he came out, before joining the forces, he was a shadow of the happy boy he'd once been. He never got over what my family had done to him. In the end, he was disinherited. Lionel ended his life a couple of years ago. He threw himself into a canal, Mr Waverly, and drowned."

"Tim, please," he said, humouring her. "I'm very sorry to hear about your brother's death, but the obvious question is: what happened with the marks? After Lionel was sent away. To the school, I mean."

"Well, as far as I'm aware, they stopped. Several coats of paint and a bit of wallpaper and they were soon forgotten, or at least hidden from view, which I suppose was all that mattered to our parents."

Mrs MacDonald gave a shrug. "Lionel knew exactly how the absence of new images appeared, Mr Wave...Tim. He still denied culpability, although some appeared many years later, after he'd left the army and returned home for a short while. Our father was dead by then.

"The images didn't return in the same volume after his return, thank goodness. I think that would have driven my brother into an even earlier grave.

"And now look," she threw her arm out to emphasise the point. "This image is identical to one I saw as a child. I'm sure of it! That must mean something, even though I've no idea what.

"Tim, *this* was the facility Lionel attended. Just yards away from home, it may as well have been in another country. This was no orphanage, although no doubt many of the boys kept here would have been orphans. Lionel had no choice but to live in this God-forsaken place."

Tim wasn't sure how to respond, or whether he should further indulge the old woman's fairy tales.

The handprint in the wall taunted him from his seat on the sofa, and he averted his eyes. There had to be a rational explanation. "Well, that was an eerie story," he said, standing. "But I'm afraid you'll have to excuse me, as I need to eat and prepare for school tomorrow. I'm a teacher you see at St Isaac's."

Mrs MacDonald, recognising that the young man had dismissed her, arched an eyebrow, and gave a little sniff as she placed her cup back in its saucer.

"Understood, Mr Waverly," she said, her tone formal as she stood up, buttoning her coat. "I know it all sounds 'eerie', as you put it, but there we are. I thought you should know. Forewarned is forearmed, as they say."

Tim accompanied his neighbour, her posture perfect, to the door. Mrs MacDonald was a smart, albeit old-fashioned, woman in her manner and her mode of dress. Her conviction about such a strange tale surprised him.

Closing the heavy front door against the darkening night, Tim felt relieved that she had left, and he had the place to himself again.

Back in his living quarters, he poured himself a large glass of wine. Despite its ridiculousness, he couldn't help but question why he had been misinformed about the building's original purpose.

"*Anthropomorphism be damned,*" he said to himself, raising an ironic glass towards the handprint. Let the old woman live her fantasies; he wouldn't be pulled into her delusions, even if she believed them.

It wasn't to be long before he found another image.

CHAPTER SEVEN

Lucy thundered out of her house, filled with the promise of the looming weekend and nervous about the evening ahead, although she would never say it.

Pig had told her he was planning to spend time at the weekend, outside of revision, concentrating on preparing his pitch to Fortean Times for a story about the many spirits manifesting in the Langham Hotel. The magazine, dedicated to the weird worldwide, might even pay for a night at the hotel, he'd told her.

Lucy was excited about the prospect of contacting those beyond the veil.

She had made sure, before leaving St I's, to confirm the parents' evening for the younger children was going ahead. Upon seeing the school hall being set up, she'd sent Pig a 'good to go' message.

The light was bleeding out of the sky as they greeted one another outside the orphanage.

As instructed, Pig was wearing dark colours from head to toe, Lucy having advised that it would help them "get lost in the shadows."

"How do you know we'll be able to get inside?" he asked.

"Angela Bloxham and Darren Parker have been coming in here for ages," Lucy answered, checking her rucksack to make sure she'd packed a torch. "To snog and...whatever," she added.

"Jeez, that's gross." The friends snorted with laughter.

The abandoned building loomed through the grey light. It seemed to suck the air from its surroundings, its high windows staring down in judgement. Even the temperature seemed different, colder in its shadow.

"This is one creepy place," Pig opined.

As they stood by the side of the building, Lucy found herself in agreement. She admired Mr W. There couldn't be many people brave enough to stay here, let alone move in.

A small alleyway was a dark mouth between the old orphanage (for that is what they believed it to be), and the side wall of the street's first house. According to Angela Bloxham, the alley provided the easiest route to gain access. Assuming Ange hadn't been taking the piss.

The alley had little light, and rubble and other detritus covered the ground, causing Lucy to stumble as they entered. Pig grabbed her by the arm to steady her and she turned to him with a smile that was lost in the darkness.

Things skittered and scurried unseen in the filth. Squirrels, perhaps. Or rats.

Nervous giggles filled the air as they walked around to the building's rear. Their frequent "sshhhing" was louder than the laughter. Had they been bystanders on Oldfield Street, they would have discovered that no sound exited the dark alley.

Lucy flicked her torch on and pointed the light up at the building. "Exactly where Ange said it would be!" she said.

The metal grille, illuminated in the torch's orange beam, was about fifty centimetres square. Lucy turned and found what Ange had described: a forgotten wheelie bin by the neighbouring house.

Pig manoeuvred the bin, so it sat underneath the tall window. He tested it, rocky on the uneven ground, but it should hold. He hoped.

"Go on then," Lucy urged, impatient. Pig rolled his eyes in the dark and awkwardly clambered onto the bin, which Lucy held onto in case it toppled. He gained purchase on the grille and, having done so, he pulled.

•   •   •

Perhaps a little too hard. The grille popped away from the wall like a cork from a bottle with a metallic CLANG! The sound reverberated through the space. Sour air escaped from the hole in the wall. The friends held their breath for a time, fearful someone might have heard.

Pig stifled a nervous giggle as he let his breath out with a slow hiss. "I'm going to go in," he said, passing the grille down to his friend. "Pray for me, I don't want to twist an ankle." He placed his torch into his rucksack, bent his knees and, with a small bounce, lifted himself towards the dark opening.

Slowly, shuffling his way over the rough sill, Pig made a feet-first leap of faith. He had no way of seeing how far he had to drop.

"*Pig*," Lucy said from outside.

"I'm okay, not too far down." He used the light from his torch to illuminate the opening. "Go for it. I can grab your legs as you come through." Moments later, soundtracked by muttered swearing, Lucy joined him.

They combined torch beams to examine the space. "Gnarly," Pig said, Lucy grunting her assent.

It was a communal bathroom. With open showers and toilet stalls, it afforded no privacy to its users, no place for a person to attend to their most personal needs unobserved. The tiled floor, illuminated by the torchlight, revealed myriad cracks zigzagging across the space, giving no clue as to its original colour. A cancerous black mould crawled up the walls and across the ceiling.

The only sound apart from their breathing was water dripping somewhere.

"Let's do it," Pig said, flashing a smile. He walked over to a light switch and flicked it on and off without success, giving a shrug.

They found some splintery old crates to use as a table and chairs and set up the ouija board. Lucy took out a pad and pen from her bag in case they wanted to make notes. "If my mum knew we were doing this, she would never let you come for dinner," she said.

Pig clutched his belly and let out a comical moan. "Nooooo!" he said, "Not that, pull out my fingernails with pliers, but don't keep me away from my victuals!"

The two of them folded over with laughter. Several minutes passed before they returned to the sombre state the experiment required.

Lucy thought that the board and planchette themselves let the side down, being cheap plastic items from Amazon, but hoped it would work. The bleak atmosphere helped her imagine something a bit more authentic looking if she didn't look too closely.

"Let us begin," Lucy intoned, and Pig fought back another giggle.

They placed their index fingers on the flimsy planchette, torches providing just enough light to see by, and moved it around the board three times. According to the instructions, doing this would help to open 'lines of communication with the spirit world'.

"Are there any spirits who want to communicate with us?" Lucy asked, forcing any humour from her voice. A long pause followed, as the pair stared at the planchette, which remained stationary.

"Come in Captain Howdy," Pig joked.

Lucy gave him a sharp look. "Behave, the board's warming up," she said. He gave an apologetic shrug of his skinny shoulders. "We're asking if any spirits wish to communicate with us," she continued.

Nothing. Frustrated, Lucy's gaze drifted into the depths of the room. Shadows danced in the torchlight and her heart skittered like a frightened animal. Dread suddenly overwhelmed her. It was as if she'd seen the future, and everything was bad.

"Did you feel that?" she asked.

Pig looked at her with shining eyes. "I can't say I feel anything much. Excited, a bit hungry, maybe," he shrugged.

She gave him a straight look. "Let's try again. Are there any spirits that wish to speak with us?"

The man's laughter made her jump. "Jesus Lucy!" Pig said with a nervous laugh. "You nearly hit the ceiling. It's just someone outside, in the street."

"I think my nerves must be getting the better of me," she said, embarrassed, her ears still tuned to the mocking laugh, now distant. "Right. Gather," she took a deep breath and let it out with a steady hiss. "Are there any spirits that wish to speak to us?"

A pause. Abruptly, the planchette moved to the YES printed near Lucy's elbow. "Woah, was that you Luce?"

Lucy felt the blood drain from her face. "What is your name?" she asked

The planchette gave off a faint vibration and moved once again. Slowly. Rather than spelling out a name, the teardrop-shaped piece of plastic travelled across the board in a lazy, circular movement.

Lucy's heart was in her throat. She watched the planchette as it continued its circular journey around the board, filled with a heady mixture of fear and excitement.

The planchette stopped circling yet continued to send that strange vibration along the friends' fingers.

"What is your name?" Lucy asked again. The planchette circled once, twice more and then moved towards the letters printed on the board.

I.S.E.E.Y.O.U

"I see you," Pig whispered.

Creepiness overwhelmed Lucy. Perhaps they should have performed the ouija somewhere else. Like Pig's house.

The planchette circled the board, faster this time.

I.S.E.E.Y.O.U

"Can you tell us your name?" Pig stepped in.

Circling again, in the opposite direction now. Once, twice, three times.

"I'm not sure I like this, Pig."

"We need to carry on, Lucy. It is creepy, but it's kind of interesting too. Please give us your name. We want to know who you are."

I.S.E.E.Y.O.U.L.U.C.Y

"Ohhhh shit," Lucy said with a shiver, "this is totally weirding me out now. If it is you, Pig, you're dead! How do you see me? Are you standing in the room?"

I.S.E.E.Y.O.U.L.U.C.Y

"Ugh!" She'd had enough and pulled her finger off the planchette as if she'd been burnt.

Despite this, Pig was determined to continue. "Please, tell me who you are," he asked.

Lucy jumped up, the crate she'd been sitting on shifting across the floor with a harsh screech.

Pig's wide eyes were fixated on the planchette circling the board.

"Pig, please stop. Pig, I'm not having fun now." Dropping her torch, Lucy grabbed her friend by the shoulders, shouting into his face. "PIG, STOP! I DON'T LIKE IT!"

Pig seemed disorientated when he pulled his gaze from the board, as if awakened from a deep sleep. "Wha…? Oh, yeah, I just wanted to know its name."

They gazed at the circling planchette as Pig reluctantly lifted his finger away.

It continued to circle. "What the actual *fuck?*" he asked.

The planchette circled once more before stopping. It moved, somehow insolent, to the letter:

K

Slowly, the piece of cheap plastic shifted sideways with no human contact, before sliding off the table and landing on the floor with a sound like the softest sigh.

Lucy, shivering with fear, stared wide-eyed at her friend. "What just happened?"

They gathered their things in a hurry, the fun of the evening overwritten by their shared anxiety. Lucy, shoving the ouija back into her rucksack, heard Pig's gasp.

"Unbelievable." His voice snagged Lucy's attention as he shined his torchlight at the back wall of the room. The words hadn't been there before. Reaching from floor to ceiling, they looked like they'd been scorched into the filthy old tiles.

I SEE YOU LUCY. WHEN YOU SLEEP.

Pig walked over to the wall, reaching out towards the words. "Pig!" Lucy exclaimed, her obvious fear stopping him in his tracks. "Let's get out of here. NOW!"

•   •   •

The moment the planchette fell to the floor of the old bathroom, cosy in the warmth of her sitting room, some*thing* stepped over Mary's grave. Her body's involuntary shudder was powerful enough that she spilled some of her tea.

Hands shaking, she placed her cup on its saucer, placing them onto the table before dabbing at her skirt with the handkerchief she kept tucked into the sleeve of her cardigan.

Mary had spent much of her day ruminating about her conversation with Tim Waverly. In hindsight, she knew she had made a mistake by blundering in and telling him about Lionel. She should have eased her story into a more general conversation.

She felt it crucial to warn the man about past strange occurrences, yet his unresponsive, albeit polite, demeanour did not surprise her.

She had handled things incorrectly. Going in all guns blazing where she should have used tact. She should have warmed Tim up over the course of a number of conversations, allowing time for him to experience more of the strangeness for himself.

What was done was done. As always, she had waded in, where angels fear to tread, and now her new neighbour would think her a dotty old woman!

Thoughts wheeled through her mind like snow before settling where she wanted them to.

Her brother, framed tumescent, obscene in the bedroom door, had been so *real,* and he'd spoken to her.

With horror, Mary recalled how she had used her bedding to muffle a scream - when she reopened her eyes, which seemed like many hours later, Lionel had disappeared.

In her waking mind, she put the experience down to an unpleasant dream, perhaps triggered by other anxieties. Mary believed in some kind of hidden world, she supposed - unsurprising, having experienced uncanny events as a little girl.

Returning to her, now tepid, tea, she considered how she'd come across to Tim Waverly.

Mary feared she cut a ridiculous figure. A doughty childless old widow, jumping at shadows and relaying tales of the uncanny like some hysterical relic from an Edwardian melodrama.

She let out a sigh. She needed to make her neighbour listen in case things escalated. But *how*?

•　•　•

Tim found a torch on the floor of the communal bathroom on Saturday morning. Two crates were pushed against the wall under the window, its grille hanging askew, and he realised someone had been in, most likely while he had been working at the interminable parents' evening.

Perhaps junkies were getting in to shoot up, or kids wanting to fool around. He suppressed a shudder. Although there was no evidence that anything untoward had taken place, and he'd seen nothing to indicate anyone had ventured into his living quarters, it would have to be reported to the Angels.

He resolved to repair the grille and make the place more secure while looking around the room for further signs of unwelcome visitors.

"What on earth?" he said, stomach lurching.

The wall that housed the shower heads was black with grease and detritus. Mouse (or rat?) droppings littered the floor.

Amidst the filth, a pair of angry eyes stared into the room. They looked scorched into the tiles.

This was no trick of the light, no optical illusion. It was quite clear.

Whitish against the dirty wall, it gave the impression of a photographic negative. The mark, about a foot across, had a significant impact, especially since the handprint in the apartment was life-size.

Tim took his phone from the pocket of his jeans and snapped a photograph. *Whoever's breaking in must be making these pictures,* he thought to himself.

His thoughts turned to Mrs MacDonald and her wild story. He assumed her brother must have been suffering from some kind of psychological impairment - after all, his desperate parents had sent him away and why else would he have drawn all over his own home?

Although discombobulated by this new mark, the level of artistry was impressive. There was depth to the image and exquisite detail. Individual eyelashes were visible, despite the dim light.

It was difficult to discern the expression in the eyes - a hint of malevolence, perhaps amusement?

Tim pondered. Where did these marks emanate from? It had to be a symptom of some natural changes occurring within the building's fabric. Despite this, he did not, could not, bring himself to touch the image, certain that his fingers would meet something cold, wet, somehow *wrong*.

Thoughts racing around in his head, he went to finish inspecting the building. He tried to ignore the battering of his heart.

CHAPTER EIGHT

On Saturday night, Michael Slade had a dream. It was so unsettling, so vivid, he was sure it would haunt him for a long time.

He lay naked and vulnerable on the bed.

Disorientated, he tried to move his extremities, but found that his arms and legs were locked into place.

The only movement possible, he discovered, was from the neck upwards. Understanding this must be a dream, he looked to the side to check his surroundings. In the sickly light from the street, filtered through the curtains, he made out the familiar sights of his bedroom.

He started shivering from the cold and yearned to be under the covers. *Should I be able to* feel *cold when I'm dreaming?* He wondered.

A faint sound was coming from the ground floor. Something thumped onto the floor, and he thought it was coming from the living room beneath him.

The thump had a wet, almost *fleshy* quality to it. It was as if someone had dropped a large slab of raw meat.

After a few moments' silence, a new sound emerged.

A sliding, slithering along the floor, slow but somehow determined - as if the cause of the disturbance had a destination to reach. Although the noise was faint, he could discern the progress of whatever was causing it.

Across the lounge, perhaps turning to avoid his armchair and through the door into the narrow hallway beyond.

The snake (for that's what it must be, a giant, fanged, nightmare serpent, dripping venom) exited the parlour and headed for the stairs.

The sound took on a new quality, *thump-bump, thump-bump*.

And now, a *creak*. The sixth stair, which creaked every time it was stepped on, had been reached. Then, inexorably, *thump-bump*, followed after a few moments by a second *creak* as the rest of the serpent's scaly body traversed stair number six.

Even though he was cold, an itchy, fearful sweat broke out across his body (*you can't sweat in a dream*) as he stared up at the ceiling.

Knowing the nightmare would disperse like a grain of sand in a storm didn't prevent Slade's all-consuming fear at that moment.

The sound had now altered once again. *Thump-bump* was no more The thing's journey up the stairs having ended.

Once again came its shuffling progress, the sound joined by laboured breathing, - "*aaarrcch-garghhh,*" it went, "*aaarrcch-garghhh.*"

Given his state of near paralysis, Slade had to force his head to turn towards the door. Whatever horror lay in this dream, it would surely find its way to him.

"*Aaarrcch-garghhh, aaarrcch-garghhh.*" The breathing came from just outside the closed door to the bedroom. "*Aaarrcch-garghhh, aaarrcch-garghhh.*"

The doorknob jolted and then turned. *So not a serpent then*, he thought, *or perhaps a serpent with* hands.

The bedroom door opened slothfully, nudged from behind.

From Slade's position, he had a restricted view, and it appeared as if there was nothing to see. The monster that haunted his nightmare remained hidden.

With the room open to the rest of the house, Slade was overwhelmed by a stench (*you can't smell in your dreams*).

Cloying and cadaverous, he felt his gag-reflex kicking in. *It's the miasma of flyblown death*, he thought, bile burning the back of his throat.

Wet slithering and the laboured *"aaarrcch-garghhh,"* louder this time with the proximity of the nightmare creature.

The monster was travelling at floor level around the bed. He looked down, gasping from the pain in his neck and shoulders, along the length of his naked body, but could see nothing in the murky light.

Then, with utter horror, what he believed must be a fingernail (*serpents don't have nails*) scraped along the sole of his bare foot with agonising slowness.

He choked back a scream. The sensation was intense and, he thought with disgust, intimate, horrible - almost sexual. His scrotum tightened, balls shrinking into his body.

This ghastly violation over, Slade heard, once again, the monstrous, unseen form, continue its slow progress around the bed.

His intense terror caused him to dissociate, something he believed was impossible in a dream.

His awareness of his surroundings receded, and his field of vision, already limited by the mean light from outside, reduced.

With almost painful slowness, the nightmarish visitor hoisted its vast body onto the bed.

Slade's vision was greatly diminished, leaving him virtually blind and unable to identify the creature. The bed groaned and protested at the extra weight asserting itself onto the mattress.

Now he felt the body of the beast as it rested alongside him, hot flesh touching the length of his body, making him shudder uncontrollably.

The smell, already bad, became almost unbearable, filling the room with its overpowering and sweet odour.

The thing shifted, undulating against naked skin. It rubbed and vibrated against him.

"AAARRCCH-GARGHHH, AARRCCH-GARCHHH."

The entity breathed heavily into his ear.

"AAARRCCHHHH-GARCHHHHHHHH."

Longing to scream, he found himself voiceless, his throat tightening from the nightmare's grip.

He wept, hot tears coursing down the sides of his face. Yet, even in his terror, his penis stiffened from the experience of something, however unspeakable, touching him so intimately.

"*AAARCCH-GARCHHH.*"

Between the glottal, hot, sickly breaths he heard The Voice, close to his ear. The sibilant hiss commanded, "Take that child."

"What are you?" he asked, his voice trembling.

"I am you and you belong to me," The Voice told him.

When he awoke, Slade lay naked and vulnerable on top of his bed, semen drying to a crust on his stomach. The bedroom door was wide open, and the smell of rotten meat hung in the cold air like fog.

•   •   •

Mary MacDonald turned the contents of the document she held in front of her around her mind. She'd lost count of the number of times she'd read the letter. Even so, she struggled to make sense of it.

The letter, written in Lionel's childish, uncertain hand, arrived a day before his death. Most of the contents were gobbledygook.

Words crawled across the page and up and down the margins. There were random numbers and letters littered throughout. When she'd first received it, her instinct had been to throw it into the recycling, just a pointless reminder of an old man's troubled mind. However, she couldn't resist the urge to keep it safe.

Her final interactions with Lionel hinted at his declining mental state, as if his very identity was fragmented.

As her brother retreated into the past, he'd shared shameful stories of his mistreatment as a teenager in that terrible place.

He had wept those last few times, as he had tried to articulate how his life had long haunted him both in that terrible institution and in his own home, and how this had "destroyed" him.

Mary felt so sad. Lionel's life had been a difficult one. Haunted was correct. Abandoned even by his beloved mother.

As she stared unseeing at the letter, she wondered if Lionel had ever known happiness or peace. Had he ever loved or dreamed of a fulfilling life?

She focussed once again on the page in front of her, adjusting her reading glasses. In amongst the hectic jumble, one phrase stood out, repeated, and underlined, across both sides of the page:

Suffer the children. They go unto him. It must be stopped.

Not for the first time, Mary questioned what Lionel had been trying to convey.

Its repetition throughout the letter (*suicide note* popped into her mind) implied that that, whatever it was, he'd felt compelled to share with her.

Given the tone of his words and the bastardisation of a biblical quote, it must serve as an instruction. To do what? To stop the children or their suffering? Yes, perhaps, but to whom did Lionel believe the children were going, and where? Whoever the 'him' the repeated text mentioned was, she knew in her heart it wasn't God. If only Lionel had given 'him' a name.

She considered the detail of the letter.

As well as this repeated passage, Lionel referred to 'the music', 'the beasts of the sewers' and, several times, the number ninety-one.

She couldn't make sense of it and wondered if it meant anything. In what was left of Lionel's mind when he wrote it, the letter must have carried meaning.

With care, she re-folded the piece of paper, replaced it in its envelope, and tucked it back into her bureau.

Sitting back, she thought. Something was happening and had been happening for a long time. She did not know what it was, other than something quite beyond her understanding.

Mary had always been busy of mind. Now it wheeled on, thoughts tumbling over themselves like a great murmuration of starlings, turning, spinning on their own mysterious current.

Her thoughts settled, once again, on Tim Waverly. Whatever had haunted Lionel hadn't died with him, she was sure of it.

Should her attempt to warn Tim have been clearer? No, after all, she wasn't sure what she was warning him about. Other than he should abandon that cursed place.

Was there a real concern for him, or simply the anxious fussing of an old woman with little life and too much free time?

Mary removed her glasses and massaged her temples. Worried, yes, fussing, no, she told herself. She was certain something very bad was happening.

She couldn't yet know what role she had to play, or if she had a role at all.

CHAPTER NINE

"Tonight goes in the fuckit bucket :(!"

Message to Pig sent, Lucy, still miffed, threw her phone on the duvet, falling back into her mound of soft pillows.

Despite the ouija experiment, Lucy, with youthful resilience, rationalised the appearance of the words on the wall. Lying awake late into the night, she'd persuaded herself that it was old graffiti, nothing but a strange coincidence. Her reaction, which she considered hysterical, embarrassed her, while Pig seemed invigorated by it all.

Tonight's second ouija session, instigated once again by Lucy, but hosted this time at Pig's, had been a total bust and not for want of trying, although she had enjoyed the dinner prepared by his mum, Dorothy.

Her friend's commitment to the cause impressed her. He had filled his bedroom with candles (albeit filched from his mum and scented like summer blooms). He'd dimmed the lights and even spread a burgundy throw over his bed to add to the gothic atmosphere.

Posters of Stormzy and Harry Styles detracted from his efforts, but she'd maintained a diplomatic silence.

All of her friend's valiant preparations had been in vain.

The plastic planchette had turned into a mountain - unmoving. It sat, as if rooted at the board's centre. As they attempted to communicate with the spirits, it had remained that way, regardless of anything they tried.

Despite her terror during the first session, Lucy was frustrated by the lack of progress tonight.

Sitting back in the bed, dark hair loosely tied back with a scrunchie, she replayed the session in her head.

They'd done everything the same as before, albeit scented with God knows what, peonies maybe, yet the ouija was silent.

She realised, with something close to alarm, that there had been one major difference - they hadn't been in the dismal atmosphere of the abandoned orphanage.

As well as being a dead loss (har de har), she'd acted like a stroppy teen by descending into a pouting sulk, and was deeply ashamed about her behaviour.

Pig, mortified, had done his best to lighten the mood, revealing a packet of biscuits from under the bed and suggesting she helped him with the submission he was preparing about the Langham Hotel story, which he wanted to pitch to the Fortean Times.

Unmollified, Lucy had said "see ya" before flouncing off, having shoved the ouija paraphernalia into her rucksack.

To top the evening off, her mum had had a go at her for being back beyond her 9 p.m. weekday curfew and not thinking to text, while her dad's eyes hadn't shifted away from the television. *What a total fuckup.*

Checking her phone, silence from Pig, Lucy opened a textbook determined to at least have a go at revising. 'Comparative Religion in the 21st Century', *ugh*, she thought, *reading material set by the teacher/neighbour. What joy!*

For thirty minutes, she grappled with various arguments around crime and punishment from Muslim, Christian, and secular perspectives.

After a while, she realised she had attempted to read the same passage at least twice. Her head lolled on her slender neck and a baby cried in the distance.

She jolted upright and settled herself back, book in hand, once again.

Minutes later she drifted off, eyelids dropping and awareness of her surroundings dimming. Yet again she snapped into wakefulness and fumbled for her textbook, determined to read one chapter before turning in.

A few moments later, the textbook was gone, as was her bedroom and everything in it.

*　　*　　*

Lucy was standing in a moonlit field.

I must've been totally whacked, she thought, shivering. *Odd, to feel cold in a dream.* Looking down, she saw she was wearing a sweater, trousers, and sturdy walking boots, none of which she recognised. The freezing conditions bit painfully at her gloveless fingers, and she pulled the arms of the jumper over them.

She must be dreaming of winter, just a few weeks away. The ground was blanketed with undisturbed snow, giving no visual clue to the field's size.

The only item visible on the horizon was a sad-looking tree. Strong winds must have battered the tree throughout its life, causing it to stand hunched over itself like a gnarled question mark.

Yielding to the dream's logic, Lucy chose the tree as her destination, a marker summoned by her subconscious for some unknown reason. She crunched her way in that direction.

After a short time, she needed to stop to take a breather. She couldn't remember a time in which she'd had to rest in a dream, but the effort of wading through the snow, which reached up almost to her knees, was taking its toll and she wiggled her frozen toes in the boots.

An unfamiliar moon, which hung high in the sky, illuminated the pitiful tree. Behind her, disturbed snow showed her passage across the field. There was no sign of other life.

As a city girl, Lucy was unsure she'd ever been to a moonlit field. She didn't know what creatures would live in such a place. Owls, perhaps, or farm animals?

Shoving her freezing hands deep into the pockets of the trousers her dream self was wearing, Lucy set off towards the tree once again.

The blanket whiteness of the scene, coupled with the lack of daylight, made it impossible to judge the distance but the tree didn't seem to draw any closer. *Hardly surprising: this is a dream*, she thought, *and I seem to be in Narnia.*

On she trudged, accompanied only by the critch-crutch sound of boots sinking in the snow she was wading through, and the halo of smoky breath that surrounded her hatless head. Her hands and feet stung from the cold, and she wanted to wake up.

It felt like hours before she finally reached the tree but, she remembered from her studies, had likely been mere seconds in the real world of her bedroom. She forced a smile; her limbic system must be firing on all cylinders tonight.

As she arrived at her destination, Lucy realised that she had been right about the tree being hunched. In fact, it went beyond that.

The pitiable, ice-encrusted thing must have spent its life being battered by the elements before finally giving in, resigned to existing as a stunted, broken tragedy. It was bent so far that the gnarled uppermost tips of its bare branches were skimming the snowy ground opposite the thin trunk, rather than pushing into the sky above.

The tree's contortions had created an archway into the field beyond, although one could only catch glimpses of it as flashes of white through its tangled branches.

The twigs and branches formed a knot at the centre of the arch. It appeared more structural than natural.

She took a few steps back into the trench created by her boots and looked again. Yes. There was something. It had not been visible when she'd first arrived at the tree.

There was no obvious movement from the branches, but the image defined itself, like a photograph from an old Instamatic.

The archway changed. Something manufactured rather than a part of nature took the place of the twisted branches. After several minutes, a closed door filled the natural arch created by the tree's misshapen structure.

She circled the tree and saw the same door mirrored on the other side.

There was now a doorknocker. An ugly blackened brass thing in the shape of a ram's head.

Finding the dream increasingly weird, even by her standards, Lucy drew a frozen hand from her pocket and knocked on the door. What else could she do?

The expected reverberation never came. Instead, there was just a muffled noise–whomp. *Perhaps the snow's changing the way things sound?* she wondered.

In true gothic fashion, however, the door swung open on its great hinges with a reluctant creek. Lucy chuckled with amusement at the cliché her sleeping mind had offered as she made her way inside.

•   •   •

Behind the door stood a long corridor.

Dim yellowish lighting pulsed from bulbs placed in sconces lining the walls along the space. The walls themselves were the deep red of dried blood.

There were no artworks or adornments. A hideous floral carpet covered the floor, patterned with twisted vines and sickly roses.

The corridor stretched off into the distance with no end in sight.

The doorway and the field were gone. Lucy couldn't see any doors leading off the corridor.

Lucy, all thoughts of the cold winter forgotten, wondered how long she'd been sleeping - it could be minutes or hours. She hoped she would feel well-rested after such a busy night's mental exploration.

As she continued along the corridor, she noted the trousers and boots were gone.

Once again, she wore an outfit she wouldn't be caught dead in, a floral dress with a wide skirt and white ankle socks. She looked like an American character from a movie set in the 1950s. On her feet were plain white (*ugh*) pumps with low, dainty heels.

As she traversed the corridor, slightly nauseated by the pulsating quality of the lights, scratchy music began loudly playing, giving her a start.

Looking around, Lucy couldn't see any visible speakers or mechanisms with which to play music, but it sounded like some old-time record played by her dad on his beloved turntable.

The sound of many instruments playing a tuneless song filled the corridor. Countless voices, those of children, joined in, although it was impossible to make out any words. Behind the music, a man's laughter. It sounded insane.

The tuneless music faded away and began once again, as if on repeat.

Lucy, fearful, was keen for the dream to finish now and moved at a faster pace along the corridor, almost running in her ghastly little pumps.

The song repeated twice, three times more. Each time becoming slower, as if played on a gramophone that needed winding. Ultimately, it slowed, slowed, and mercifully stopped.

A drumroll reverberated like thunder along the corridor, BRRRRRRRRRR-TISH-ah!

A mime suddenly appeared in front of Lucy, causing her to halt in confusion.

It was a man.

White makeup caked his ageless face in a thick layer. He was wearing a black suit and tie, a blood-red shirt, and a top hat. His eyes were the blue of a frozen lake.

With a slight bow, the mime conjured a handful of silk flowers. Her fear forgotten for the moment, Lucy giggled and took them from his outstretched hand.

Next, he stared at her with an expression of unnerving intensity.

Then he changed his hold on his body, seeming to become larger, more muscular, and his jacket strained.

Holding up a finger, he shot her a quizzical look.

Standing back, he performed a flicking motion, and with slowness and a pained expression, demonstrated the slashing of his wrists. As he did so, he pulled a length of red silk handkerchief from each sleeve to signify the flowing blood.

"Cutting your wrists?" Lucy guessed, disturbed now.

The drumroll again, BRRRRRRRRRR-TISH-ah!

He placed a finger on the end of his nose and pointed at Lucy with a broad smile. His grin was a little too wide, his teeth a jaundiced yellow.

Next, the mime opened an invisible bottle and started pouring the contents into his mouth. After a few moments, he dropped the bottle and started clutching his stomach, wincing as he did so.

"Er, stomach ache?" Lucy said.

An invisible klaxon blared - UGHHH-ARRH!

His mouth drooping with sadness, he repeated the performance. Lucy thought for a moment. "Overdose?"

BRRRRRRRRRR-TISH-ah! The mime placed a finger on the end of his nose and gave a little bow.

Now a third scenario was underway.

He abandoned the larger persona and squatted down on all fours. The mime sniffed around the floral carpet, circling her in a way that made Lucy feel like her personal space was being invaded.

"Dog?!" she guessed. UGHHH-ARRH! roared the klaxon.

With his sad expression, the mime stared up, blue eyes watery and shot through with red. He placed a hand on his lower back and circled it three times.

"Oh, of course, Pig!" Lucy said.

The mime glanced up from the floor with a wink and his yellow smile.

He continued scurrying around and snuffling at the carpet as if seeking truffles. He then stopped, clutching his neck.

His body vibrated, and Lucy stepped back reflexively. His head shook from side to side, preternaturally fast.

Remaining silent, the mime clawed at his throat as foamy spit dribbled from his mouth.

As he convulsed, the foam-flecked spittle splashed against the walls on either side of the corridor. Lucy gasped with shock as a blob of thick phlegm, flecked with bright spots of blood, spattered the tops of her white shoes.

After what seemed forever, the mime's seizures began slowing before his chest stopped the rise and fall of life.

The white-painted face was a death mask, and those vivid blue eyes, half closed, stared sightlessly at the ceiling.

Lucy stared, panting with shock. "Pig dead?" she asked.

BRRRRRRRRRR-TISH-ah! echoed the drums.

•   •   •

Lucy awoke to a cold, drizzly morning.

Grabbing her phone from the floor, where it and 'Comparative Religion in the 21st Century' had fallen, she thumbed an urgent message to her best friend.

CHAPTER TEN

Sanjay felt like a big boy.

Harried, Anita allowed him to go to the mini mart alone for the first time. In truth, it wasn't much of an expedition. The corner shop was only twenty yards from their block, Oldfield Court, on the same side of the A-road. Sanjay wouldn't need to cross any traffic, but it still felt far from home.

In order to be allowed to fulfil his mission, he'd half-listened to his mother's lengthy lecture about road safety and 'stranger danger' and about the need to come straight home when his quest, to buy milk and eggs, was complete.

He'd been extra-excited when she'd passed him a five-pound note, telling him he could put any change in his Paw Patrol piggy bank. He was saving for Lego Batman figures.

Sanjay thought this to be an important moment in his life. He got ready and left the flat with the money carefully folded in his jeans' back pocket. He fastened his coat against the cold, had a pee before he left home.

He was excited to be allowed to perform such a grown-up task.

•   •   •

Slade had been drinking. Hard.

The Voice had taken over his life. He no longer visited the Dark Web or communicated with his online network. He stopped responding to messages from those who shared his own specific interests. He had no interest in his window-cleaning round.

The Voice was his constant companion.

It spoke to him in his dreams, wheedling about the importance of the Mistry boy. It shouted him awake and muttered while he ate. It made its demands when he was taking a shit.

He hated it and yet, in a strange way, he loved the rare sense of companionship it brought to his life.

Michael had started talking back. This was something he wasn't aware of, but it came naturally. Initially, he argued with The Voice, repeatedly emphasising that he would never harm or approach a child, no matter how much he longed to. He wasn't a monster.

His resolve was cracking. The Voice assured him that no trouble would arise since no one, including the police, could find the child or identify Michael as the kidnapper. This, it told him, was a solemn vow.

It was tempting.

If The Voice was being truthful, he could take the child without consequences. He could be happy for the first time in his life. Not alone.

No. He would never hurt a child. He held the whisky bottle up to the light, dim through the closed curtains. Squinting, he saw it was almost empty.

He needed to go to the shop.

•　　•　　•

Sanjay was having the best time. Yes, he knew his Mummy thought the Lo-Cost an ordinary place. But not for him.

Today he was Sanjay the Superhero! His quest? To find the magical milk (pint, skimmed) and jewelled eggs (half a dozen, medium), could only be accomplished by stealth. If he went into an aisle and saw another shopper, he'd have to find a different route.

Shoppers with trolleys were a particular danger, and he needed to avoid them at all costs. They were servants, collecting food to give to the dinosaurs hidden at the rear of the shop. In the alcohol aisle (Bad) he fancied he could hear Drunky, the fire-breathing dragon. Sanjay the Hero let the monster sleep and departed, leaving its snores in the distance.

He secured the milk and held it aloft, much to the bemusement of other shoppers. The first part of his quest was complete!

Now for the eggs, which would mean facing the danger of Cannibal Chicken.

•   •   •

Michael Slade had to dig around for his debit card, which he found in the dust-filled wasteland underneath the sofa. He'd buy three bottles of Scotch today, which would limit his need to leave the house. Maybe some beers too.

He was frightened about what he might do. Since The Voice had made itself known to him, he trusted himself less and less. The desire to take a child consumed him. To *play* with them.

As he shoved his feet into an old pair of trainers, pushing down the heels, he set the alarm by the front door. "You can't be too careful," he muttered to The Voice. "There are people who'd break in if you're only out for ten minutes."

The response came after a moment's silence, dripping with malice. "Bring me the child."

•   •   •

"Awright *indybum.*"

Sanjay's elation at having fulfilled his quest was short-lived. Peter Eames and his friend, who Sanjay thought was called Liam, were standing outside the mini mart waiting to pounce.

Peter, in the year above at school, was Bad and Sanjay did everything he could to avoid him in the playground. Now the boy, in a red hoodie and trainers which might have been white a long time ago, sneered, running his hands through greasy brown hair and pulling himself to his full height, rocking back on his dirty shoes.

"Is this your dad's shop then indybum? Does he live to *serve* the rest of us?"

Sanjay gave a small shake of his head. "Can't you speak English then?" Peter demanded.

"My dad's an account manager," Sanjay answered, no longer feeling like a hero. He was a small boy again. He hefted the carrier bag and started up the street.

"Don't go indybum, we're only havin' a chat with ya." Peter and the other boy, who remained silent, fell into step with him.

"There's lots of your sort round here, innit," Peter said. "Too many, that's what my dad reckons. I tell my dad, 'No, that's wrong. We need shopkeepers and people to clean up after us, right?'"

Sanjay walked faster, almost reaching the side of his building. He gave a small cry as Peter took him by the arm, pinching the sensitive skin just above his elbow.

"You're not going home, you indy*cunt*," Peter said. Maybe-Liam, silent, took Sanjay's other side, the older boys flanking him as they steered him along the A-road.

When they got to Oldfield Street, the boys manoeuvred Sanjay, who was blinking back tears, across the road. He prayed his Mummy could see him through the window. She must be keeping an eye out.

Arriving at the alleyway which ran behind the abandoned building, the place which invaded Sanjay's dreams, they came to a halt.

Peter Eames looked down at him. Sanjay, terrified, didn't have space in his mind to think about attempting to run the short distance to the doors of his building. "My dad," the freckled boy sneered, "says that people like you should live together in places like this," he gestured at the empty building.

"What do you reckon, eh? I think it's a good idea. I think you should move in there with all your indymates and eat curry, yeah." Maybe-Liam gave a snotty, wet snigger.

Hot tears streamed from Sanjay's eyes as Peter snatched the Lo-Cost carrier bag, which was still hanging, forgotten, from his fingers. "Oh, nice," the older boy said, "eggs."

After checking that nobody was around, he plucked an egg from the box and whacked it into the smaller boy's forehead. Sanjay's pain and humiliation were intense as the contents of the raw egg mingled, sticky, with his tears.

Peter laughed, pushing himself into Sanjay's dripping face. "You're a right egghead, ain'tcha?" He dropped the shopping bag, took Sanjay by the shoulders, and started shoving the smaller boy into the entrance of the alleyway, laughing and pointing at the wetness that had appeared on the front of the Sanjay's jeans.

•   •   •

Slade couldn't believe the opportunity presented itself.

He had checked and rechecked the lock on the front door as he left the house to fetch his whisky. As he closed the front gate, he walked with a slight swaying motion and needed to blink several times in order to focus his vision on the street in front of him.

Three boys were playing at the bottom of the road. He wished that he had his phone to hand in order to take a quick picture of their roughhousing. It was only as he drew nearer that he realised this wasn't a group of young boys at play.

He recognised Sanjay with a jolt, The Voice, screaming in triumph, searing into his mind like a brand. The smaller lad was crying as the others tried to push him into a dark alleyway.

Poor little mite, he thought to himself and let out a great roar, thundering towards the trio with surprising grace.

One of the other boys, an aggressor he was sure, looked up, alarm etched onto his broad, freckled face. He let go of Sanjay, nudged his friend, and gestured towards Slade, giving him the finger. The other boys then ran off, turning the corner onto the A-road, shouting obscenities, and left Sanjay alone.

"Hey, hey," Slade said as he reached towards the boy ("take him NOW!" The Voice shrieked), "you're okay. It's all over. What did they do to you?"

Sanjay looked up and tried to speak through hitching breaths. Slade knelt down and gazed at the boy. His beautiful face was streaked with tears and egg. "We need to clean you up, Sanjay," he said.

The boy's gaze held a mix of confusion and relief as he looked up at him.

"We don't want your mum to see you like this, Sanjay. She'll be angry. And you broke her eggs. I tell you what, come back to mine. We'll get you tidied up; she never needs to know you got in such a state."

Slade knew he'd crossed a line, that he'd gone further than he'd only ever dared to imagine, and he experienced a strange tangle of emotions, elation mingling with fear. The Voice was silent. All he could hear was the thunder of his own blood.

"Once you're fixed up, your mum won't need to be angry about what's happened. I'm bound to have some eggs we can swap in my house," he pointed, "it's only over there, Sanjay, with the red door. This can be our special secret. What do you think?"

When the boy didn't respond, Michael placed a large, gentle hand on Sanjay's narrow shoulders. "We can," his voice caught, "get you out of those wet trousers, run you a bath."

Sanjay placed his small hand in Michael's large palm as they turned towards the house.

Slade's excitement was to be short-lived. As he and his newfound friend had started towards the house, a faint sound came from behind them as someone cleared their throat. Turning, he was dismayed to see the determined expression on the MacDonald woman's wrinkled face.

"Oh, hello Mrs MacDonald," he forced a smile, "young Sanjay here was being bullied something awful, and I'm popping us to mine to get him cleaned up." He lowered his voice, "He's, you know, had a bit of an accident."

The woman stood and stared, unblinking, at his hand encircling the boy's, and he let go under the strength of her steely gaze.

"How kind of you. It's Mr Slade, isn't it?" she said. "Yes, very kind indeed. That said, it's clearly been upsetting for the boy, I'm sure, and he's so close to home." She shifted her gaze to the child and smiled. "Your mother will be pleased to see you, dear, and she'll not worry about you having got a bit grubby."

Slade wanted to protest but couldn't form the words. His excitement drained away; he was going to lose his prize so soon. In his head, The Voice cursed the old woman.

"Now, I think you live in Oldfield Court, young man. Do you know the number of your flat?" she asked.

Sanjay nodded up at the old lady and smiled. "Very well," she said. "I suggest you and I find your mother now. She will be pleased to see you. Thank you, Mr Slade, for being so kind. Come along."

Michael Slade stood slack jawed as the meddling old bitch steered Sanjay towards home. He feared he'd missed his chance for good.

•   •   •

Returning to his house, all thoughts of drink forgotten, Slade slammed the front door and disabled the alarm before The Voice raged.

"FOOL! USELESS IDIOT! THWARTED BY A PATHETIC, MEDDLING OLD WOMAN!" it screamed.

Michael sank onto the filthy sofa and closed his eyes. The Voice remained silent for a long time.

When it came again, it was no longer shouting. It was chatty almost. The Voice explained that Michael had run out of road. That there was nothing left, that's all she wrote, time to check out.

Opening his eyes, he stood up from the sofa and, blinking in the murky light, walked to the kitchen and filled a pint glass with tepid tap water. He then slowly swallowed the paracetamol he'd been stockpiling in case the authorities started taking an interest in him.

He kept a running total, losing count after he'd ingested thirty-six tablets. Taking more might trigger vomiting, and he didn't want to risk it.

The Voice instructed him to look at the coffee table. There was a straight razor he had never seen before. The Voice promised him that this would serve as the ultimate guarantee to end his useless life.

Sure, the paracetamol would do the job, but it wouldn't be fast or foolproof. If they discovered him before the end, they might pump his stomach and unearth his secrets.

Michael realised The Voice wasn't in his head anymore. It came from just behind his shoulder.

"Go on, you useless nonce," it urged, "get it over and done with. Just a slice down each arm, Michael. Starting below the elbow will be most efficient."

It paused. "I'm going to give you the time of your life. You are mine now."

Tears rolling down his cheeks, Michael Slade could only comply. The end, when it came, was quicker and less painful than he deserved.

CHAPTER ELEVEN

Several weeks went by and autumn landed on Oldfield Street like a bomb. The temperature dropped, the sky grew dark, and by Halloween, residents adorned various houses with carven pumpkins and leering skulls.

In the grey light of her kitchen, Mary sipped at her morning cup of tea and noticed that her hands were shaking. She gave a small, tired sigh and put the cup down on the counter.

Her night had been troubled. Of late, they all were.

She was often awakened by strange noises. Crying babies, tuneless music, the sounds of machinery of some kind, and the snuffling of unseen animals.

In her night-time imaginings she'd conjured many strange images to accompany the noises she'd heard (soon she would know close these had come to reality) and, in doing so, had scared herself half to death.

Despite her tiredness, Mary's mind spun around busy as ever, Lionel's *instruction* pressing itself once again to the forefront of her thoughts. She had re-read his letter the previous evening, trying in vain to parse meaning from his strange ramblings.

And as for Mr Waverly, what next?

She would need to speak with him further and, perhaps, she should share with him Lionel's letter. Yes, this seemed a sensible approach.

Despite the passage of time, she was none the wiser as to what Lionel had been seeking to impart (she had never considered sharing it with her sister, Cecily, whom she disliked). Perhaps Waverly would bring new insight. He was certainly an intelligent young man, albeit a little closed-minded, perhaps.

Decision made, Mary felt a little better. Actions, not thoughts, were required.

Throughout her life, she had been a woman who had confronted the challenges that manifested themselves. She was determined not to turn into an old woman quietly knitting in the corner just yet. Yes, Tim Waverly might seek to disengage, but that was something she needed to manage as and when.

Taking a long drink of tea, the word *haunting* came to her.

Despite the many strange occurrences that had taken place during her childhood, including the appearance of various other-worldly images in her own home and the swirling rumours about that terrible building at the end of the street, Mary had always resisted the notion that her house or her family were haunted.

After all, the strangeness stopped when Lionel left, but there was some activity when he briefly returned home years later.

But was it a haunting in the traditional sense? Surely things should be falling off the wall as if pushed by an invisible force, not pressing through from, well, somewhere else.

Perhaps *infection* might be a better description.

Yes. Something infected that building, and, for whatever reason, the virus was spreading and mutating. She pushed away the thought that Lionel had been the source of that infection.

This last led her to consider the spread of the disease. Where would it end? What dangers did it bring?

•　　•　　•

How fitting, Tim thought, that Halloween should begin with a fright.

Refreshed from a rare decent night's sleep, he was greeted by a new image.

Directly opposite his bed, a finger gestured, as if beckoning him into the wall. He did not know how or when it had got there. He was certain he could not have slept through intruders in the apartment.

He had spent the morning drinking too much coffee, feeling the flutter of his heart and the tightness of a tension headache. He sought to rationalise, once again, what was happening.

There must *be* a rational explanation.

Perhaps his occupancy and temperature fluctuations may have led to the marks bleeding through the walls. This made some sense, he told himself, as he started thinking about lesson prep for the upcoming school week.

Walking along the street the previous evening, he had noticed that several neighbours were getting into the spirit of the season. Carved pumpkins and various sprites adorned people's front gardens and Louise Sanglin had festooned her place with fake spider webs.

These 'webs', he noted with amusement, were filled with plastic spiders ranging from the tiny to the downright grotesque. Sure to give some of the local children nightmares, and some parents, too.

Smiling to himself, he determined to spend his Halloween evening with a bottle of wine, a takeaway and Netflix and, he hoped, free of trick-or-treaters or those trying to get into a creepy old building for a dare. In order to reduce the possibility, he had double-checked any window grilles that were easily accessible from ground-level.

Late morning, as he girded his loins for a visit to the DIY store, bound to be mayhem, he heard a sharp rap echoing from the main door. The quality of the knock was such that he fancied he could guess the identity of his visitor before seeing them. He was correct.

"Halloween, tsk," Mary greeted him, clad in a plaid poncho and jaunty green beret, "ghastly American import."

"Actually, the Scots and Irish imported it *to* the States," Tim said, beckoning her inside. "It's been re-imported."

Mary raised an eyebrow. "Thank you for explaining that to me, Mr Waverly."

Tim smiled and held up his hands. "Sorry, teacher - occupational hazard, I'm afraid. I expect you'd like a cup of tea?"

"I could murder one, you're most kind."

•　•　•

Making herself comfortable on the sofa, placing her handbag next to her, Mary tried and failed to ignore the defacement on the wall. She considered it for a few moments. *Yes, the mark is more defined,* she thought, with an involuntary shiver.

She imagined the hand, clammy, around her neck. Squeezing the breath from her body.

A clatter of teacups interrupted her train of thought, and her new neighbour called over that he would be civilised and make a pot instead of throwing teabags straight into a mug. "To do what do I owe the pleasure?" he asked as he poured the tea and offered Mary a biscuit, which she declined.

Mary had a sip of her tea and took a breath. "Mr Waverly, Tim," she began, "I've been thinking of what to say for some time. Now I'm here to say it. I want you to do me a favour."

Tim sat back in his chair. "Yes, of course," he said, with the hesitance of one who doesn't know what's being asked of him.

"I want you to listen, Tim," she went on. "I want you to listen without interruption and, if you have questions, would you be so kind as to wait until I've finished speaking?"

She smiled. "Put yourself in the shoes of one of your pupils." He nodded his assent and dunked a biscuit into his tea.

Mary placed her cup and saucer on the low table next to her. "I may be old, Mr. Waverly, but not foolish. I'm not prone to flights of fancy.

"I consider myself to be a pragmatist. Nevertheless, I can see that something's badly awry. And it is, oh yes, most certainly. Look around you, Tim. I'm sure you've found other images, marks that you cannot easily explain?"

He nodded.

"Perhaps the place is defective somehow, you ask yourself. Possible but, I would say, improbable however much you might hope it to be the case." She paused and took a sip of tea.

"Lionel was my brother, and, for all his troubles, I loved him. Until the end of his life, he remained alone, living off a small forces pension and welfare payments. He became reclusive, a shut-in, as they call them now, refusing to take any support from me or our sister.

"He was a product of his lived experience, like the rest of us. His life had been cruel in many ways. Loved and then shunned by his...that is to say, *our* family. For no fault of his own, in my belief. Thrown out of his home and institutionalised, most likely abused, at an impressionable age. After the family's rejection, Lionel's lot in life was to remain lonely and without love.

"After my husband died, I implored my brother to move in with me. We could have kept each other company. He refused.

"I was disappointed. He told me that what he'd experienced in the house terrified him so much, that the impact on his life had been so negative, he couldn't risk it.

"These images," Mary gestured at the handprint opposite, "*consumed* him. They ruined *everything*. They wrecked his childhood and destroyed his life.

"I already explained that, when Lionel was sent away from home, the images faded away. And they started appearing here, in this god-forsaken place. I only learned this sometime later.

"I can see your expression, Tim. My eyesight remains quite sharp. Now, here's the thing. I don't especially believe in hauntings, ghosts and all those fripperies. At least not in the traditional sense. I've always trusted in the tangible and empirically supported. I'm not about to suggest placing salt in your doorways.

"Nonetheless, you really must accept that strange things are happening, things which defy any obvious explanation. I understand, believe me, I do, the importance of finding rational ways to explain things. I've wrestled with it myself over a number of years. Yet now, with Lionel in his grave, it's all starting again.

"Well, then. I've said my piece, and now I'm sure you wish to have me carted off to the funny farm. Be that as it may, before I go you need to take a look at this." Tim was obviously working hard to keep his face neutral as she snapped the clasp on her handbag, drawing out the crumpled envelope which she handed to him. "I received this from Lionel just prior to his death."

•   •   •

The paper Tim took from the envelope was creased and faded. It was unlike any letter he'd ever seen.

Dense writing filled the page on both sides, crawling up the margins and in the spaces between lines.

He had a strong mental image of an old man desperate to impart his final thoughts before it was too late. Tim thought it a small and very personal tragedy. Peering at the text, he made out numbers alongside the words. *91* appeared several times throughout, often underlined so hard the pen had almost torn through the page. It must highlight some meaning, significant only to Mr Bracken.

There were other repeated phrases:

"Must not write K-----. It is a source of yet greater strength."

"Suffer the children. They go unto him. It must be stopped."

"I am a prisoner," Tim muttered, looking closer. No, that wasn't it, "I am a *prison*," he said.

"Well?" He looked up when Mary spoke. Lost in the document, he had almost forgotten her presence. She stared at him now with a beady expression and a half-smile.

"You'd better come and see the others," he said, returning to her the final ravings of the brother she had lost.

•   •   •

Michael Slade's body lay leeching gasses, where it had fallen to the floor facing towards the curtained windows.

The carpet, cream when new and latterly grey with dirt, was stained burgundy with the blood pumped out by Slade's dying heart when he'd opened his wrists.

An expert could have determined the timeline of death from the state of the cadaver. The lack of oxygen in the body had caused the cells to seize up. This, combined with the body's mottled complexion, gave the impression of a waxen model rather than that of a human being.

Given the fact nobody cared enough about Slade to notice anything was amiss, he would soon become a veritable feast for a host of insects (attracted by the intense aromas of congealed blood and voided bowels) and microscopic bacteria. Dead, he was destined to provide more enjoyment for one cohort of Earth's creatures than he ever did in life.

Like most people, Michael had wondered what death would feel like.

When it happened, he hadn't witnessed his miserable life flashing before his eyes. There was no golden tunnel. The voice of his long-dead mother didn't call out, pushing food on him.

What he experienced surprised him. A tug. Just as he lost consciousness, and the pain of dying was starting to recede. It wasn't small, more of a *yanking*, like powerful hands pulling head from neck. Once, twice, then three times the pulling, tugging, and yanking, followed by the bizarre sensation of bursting out of himself.

Michael, in his dying moments, heard The Voice again. It was not the voice of any god.

"Come along now, much to be done."

•   •   •

Mary, standing in the grim old bathroom, tutted to herself.

Like the images from her childhood, the smile had the appearance of a burn mark. The detail was quite astonishing in its way. She could almost *feel* the rictus of the lips pulling back from the uneven teeth.

A long nose, jawline and chin suggested something almost Punch-like and gave a greater illusion of depth - increasing the impression that it was *pushing* from within the bones of the building.

"At first it was just the eyes, which were unnerving enough," Tim was saying. "The rest is new."

She leaned in closer and gave a small gasp. "There's colour here!"

"What? There can't be."

There was. An ever-so-faint, yellow staining to the teeth. In addition, there was a redness to the preternaturally stretched lips.

"This is a new thing. There was no colour before," he said. "All the other marks are colourless, I'm sure of it. It's utterly bizarre."

Tim rushed out of the room. Mary glanced at the image one last time with a small shudder. She had an irrational desire to change her own expression, to mimic the grin on the wall. Biting on the inside of her cheek, she followed Tim from the room.

She found him sat, head in hands, in the armchair in his apartment. Looking up, deathly pale in the grey light leaking from the mean windows, he pointed to the handprint, "Colour in this one, too." Mary gave only a cursory glance, knowing it to be true.

"Regrettably, Tim, I was right," she said without satisfaction. "Whatever is happening, it's escalating."

He appeared despairing. "I just can't understand it. I consider myself completely level-headed, yet I now believe I've got ghostly marks appearing all around me. What the fuck am I supposed to do?" Mary tutted at his language. "Sorry Mary," he said, "I feel like my head's about to explode."

She gently patted his arm and suggested more tea.

•   •   •

Sanjay was fed up.

He'd been looking forward to trick or treating, only to find neither of his parents was prepared to accompany him (Anita had told him she had her "mummy pains" and wasn't going *anywhere*. She'd forgotten to see if any other parents would help. Chetan, tired from work, wasn't interested). Given his state upon returning from the shop the other week, there was no way they were letting him out without adult supervision.

Sanjay made do with watching the festivities from his perch in the front room. Loads of witches had passed by, some of whom he thought were properly scary. There had also been a couple of teenagers in hockey masks waving plastic machetes and a brace of spacemen. Nobody had rung their buzzer, no doubt mindful of the fact his flat remained undecorated, despite his pleas.

A giant snagged his attention.

Well, not a giant, but a very large man. The giant stopped in the street opposite, his wide back turned. He seemed fixated by the old, abandoned building that Sanjay always felt drawn to. Sanjay found his focus homing in on this one character, and he was oblivious to the Simpsons walking past with a Walking Dead, all screaming and laughing.

The giant was undoubtedly the most frightening thing Sanjay had seen tonight, or maybe ever. His young mind couldn't explain why. Slowly, the giant rotated his bulk, refocusing his attention until he seemed to look directly through the window at Sanjay.

The giant's face, barely illuminated by the streetlights, was impossible to make out, yet his eyes stood out, glinting red in sharp relief amid hidden features. He was familiar, but where from?

The shape lifted a hand and waved, long fingers waggling. Whoever it was, Sanjay knew he was Bad. He ducked beneath the window-ledge and took his time counting to ten.

When he looked out of the window once more, the giant was gone.

•   •   •

"It's Wednesday Addams!"

Lucy, swathed in her usual layers of black and purple, heard the shout as she entered the recreation ground. She turned around - surprise, surprise, Angela (never Angie or, God forbid, Ang) Bloxham and her posse of mean girls were standing at the entrance vaping, bottles of cheap cider in hand. Angela was wearing a virtually translucent witch costume.

"Hello Ang, you must be cold, I can see your nipples!" Lucy called back, smiling sweetly, satisfied with the look of irritation that passed across Angela's slightly too-broad-to-be-pretty face.

Pig, having decided they were too old for knocking on people's doors, had told her some of the St. Isaac's kids were congregating here this evening. She found him by the mosaic jubilee bench, next to the children's play area, noticing a bunch of St. I's lads were making use of the swings.

Pig passed her a small bottle of lager and she took a sip, screwing her eyes shut at the sour flavour. He shook a bag of Frazzles at her, which she declined. He, shrugging, upended the bag and tipped the remaining contents into his mouth.

"You're disgusting!" she said with a laugh. He grinned at her, his smile bright and reassuring in the evening's gloom.

Like her, Pig hadn't donned a costume, his sole concession to the spooky festivities being a heavy layer of dark makeup around his eyes, which gave him a hooded, moody appearance. Lucy was always struck by his good looks, especially since he was completely unaware of them.

They clinked their bottles. "Over your dream yet?" he asked, knowing her reaction to it had left her embarrassed.

"Weirdest mind-fuck ever," she said. "Probably something I ate round at yours; I blame your mum's cooking." He laughed.

Lucy thought it was a pleasant way to spend a Halloween evening, as she and Pig drifted around chatting to various kids from school. As the night wore on, the shouts of smaller children faded away as their parents took them home, too wired for sleep from scoffing treats.

The St. Isaacs teens became louder with drink and the odd sneaky cigarette or joint, running up to one another screaming "boo!" and grabbing their friends in the dark.

By 10:00 p.m. the crowd at the rec. was thinning out. Teenagers were drifting off and, mindful of parental curfews, they chewed gum to hide the smell of drinks and smokes.

"Oh, bloody hell he's creepy!" Lucy and Pig were the last left at the bench as she gave him a sharp nudge in the ribs.

"Ouch, fuck Luce, watchya do that for?" he asked, slurring.

"Glance, but don't *stare*," she instructed.

•   •   •

Sanjay sat up in bed with a start. He had been dreaming of the giant. He thought he recognised the man, but in his dream, the man's face was blank, apart from those scary eyes.

•   •   •

Ignoring Lucy's warning, Pig stared, sobering up. Silhouetted against the night sky, a tall, broad figure was standing stock-still by the fence outside the play area, a few metres from some oblivious St. Isaac's kids staggering their way home. The man had his hands inside his trousers, as far as he could tell. *Gnarly*, he thought.

Pig jumped up onto the bench for a better look, ignoring Lucy's protestations, "Pig, he'll see us!"

A voice sliced through the night air. "Lucy and Piggy playing in the dark," it called, "wary of strangers lurking in the park." There was a high-pitched, almost girlish giggle.

Pig, filled with the bravado provided by cheap supermarket lager, decided he was not having this. Leaving Lucy, he leaped, stumbling, off the bench and made his way across the dewy grass to confront the strange man. He heard Lucy calling out, telling him to leave it alone.

Odd, he thought, arriving at the play area's far side where the stranger had been standing. There was no one there. He glanced around and spotted the figure illuminated by moonlight on the opposite side of the rec. Pig was confused. *Nobody can move that fast,* he thought, giving chase.

As he ran, he saw the man flash a smile, lifting his hand in a brief salute before turning and walking away. Pig spotted his chance. The only exit on that side of the park was onto Brudenell Road. He could catch up with the weirdo as he made his way from the rec.

Having achieved a turn of speed he was unfamiliar with, Pig was unaware of Lucy catching up behind him. Seeing the man's slow walk into Brudenell Road, he followed at a jog. Making it to the park exit, he vaulted over one of the bollards, which kept cars out of the recreational area, shouting "Oi, perve!"

A dog, roused from slumber by the boy's yell, barked from somewhere up ahead as Lucy pulled alongside him, panting. An artificial spider web drifted lazily in the breeze and a dying candle flickered in a gutted pumpkin, carved into a leering obscenity and propped on someone's wall. Of the stranger, there was no sign.

"Home time," said Lucy with a sigh.

CHAPTER TWELVE

Tim Waverly found himself in an endless corridor. The walls were blood red, lined with dark flock wallpaper with a brocade relief. Dim lightbulbs, pulsating, spilled sickly yellow light like that of dusk on a stormy day.

He realised he could feel carpet under his feet, which were bare and, looking down, he could examine its chintzy pattern of swirling vines and gaudy blooms. *Oddly specific for a dream,* he thought, bemused, digging his toes into the weave.

Tim gave a start as a whooshing, clanking sound reverberated across the space. It sounded, he thought, something like a vast boiler cranking into life.

From afar, a faint voice whispered, "Hello? Is someone else here?"

· · ·

Lucy felt disconcerted to find herself, once again, in the mime's corridor. Just like her previous visit, she looked around. There were no doors, windows, or entrances (or exits) visible, only flickering bulbs in sconces. She was taken aback to find herself dressed in her loathed blue and yellow St. Isaac's uniform, a uniform she could finally leave behind once she started the 6th form.

Lucy knew recurring dreams were a function of her subconscious mind (she couldn't blame the food at Pig's for this one) and she'd have to let things play out. She refused to allow herself to be scared anymore.

Although there was no sign of the creepy mime, awareness dawned on her that she wasn't alone in the corridor. She turned, looking behind her. Nothing. Despite that, the sense of someone close by persisted. It was almost comforting - benevolent.

A great whooshing noise crashed its way through the space. It reminded her of a sound that always made her jump - when travelling in a high-speed train that shoots through a tunnel - and her stomach lurched. Silence descended once again, although she could hear the sound of the 'train', faint in the distance.

There! In the corner of her eye, someone else - a movement, little more than a flicker of another person (a man perhaps?) a shade, gone almost as soon as she'd registered it.

"Hello?" she asked, her throat dry. "Is someone else here?" She waited in vain for a response.

·   ·   ·

The unknowing companions, teacher and pupil, travelled the corridor together. He barefooted, the patterned weft of the dirty carpet crunching under his soles, she in ugly/sensible black school shoes, badly in need of a polish.

The journey was long and tiring.

Strange sounds filled the space. A high-pitched crying, that of a baby perhaps. Farmyard animals, cows lowing, sheep bleating and the scream of goats. It was impossible to determine from where these sounds emanated from, but they appeared to be traversing the corridor.

At one point a scratchy old-time record played, loud as if from hidden speakers. It was impossible to discern a tune. Many instruments played out, joined by the voices of a multitude of children. The effect was as unsettling as it was disorientating.

The song, if it could be called a song at all, repeated three times, the third echoing round the space. It slowed, as if played on a gramophone that had run out of motor, before ebbing away into silence.

The atmosphere in the corridor changed. Its uniform appearance: red walls, patterned carpet, flickering bulbs, made it impossible to know how far the dreamers had come, but the space narrowed. Each of them was certain the walls were closer together, the ceiling lowering towards the floor. The impact was mildly claustrophobic. It was like having a change in perspective forced upon them.

As well as registering this shift, Tim could feel a change underfoot. Although the ugly carpet was still there, it was no longer crispy under his feet - it was hard and cold.

In her dream, Lucy gave an involuntary gasp. In his, Tim fell to his knees.

Just ahead the floor, walls and ceiling slowly *knitted* themselves together. The effect like time-lapse photography was almost organic and disorientating. Vines which were woven into the carpet merged with the brocaded walls, bulbs popped, and the light dimmed further. The endless corridor was ending *itself*.

They stepped forward.

•　　•　　•

The corridor's violent change was complete. Before them stood a large metal-studded oaken door, blackened with age. In the centre of the door, a ram's head doorknocker, pockmarked with verdigris.

Simultaneously the pair, still hidden from one another (although each had seen the occasional movement, a tiny moth-like flickering from the corner of their eyes), reached out with a trembling hand and pressed against the cold surface of the door. Both registering a sound very much like a grief-stricken sigh as the great portal opened before them.

The space beyond was vast.

The corridor and the door through which they had entered were gone. A great vaulted ceiling, like the dome of a cathedral, soared above them, suspended by thick wooden beams. The floor consisted of filthy blood red tiles, cold and gritty against Tim's soles.

Lucy turned around in the (her) space. The room was so large she could just make out its distant walls. The ceiling soared hundreds of feet above the red floor.

Strange metal structures of varying sizes littered the room. These appeared to be machines, or pieces of machinery, their purpose unclear.

Walking forward, Tim gingerly, the detritus on the floor cutting painfully into his feet, it seemed there was something almost domestic about the space, a pastiche of a home.

In one area, two old leather Chesterfields sat facing one another, a dirty, faded rug filling the space between them, a dead pot plant on a stand. In another stood an ancient bed, its stained mattress supported by a somehow vicious iron frame (Lucy imagined being chained to it and shuddered). Tim was reminded of the old beds in the orphanage - the stains resulting from bodily fluids.

Something resembling a kitchen stood near the possible centre of the room. It was nothing as welcoming as a real kitchen. This was not the heart of a home. Utensils, pots, and pans were hanging from lengths of rope anchored to the vaulted ceiling high above. A nightmarish metal range cooker banged, clanged, and hissed; waves of angry heat pushing out into the room.

Lucy found herself terrified.

The tiny hairs on Tim's arms stood up.

Footsteps echoed around them. They both turned around to locate the source. The sound of the steps bounced around the space, merging with the roaring range and the sudden shriek of a baby's cries.

Silence fell. It was louder, somehow, than the cacophony that proceeded it. From an unseen source, a bright spotlight highlighted a distant area of floor. A dark-suited gentleman stepped into the pool of light and gave a genial wave. As he stepped forward, making his way to each individual visitor, the spotlight moved with him.

As he got closer, it became easier to make out his features. The man was *old* (Lucy) *distinguished* (Tim). He appeared to be about six feet tall. Sparse grey hair swept across a mottled scalp, receding from a strong, deeply lined forehead, and his eyes flashed the blue of a robin's egg. The man's well-fitted suit was black, his shirt red. A tarnished silver pin, shaped like a ram's head, held a black tie in place.

This man smiled; his teeth were tinged yellow.

"Greetings," he said in cut-glass English, voice stentorian, with a little bow. "Welcome to my house! Enter freely, go safely, and leave some of the happiness you bring."

He chuckled as he stepped up to them, somehow too close.

•   •   •

"How thoughtful of you to drop by Tim," the stranger said with a wide smile, blue eyes locking onto those of the young teacher. "I hope I may call you Tim as opposed to Mr Waverly; we don't stand on ceremony here."

Tim, his head spinning, nodded with a weak smile.

There was an awkward pause and, realising the man was waiting for him to speak, he nodded once again, adding, "Tim's fine. What should I call you?" There was no answer. The man's eyes travelled the length of his body.

"Goodness, but your attire!" the stranger said. "You're a teacher, not a ragamuffin." He sniffed, the corners of his mouth turning down. "You're like a little shoeless savage. My goodness, hardly appropriate dress in which to pay a visit."

With a final, dismissive glance, the stranger walked towards the kitchen area.

• • •

At the same time, the dream man greeted Lucy.

"How nice of you to swing by Miss Lucy Warwick," he said, "and in your dinky uniform too. Better than that black and purple getup you seem to favour." His gaze went to the floor. "And wearing shoes, no less. Would you believe some people pay a visit without their shoes?" he tutted. "So disrespectful. This is my home, not a beach. Although I think, perhaps, there might be a beach around here somewhere. All sand and screaming gulls."

Lucy stood, frozen with shock. The moment the strange man had greeted her, she recognised his voice. It was the voice she heard in her bedroom, the one Pig referred to as the "horny ghost." Now he was invading her dreams.

"I'm going to have some fun with you, oh yes," he went on gleefully. Lucy had a twinge of nausea at the sight of the old man's pointed yellow teeth so close to her face.

"Will you have fun, Lucy? Shh, don't answer that."

He pressed a long finger, cold, to her lips. "I'm afraid you won't have any fun at all. You and your special friends, including those you have yet to meet, will have a terrible experience. Honestly, rotten. Your presence in this place was not required; my endeavours are not for the likes of you." He clapped his hands together. "No matter, it's not about you at all. This time is all about me."

Blue eyes sparkling, the man gave a cheeky wink, turned, and walked toward the kitchen area.

• • •

The pair, standing so close and yet unseen to their companion, watched as the man strolled at a leisurely pace, highly polished shoes tapping on the grubby floor, into the kitchen area.

He stood, facing them, behind a roughly hewn stone island, in front of the roaring stove, and lifted his arms.

"I am Dr Cresta," he proclaimed. "With a K."

Lowering his arms, Dr Kresta smiled at them, it was almost a sneer. Once again, Tim felt the hairs on his arms prickle.

"It's sooooo good to be back in business!" Kresta surveyed his nightmarish domain.

On the stone countertop in front of him, which had been empty, stood a vast pile of vegetables. Peeled potatoes, leeks, onions, parsnips, cauliflowers and more. Lucy's stomach gave an involuntary rumble.

Kresta removed his jacket, throwing it into the darkness beyond the spotlight. Rolling up his shirtsleeves, he revealed sinewy forearms dotted with wiry grey hairs. They watched as he threw vegetables into a great metal container, which he slammed into the fiery range.

"Come closer. You may assist me with the main course," he commanded. They were compelled to walk to the island. They had no choice. "Now," Kresta smiled, "some meat to go with the veggies, I think. Something chewy and *plump*."

Reaching beneath him, he came up with a cloth-covered bassinet carved of rough black stone. Grunting, he settled the bassinet onto the worktop and with a flourish, removed the covering. Coddled within was an infant, a baby boy, hairless, pink, and podgy. It smiled up at Kresta, gurgled, and raised its fleshy hands toward him. Turning to his horrified guests, Kresta said, "I do hope you're as hungry as I am."

Standing back from the island, he locked his eyes on them. *They're so blue*, thought Tim, madly.

"Put the baby in the oven," Kresta commanded.

Both resisted with every fibre of their beings. It was futile. Once more they felt compelled, *pushed* into fulfilling Kresta's wishes. Both, straining, found themselves forced to lift the heavy stone basket, the baby staring up at them vulnerable, starting now to cry, confused.

They placed the bassinet onto the top of the cooker before reaching down to open its heavy iron door. Both reeled at the hellish blast of unbearable, unimaginable heat and smoke from the cooker's clanking innards.

Weeping, they heaved the bassinet from its position on top of the cooker and placed it in the oven, its door closing with a booming metallic clang like the bell of some nightmarish Satanic church.

From within the oven, the baby's screams became inhuman, the soundtrack of the slaughterhouse. Its howls rent the air. The entire universe must have been able to hear its agonies, a scream that would reverberate through the ages.

Lucy and Tim, their own screams joining with those of the baby, found themselves locked in Kresta's icy stare. "I like it slow roasted," he said. "It's best when the meat falls off the bones."

He emerged with another bassinet from beneath the counter. "Too hungry to wait," he intoned, his voice now changed to something dark and monstrous.

He looked over at them, thick threads of saliva running down his chin. "Here's one I prepared earlier," and whipped off the cloth covering.

• • •

Lucy awoke, a scream fighting to dislodge itself from the back of her throat. Her pillow was wet from her tears.

• • •

Tim fought his way from the depths of sleep. He was like a man struggling not to drown. Wakefulness came in increments, and at last he recognised his bed and lodgings, illuminated in the glow of the streetlights.

Reaching over, blood rushing in his ears, he switched on the bedside lamp and eased his legs from under the covers. They cramped as if he'd been for a long walk. His feet were filthy and bloodied as if from walking on a dirty stone floor. Feeling the moisture on his face, Tim allowed the tears to fall.

• • •

At Oldfield Court, Anita Mistry ran into her little boy's bedroom, having been shaken from a deep sleep by his screams. Sitting on the bed, she shushed him, stroking his hair and reassured him he'd had a nightmare; everything was safe.

With a single glance, Sanjay's frightened eyes spoke volumes, cracking her heart. "They put a baby in the cooker," he whispered.

CHAPTER THIRTEEN

Over the following week, various events happened on Oldfield Street, with most being unremarkable and commonplace. With Halloween and Guy Fawkes' Night over, the residents' thoughts had turned to Christmas.

The council finally dealt with the fallen leaves. Rain and an unusually hard frost for London turned the pavements into something approximating an ice rink. Mary MacDonald had taken a tumble, an incident which made her feel every one of her years. Consequently, she had resorted to carrying a walking stick with her on any excursions from the house.

Sean and Andrew, Shandrew, had a panic attack after their beloved dog, Molly, was taken ill, requiring multiple visits to the local vet, and causing the cancellation of all their planned social engagements. The vet suspected the dog ate acorns while out with the walker. A strict no-acorn diet brought relief to both the dog and the couple.

Sanjay Mistry forgot the details of his nightmare, so that was a blessing. In order to avoid a repeat of his fear, he spent a few nights sandwiched between Anita and Chetan in the (relative) safety of their bed, much to his parents' mutual irritation.

Tim's expectations and fears came true as the ghostly smile turned into a complete face. The face, in its entirety, was grotesque. It put him in mind of a grinning death mask. Over several days, the amount of visible colour increased and revealed the unmistakable features of the man from his dream, Dr Kresta. Blue eyes, vivid and teeth, yellowed, stared from the wall. The lips were stretched in an unhuman grin.

Tim drove his Kia to the DIY warehouse for paint but gave up on the idea. He thought covering the marks would only provide a temporary fix. He didn't alert the Guardian Angels. He needed to avoid eviction and being forced once more into expensive accommodation which he could ill afford.

On the Friday, Tim forced himself to go into town and spent a drunken evening with a bunch of acquaintances from his teacher-training days. Over multiple drinks, they had shared horror stories about timetables, angry teens, and passive-aggressive colleagues. Someone ribbed Tim over his move from the state sector and into a fee-paying school ("That's not teaching, it's babysitting the precious offspring of the idle rich," someone else had tipsily opined, punching Tim on the arm).

Returning home drunk, he noticed that the handprint in his apartment was joined by its pair. The hands reached from the wall as if seeking purchase around his neck. "Oh, fuck off!" he'd grumbled before collapsing, fully clothed and paralytic, onto his bed.

During the same week, Lucy and Pig had, at her behest, given up on plans for further sessions with the ouija board. Pig had been a bit put out. He loved the excitement and creepiness of it all, but, after Lucy described the horrors of her dream, he'd been compelled to comply with her wishes.

She had been so freaked out that she arranged a sleepover at his house. Fuelled by Pig's secret snack stash, they had concluded that her dreams were a symptom of stress about the first ouija session and her continued inability to knuckle down to her studies.

At number fourteen, bills and takeaway flyers piling up inside the front door, food spoiling in the fridge, the remains of Michael Slade continued to rot, hastened by the unceasing on-off cycling of the heating system.

• • •

Leaning on her hated new walking stick, Mary checked the seal and stamp on the envelope before popping it in the letterbox. *There, done* she thought, with a measure of satisfaction.

Made aware by Tim of the increasing number of images he was seeing in the old institution (he had chosen not to mention anything about the dreams), Mary considered it best to act.

She was sure that her late brother Lionel must be at the root of what was happening, or, at the very least, the strange letter he'd sent her before his death implied some kind of insight into events.

Given this, she had taken it upon herself to write to her ghastly sister who lived on the Isle of Wight. Lacking her email address, she decided a well-worded letter would be the appropriate means of contact. Although she had disliked her sister since childhood, Mary recognised she had been influenced by Lionel's accounts of his twin's behaviour toward him. She and Cecily rarely spoke, contact limited to birthday and Christmas cards, and had never discussed Lionel's childhood or incarceration in that benighted place.

As she wanted to elicit information, she had elected to be direct. She asked whether their brother had ever kept a journal, or a record of the strange events that shaped his childhood and later life.

She was determined to discover how much her sister knew about the uncanny occurrences and, with faint hope of a response, had included her email address and social media handles.

Now, she supposed, as she made her careful way back along the street to her home, pausing for a brief chat with Shandrew, walking a much improved and boisterous Molly, it was a waiting game. Would Cecily ignore the letter and tear it up? Probably, but Mary hoped this appeal to her sister's better nature, if she possessed such a thing, would pay dividends.

Returning home, she put the kettle on to brew tea, her thoughts turning once again to Tim Waverly.

She was concerned about him. When he had knocked on her door a couple of days ago, his face had a haunted, sunken look as if he had experienced rapid weight loss or a period of ill health. His mousy hair was in disarray and in need of a barber's attention and, Mary noted, his sweater was inside out.

Truth be told, she thought, taking a warming sip of tea, she felt sorry for him. Tim, a good man, faced horrendous circumstances that would make anyone feel disheartened.

Despite her reluctance to interfere, she felt it was the right thing to do. The bizarre occurrences were not confined to that awful place, she was certain. Tim shouldn't face things alone.

Regardless, she had stepped in now. Mary was not a woman prone to regret her actions. The letter had gone and, she prayed, might trigger a response from Cecily. Until then, she would watch and wait before deciding if further action was required.

•   •   •

Later that evening, around 10:00 p.m.:

Mary sat, propped up in bed with her Kindle, lost in Louise Penny's snowy Canadian landscapes.

Back in the apartment, Tim had concluded his rounds through the building and was concentrating on lesson planning, fortified by a bottle of supermarket plonk and Spotify. He did his best to ignore the image of a smartly shod foot. It appeared to seek an escape from the wall.

•   •   •

The Sean half of Shandrew ambled along Oldfield Street on his way to the rec. an excited Molly straining at the leash.

The earflaps of Sean's woolly hat (which Andrew always laughed at) hung over his ears, the cold spell well and truly bedded in. His breath haloed his head and merged with the fog of the evening. Sean

had left Andrew at home on the sofa tonight, nursing aching legs–
well, if he will do squats. He smiled to himself.

Arriving at the rec., the space shrouded in darkness, Sean scanned
the place for danger as city-dwellers are wont to do after dark.

A few streetlights were scattered around, with some venerable
trees looming through the fog. Voices and laughter echoed, muffled,
around the space. Sean imagined it was the street drinkers who
frequented the facility after dark, when the mums and dads and their
babies slept, tucked up safe and warm at home.

He crunched across the frosty leaves to the jubilee bench, the same
spot where Lucy and Pig had hung out at Halloween. Sitting on its
cold, mosaic tiled surface, Sean fumbled through his coat pockets for
cigarettes and lighter, mulling over how irritated Andrew would be if
he found out he had fallen once again from the tobacco wagon.

Contraband found Sean removed his gloves and, after switching
on her flashing collar lights, freed Molly from the lead. Despite her
breed, she was a good girl and never strayed far. He lit the cigarette,
taking a long draw. Within seconds, he experienced the pleasant light-
headedness that tempts struggling ex-smokers and sighed with
satisfaction.

Molly snuffled around the bench, squatting for a wee with a
satisfied chuff.

Christ, that was so good and yet so bad, Sean thought, finishing the
cigarette. He extinguished the remains, making sure it was dead, and
pocketed the stub, placing a stick of gum in his mouth.

Just ahead, Molly circled around a Victorian streetlight. He
checked his watch, deciding to give her another five minutes.

He could no longer hear any voices. Perhaps the street drinkers,
having run dry, were off seeking new bounty, or perhaps the
thickening fog muffled signs of their presence. He put his gloves back
on, clapping his hands together for warmth with a wumfh.

Unusually, for such a calm dog, Molly growled. Sean stood and
glanced over. "What's got into you, Mol?" he asked. The dog dashed

further into the park, leaving Sean to shrug. Probably a squirrel or a fox.

A man emerged into Sean's eye-line, bathed in the streetlight now vacated by his dog, whom, he realised, wasn't in view. He couldn't see the flashing pulse of her night-time collar. He gave a soft whistle to alert her it was time to be coming along, squinting at the man. *Odd*, he thought.

Spot lit, the man struck Sean in several ways. For starters, he was big. Sean didn't consider himself sizeist - the man seemed tall and broad, solid rather than fat. Anyway, Sean was conscious of being chunky himself, a consequence of a desk job and an abiding love for craft ale, but the stranger facing him cut an imposing figure.

The man seemed coatless. No breath wreathed his head–it was almost as if he wasn't using his lungs. In fact, had he not seen him hove into view, Sean might have mistaken the man for a cardboard cut-out or a mannequin, propped up to give park-goers a fright, a leftover teenage prank from Halloween.

Sean looked behind him, checking the children's play area for signs of Molly. She wasn't there, the swings moved lazily in a soft breeze. He turned back. There was no one there.

No Molly. Sean whistled again, louder this time. He was mindful that being too loud might trigger barking across the neighbourhood. He heard a familiar bark, faint, up ahead.

It was freezing. Sean's fingers throbbed despite his gloves, and his nose was a block of ice.

Moving from the bench, he noticed how the fog and chill obscured his awareness of the surrounding city. He was utterly alone, as if abandoned on a deserted island, even though his warm home and the person he loved were just a short walk away. The wintry night rendered this place alien and unfamiliar.

He arrived at the light where the man had been standing moments earlier. Squinting, Sean stood in the approximate position where he'd seen the man.

Yes, you could see the jubilee bench, although it was pretty faint under the lamp's sickly yellow wash of light. He chided himself for being silly. The man hadn't been staring at him after all, rather he'd been looking in this general direction, perhaps lost, literally or in his thoughts.

Maybe it had only been a homeless person, looking to secure a spot to sleep.

Sean struggled to pinpoint a sudden, intense feeling that snatched away his thoughts. Heart racing, an unrelenting sense of *dread* overcame him.

The feet of countless insects skittered along the length of his spine and a soft breath chilled the back of his neck. A realisation dawned upon him that terrible events were happening. Events which he, his husband and their beloved dog must avoid becoming caught up in, at all costs.

Things were happening which, he knew in his soul, would cost lives.

His heart slowed, and the dark feelings dissipated when he heard a jolly huff and chuff approaching from behind. "Where have you been Mol, you lovely girl, not eating acorns again I hope!" he said, voice shaking, as the dog's flashing collar came into view, tail circling in the fog and breath wreathing her velvet ears.

Gloved fingers attaching the leash to Molly's collar, he rubbed the soft fur behind her ears. No more exploring in the dark. Not on that terrible night.

"Home time," he said, deciding to steer clear of the rec. for a few nights.

CHAPTER FOURTEEN

Pop quizzes are a useful tool in the teacher's armoury. There are few such simple ways to pull together an overview of whether their teaching over a period of weeks has sunk in and they require minimal effort by the teacher.

Tim considered this as he looked out across the bent heads of his teenage charges. When he'd announced the test, a muted groan had gone up among the students.

He'd been focussing on comparative religion and the question of morality in recent weeks and some students had struggled to grasp the weightier concepts or had simply chosen not to. The quiz would enable him to understand which of the teenagers needed additional support.

Choosing to ignore the murmurs at the back of the class, Tim rocked back in his chair, its front legs lifting from the floor.

Truth be told, he was exhausted. The orphanage, he couldn't bear to call it anything else, felt like a psychological battlefield. The strange pictures had continued to appear, smiles, icy eyes, many fingers beckoning.

The older images were sharper and more defined, with muted colours developing like secrets being brought out into the light.

Sleep was becoming a rare and troubled thing. Every night, he was shaken from slumber by the agonies of a dying baby, the memory forever imprinted in his mind.

Tim didn't know what to do. He didn't want the Guardian Angels to think him mentally unfit, and he needed somewhere to live. Regardless of everything, he felt a strange commitment to protect the building and halt what was happening. He sighed. Something needed to be done, but what?

"SUCH A LARK TO BE OUT AND ABOUT!"

The shout was deafening, almost painful to the eardrums.

Heart pounding, Tim shot backwards in his chair, almost losing his balance. Dr Kresta, patrician in his dark suit, stood by the back wall, his face splitting into a yellow grin.

Kresta's eyes bored into him; the feeling of malice so strong it was almost physical.

•   •   •

Lucy, struggling to focus on the quiz, heard the shout as if someone was about to pounce.

Her body, wanting to take flight, shot up from her seat and she registered that she'd given a small scream. She noticed, despite her confusion, Mr W. rocking back in his own seat, a look of abject terror on his face.

The class erupted in chaos, some of her classmates jeering while others laughed. "What the fuck, Warwick?" one boy sneered at her as she resumed her seat. Lucy gave him the finger.

Mr Waverly, shocked and dazed, attempted to restore order. Kresta was gone. She convinced herself he couldn't have been there.

•   •   •

Pig, bundled against the chill, sat behind the gym, eating a Twix, lost in thought.

"That's just a whole new level of weird. There's no other word for it," he said to Lucy in between mouthfuls.

"I know, right? I'm sure Mr W heard it. You should've seen the look on his face. It was like someone had assaulted him or something."

The rest of the RE period had had a strange atmosphere, she told him, as if the class had lost respect for their teacher. Lucy's classmates lost concentration on the quiz, with nonstop murmuring and giggles until the bell signalled the lesson's end.

As for Pig, while he appreciated Lucy was having some startling experiences, in his heart of hearts he felt guilt for being disappointed that none of these had revealed themselves to him. Even the strange seance in the abandoned building revolved entirely around her.

He had listened to Lucy's recounting of her strange dreams with rapt attention and understood that was struggling to sleep. Her increasing grumpiness coupled with the dark circles underneath her eyes, gave it away. In contrast to his friend, Pig was enjoying the best sleep of his life and struggled to emerge from his bed in the mornings.

"If Mr Waverly experienced anything, that's got to mean *something*," he said. "I think you're going to have to speak to him?"

"And say what, exactly?" Lucy said. "Excuse me sir, have you been having nightmares starring a psychotic cook too?" She rolled her eyes.

"I get what you're saying, but I think we need to try to find out if he knows something," Pig reasoned. "After all, it will prove you're not going crazy, at the very least." He was glad to see a faint smile pass across Lucy's lips.

"You're right," she said. "I *am* worried Pig and I'm afraid I might lose my mind. I can't think of a way to speak to Mr W without sounding stupid. It's just a few nightmares, after all. They probably got sparked by the ouija board and I might be stressing about my GCSEs. Well, deep down at least.

"Also, I might have just imagined that he looked scared. I was pretty freaked out myself."

"Hmmm," Pig sighed as he folded his Twix wrapper and placed it in his backpack. Fumbling for a moment, he unearthed a packet of cheese and onion crisps.

"We need a plan," he said, tearing open the packet.

•   •   •

Less than half a mile away, at Oldfield Street, a freak wind coincided with the precise moment Tim sighted Dr Kresta at the rear of the classroom.

It ripped, roared, and rampaged down the street, as if sent by a furious god. The few remaining leaves were dislodged from the trees, their hope for prolonged life ended. Along the length of the street, branches came crashing down, one landing on Michael Slade's Pain Free Panes van. Not that he'd be needing it.

In her front room, the bay window shook with such violence, accompanied by an unearthly howl exploding from the chimney, that Mary, startled, dropped her teacup onto the carpet.

At Louise Sanglin's home, her heavy wooden garden furniture lost its tarpaulin cover, which would never be found. The table rocked in the tempest, chairs flew across the patio, one smashing as it fell.

Andrew, walking home from the Post Office, tried in vain to keep the beanie on his head as the wind almost blew him from his feet. He was kept upright only by the painful smashing of his body into the gnarly trunk of a London plane.

He told Sean later that the gust was so violent he could not breathe for a frightening few moments in its wake. As the only person outside in the street during the freak weather, Andrew fancied he could hear strange music carried along with the howling gale, and a pestilential stench riding on its back brought gorge to the back of his throat.

It was over as soon as it had begun. Only the trail of damage remained, a silent reminder of its existence.

Bins lay on their sides, their contents disgorged onto the pavement, and several of the homes had broken windows and downed fences.

The sound of alarms blaring from the cars parked along both sides of the street, and birds shrieking angrily in the sky above, replaced the wind's roar, and the hellish music.

The Oldfield WhatsApp sprung to life as the street's residents emerged, like vulnerable animals startled from hibernation.

Looking out of her front window, mercifully undamaged, Mary MacDonald ignored her phone notifications. *It's an ill wind that blows nobody any good*, she thought.

• • •

With her oversized glasses and petite frame, Charlotte Woodbury had an unfortunate insect-like quality - she was referred to as Charlotte Woodlouse by both students and staff. It was through these glasses that the St Isaac's headteacher peered at him, eyes magnified so much it was like being under a microscope.

"I don't know what stresses you're under outside of school, Tim," she said, tone not unkind, "but, as a fee-paying institution, our parents and students have high expectations. Expectations which we have a mission to deliver in the form of *exceptional* results."

Tim, certain that Charlotte had delivered this lecture before, decided it was best not to interrupt. "Things are getting…sloppy," she went on, her speech clipped. "You look like you aren't sleeping and, my sense is, you aren't entirely *present*. I wonder if your unorthodox living arrangements are having an impact. And that brings me to today.

"Our students need, above all, to have respect for the teaching staff. They must be confident they are getting the *best education* that money can buy."

Her eyes softened. "Tim, you're a good teacher, the kids, and their parents, like you and, goodness knows, RE teachers aren't exactly queuing around the block. I know from your file that you've struggled with your mental health from time to time and I have every sympathy."

He knew what was coming. Of course he did.

Today he'd lost control of the class. Yes, it was a few brief moments, but he'd been at St. I's long enough to recognise that this was considered a major failing. The school leadership reacted badly to anything untoward being reported by the students to their parents, however insignificant that might be.

And here it came.

"I'm going to suggest you take a leave of absence, on full pay, of course, at least initially." Tim knew this wasn't a suggestion at all, and took a deep breath. Woodlouse removed her glasses and gave him a look which was surely the product of an empathy training day.

"Take some off. Get some sleep for goodness' sake, perhaps find a proper home too," she said, staring, it seemed, deep into his soul. "I'll make a note to catch up with you in the near future."

Spectacles back on Charlotte returned to business mode. "I, we, don't want to lose you, Tim. But you need to sort yourself out. Take a break, I can organise cover, and I'm sure you'll come back raring to go."

Taking his leave, Tim thanked the headteacher, aware of the irony given she'd suspended him like a disruptive student. Perhaps it was for the best. Charlotte hadn't been wrong. He needed to get his shit together and was too distracted by the weird circumstances in which he'd found himself since his move into the orphanage.

Leaving the building he was struck by events earlier in the day. He could only imagine that he was experiencing some kind of mental disturbance, a thought that he was anxious about given his history with anxiety and depression, now added into a toxic mix by lack of sleep. How, though, would this explain Lucy Warwick's reaction to the appearance of Kresta, assuming this wasn't a mere coincidence?

He couldn't know that he'd taught the last lesson of his life.

•   •   •

Lucy, standing in the St I's car park with Pig, saw him first. She thought Mr Waverly looked lost and forlorn. His dishevelled hair and worn-out trainers gave him the appearance of a student. Most of the teaching staff were in avuncular middle-age.

Pig, looking up from his rucksack, gave her a prod. "I know," she said, "just psyching myself up."

Pig rolled his eyes and strode towards Mr W, who was almost outside the wrought-iron gates which marked the school's boundary. "Oh, fuck me," she said, following in her friend's wake.

•　　•　　•

"Sir!" Hearing the shout, Tim looked around to see Korrey Amari speed-walking toward him from the far end of the car park, his long, thin legs moving at pace. Lucy Warwick was bringing up the rear in a slouch.

At fifteen, Korrey had surpassed Tim's height, and, with his skinny frame and shock of Afro hair, Tim thought he was likely to break a fair few hearts, Lucy's potentially being the first of them.

"Sir," Korrey repeated, "Lucy and I were hoping we could have a word?"

"If it's about Lucy's pop quiz, no, I haven't been through them yet and, erm, I'm taking a few days off." Tim wasn't sure why he needed to explain anything to the boy, who everybody called Pig for some reason. Lucy Warwick had, with obvious reluctance, joined them.

As if by some unspoken agreement, the trio moved away from the school gates to escape the throng of younger children and parents congregated there. Lucy realised they were heading for Oldfield Street.

Pig broke the uncomfortable silence that had fallen among them. "Sir, about what happened today?" he said, turning the statement into a question.

"Cramp, embarrassing," Tim answered without a beat, hiding his irritation. "I'm prone to it. It always catches me by surprise. I think I need to do daily stretches, maybe eat more salt." He gave them a forced smile.

Silence descended once more. In the darkening light, there was a light dusting of frost on the pavement beneath their feet.

• • • •

Planning to talk to Mr W was easier than actually doing it. Face to face, Lucy felt embarrassed and found herself unable to speak. Of course, her teacher wasn't experiencing anything strange. He'd got cramp as he had said, that was all.

She felt trapped. Oldfield Street was a good fifteen minutes' walk, and she wondered if she and Pig could peel off on some pretext.

Waiting for an ambulance to streak past them, sirens screaming and flashing lights bathing the frosted pavement in blue, it was Pig who broke the silence once again. "Kresta," he said.

Mr Waverly stopped walking.

CHAPTER FIFTEEN

If Mary MacDonald was prone to expressions of excitement, she would have leapt, whooping, from her seat. As it was, she allowed herself a thin smile.

Cecily's email was short and to the point, but Mary was astonished to have received any response to her letter.

Her sister wrote that Lionel hadn't left a journal and, to the best of her knowledge, had never kept one.

This was a blow. *What better way to get to the heart of the man?* Mary thought. Despite this, it was encouraging that Cecily suggested a meeting. "I don't know quite what it is you want to find out, but I am travelling up to town for Christmas shopping, and I'm prepared to spend thirty minutes to meet," she'd written.

Familiar with her sister's attitude towards others, Mary imagined thirty minutes meant just that. She'd have to plan her questions carefully to get useful responses.

Settling back on the sofa, she pondered. Her sister knew about the frightening images, having lived with them as a girl. Cecily saw her twin as either a vandal or mentally disturbed.

How should Mary raise what was happening?

Uncertainty clouded her mind, but she knew better than to openly speculate about unnatural possibilities–her sister would disapprove. Taking everything into account, Cecily's agreement to meet was a win. Now she could ponder how to approach it.

The next challenge on her path was Tim Waverly himself. Lately, she had only seen him in passing and feared for the poor man. He looked tired, drawn and, well, haunted.

Mary, having tried to support Lionel for years, understood the difficulties of helping shut-ins. She was determined to do her utmost to ensure Tim didn't succumb to the same dismal fate as her brother and was concerned the young teacher was already withdrawing into himself.

She'd heard it said that a person would only agree to be helped when they accepted they needed help. As the product of an older generation, Mary thought such self-help notions to be foolish. Of course, Tim needed help, and she was utterly determined to give it, invited or otherwise.

She knew not intervening could have serious consequences. She refused to be a bystander.

It's time he faced reality, she thought.

•   •   •

Had anybody been there to smell it, the stench in Michael Slade's home was an obscenity, an assault on the senses. The neighbours smelled it in their homes and called an exterminator, worried about rats.

Slade's nails were pulling away from their beds and his eyeballs had dried to gritty, desiccated husks.

The state of decay advanced, hastened by the heating system still running each morning and evening. His body was collapsing in on itself, liquefying. Seeping fluids drained into the carpet and merged with the building's fabric.

As for Michael's revenant, he (it) had remained away from this place, despite being given the means to travel through the earthly realm. He lacked interest in the decaying remnants of his former self. Instead, he had no choice but to spend his time watching his new playmates and listening to the one he called The Other. Michael couldn't grasp The Voice's nature. He called himself Kresta but, to Michael, he was other than a man.

Michael was afraid of The Other, who was revealing himself to Michael's new friends. Sometimes, he found himself *pulled* into The Other's domain, a place of endless corridors and unfathomable rooms, where he was forced to listen to stories from The Other's long history - tales of great pain and pleasure which left Michael both titillated and confused.

He questioned The Other about his plan for the street's inhabitants. This had elicited deep and resonant laughter. "The street?" The Other had chuckled with a flash of yellowing smile. "Dear boy, I am a devourer of *worlds*. Your puny street, your tiny city, is but a mere morsel. An amuse-bouche for the likes of me. This is only the start; I and others will stride across this world and destroy everything in our path. When I reach full strength, I will be unstoppable."

Despite further probing, Michael had failed to glean anything more. Overwhelmed by questions, he was left alone in the liminal spaces that became his new home.

•   •   •

"Kresta."

One word, a strange name, uttered by a teenage boy on a wintry London street, punctuated by the plaintive wail of a siren. It rolled around Tim's head like ceaseless thunder, intruding into his every thought.

When Korrey Amari had voiced the word, it had stopped the teacher in his tracks. He'd looked first at the boy, then at Lucy Warwick, trying to find an appropriate response, the correct words.

In the end, unable to find anything to say, he had simply walked away, shoving his hands deep into the pockets of his coat, and directing himself away from Oldfield Street and ignoring their calls, "Sir! Mr Waverly!" - their voices merging with the endless soundtrack of the city. He felt pleased that they had chosen not to follow him, yet deeply ashamed for leaving them there. The moment he walked away, the questions started.

Surely the man was a mere fragment of his nightmares? He might have been conjured by anxiety or bad food. Tim tried and failed to tell himself he'd misheard, and that Korrey had said something similar but unrelated. He knew it wasn't the case.

Returning to the orphanage, he noticed some window grilles hanging loose, as if forcefully torn away. Or pushed by some force from deep within the building. After his strange vision and suspension from his job, he had no appetite to engage in repairs after dark.

Tim took a sip of strong coffee. He'd struggled with his mental health over the years, coped badly with the loss of his parents, and had now fallen into the depths of a black mood. However hard he tried to avoid them, thoughts of Kresta intruded into his mind when he was awake or searching for the sleep that would not come.

He wasn't sure if he could cope.

Korrey's utterance, while disconcerting, had to *mean* something.

These kids couldn't possibly have knowledge of his dreams. He asked himself if walking away had been the correct response. He could have asked his own questions instead of leaving.

Looking around himself, Tim experienced a momentary disconnection. This dreadful building, pregnant with secrets, was nothing like a home. Waking nightmares and fear of the unknown consumed his world. And now this deeper mystery: two kids, schoolchildren, seemingly aware of Kresta. Although he resisted it deep inside, Tim knew he'd have to speak with them.

A knocking at the main door disturbed him from his thoughts. The sound echoing through the near-empty building brooked no argument.

•   •   •

When Mr Waverly answered the door, Mary was taken aback. He'd aged considerably in recent weeks. There were dark circles under his kind eyes, and he gave off an air of nervous exhaustion. She sensed her visit was unwelcome. So be it. She had things she needed to say.

She was truly shocked when he ushered her into his apartment with a promise of tea. She could not prevent a slight gasp, a sudden intake of breath as her neighbour invited her to take a seat on the sofa.

The walls were massed with images which brought to her mind that strange and chaotic last letter from her brother. The marks were randomly positioned, lacking any clear sense, like Lionel's words and numbers. As Tim made the tea, she examined the room.

The marks, some sharp, some blurry, others incomplete, filled the wall.

Numerous eyes, the vivid blue of a Greek sky, gazed from the plaster. Some looked amused, others angry.

Hands reached out as if to grab the living, to drag them to a place from which they could never return. She gave an involuntary shudder.

"Perhaps Mr Waverly. Tim," she said as he returned with her tea, "you might think about staying somewhere else for a while."

"I have been thinking about checking into a hotel," he said, taking to his armchair. "I have to admit it's becoming difficult to cope, stuck in here. It's…" he searched for the correct word, "…it's *isolating*, I suppose. Not much of a guardian angel, am I?" He gave a mirthless chuckle.

"It must be very isolating indeed." Mary nodded her assent, taking a sip of her tea. "Remember what I told you about poor Lionel, a virtual recluse for years?"

She stared directly into Tim's eyes. "Whatever happens, whatever is coming, whatever all of this means," she gestured vaguely at the surrounding room, "you mustn't make the same mistake. You can't let it *control* you."

The floodgates opened; he couldn't stop it. Reassured by her presence, Tim, eyes shining, began to tell her about his experiences.

He shared his night terrors and the appearances of Kresta, first in a dream and later in his classroom. He told her of his suspension from the job he loved, and the deepening anxiety that was overwhelming him. Finally, he confessed to walking away when two students had hinted at some knowledge of events.

Mary sat in silence as Tim shared his experiences. She was pleased he had opened up to her and didn't want to interrupt, lest it triggered a return to his earlier reticence.

Observing him, she watched the way his hands trembled as he spoke and noted the moisture in his eyes which came so close to cascading down his cheeks. She pitied him. At the conclusion of his account, he gazed at her with a grim expression.

She pushed her emotions to one side, knowing they served no useful purpose in the present circumstances. "There's no point in self-pity," she said gently. "I'm pleased you've shared everything that's been happening to you, but you need to act. It's not good to sit alone in this terrible place.

"You must speak to those children and find out what they know."

Tim nodded, seemingly encouraged by Mary's no-nonsense approach to the problem. Now that he had recounted his tale, she explained about the letter she'd sent to her sister and her surprise at getting any response at all.

"I've got to approach it with care," she added, "but Cecily *must* know more than I ever realised–the subject's always been off limits. She was Lionel's twin, after all. I was too young to understand what was happening."

Mary sat back and saw the pressure falling away from him slightly, his desolate mood lifting now there was a decided course of action. He would track down the students while she would try to elicit information from her sister. Both were terrified, but knowing *something* would help.

Mary allowed herself a small smile as Tim called the local Holiday Inn and booked a room.

CHAPTER SIXTEEN

Sanjay Mistry, back in his own bed after several nights squeezed between his parents, could not sleep.

He thought this was strange. He had a busy day at school, running around quite a bit. All the activity helped, because it was so cold.

Over dinner (veggie escalopes with peas, not much better than tofu curry) he had tried to persuade his mother to let his best friend Jacquie sleep over at the weekend. Mummy was unenthusiastic, and Sanjay, a bright boy, knew when to let go.

Back in his own room, his thoughts were tripping over themselves, preventing him from getting to sleep.

He had resumed his vigil of the street between getting back from school and his dinner and seen nothing especially strange other than a few branches scattered around the ground. The pretty girl with the dark hair had walked home, head down, lost in her music. In the chilly darkness, he was excited to spy a fox running along the pavement.

Opposite, a familiar old lady had said her goodbyes. He liked Mrs MacDonald because she had helped him after his run-in with Peter Eames and had spoken to him like a grownup, which was always worth a gold star in Sanjay's mind. Mrs MacDonald told Mummy all about it, saving him from getting scolded for the broken eggs.

While Mrs MacDonald and the unfamiliar man spoke on the doorstep, Sanjay sensed an unsettling aura from the building. He couldn't understand how a building could be Bad.

But it was.

He leaned from the bed and tapped his red Lego alarm clock. It blinked at him, 11:23 p.m. His parents had gone to bed a while ago and all was quiet save for the hum of traffic on the A road.

Squeezing his eyes closed, Sanjay listened extra carefully. No sound came from the young couple next door. They mustn't be playing tonight.

It wasn't working. His eyes sprang open, sleep remaining out of reach. Gazing around his bedroom, Sanjay could see the outline of various toys, including his favourite, Oscar the bear, which he'd had as a baby and still loved. He would never admit it, afraid of sounding childish.

Whack! His hand on the clock again, 11:37 p.m. The last time he'd checked seemed like ages ago. He sat up in his bed, confused.

If sleep refused to come, what would he do? Would he fall asleep in school, which might get him in trouble and cause his classmates to laugh at him? Peter Eames would go on about it forever if he heard about Sanjay falling asleep in a lesson, because Peter was a very Bad boy.

Once again, he checked the room. As far as he could make out in the dim light, everything was where it belonged. Mummy was strict about such things, and he was a neat child.

The giant from Halloween was standing at the end of the bed.

Most of the space between the bed's foot and the wall was taken up by the stranger. The giant swayed from side to side as if he was standing on the deck of a boat. His eyes, the only part of his face that could be seen, glinted and stared at Sanjay.

Sanjay started to cry. He was afraid to scream and determined not to. He had picked up on his parents being fed up with him sleeping between them after his last nightmare and was sure he must have finally fallen asleep and started dreaming.

The giant's breathing was an angry, heavy, liquid gurgle, which sounded painful to the child's young ears. Slowly the stranger lifted both hands and gave his jolly wave. "Hello, little Sanjay," the man said. "We're going on an adventure, just you and me."

The tears slipped down the little boy's soft cheeks. How he longed to be stroking Oscar's soft fur.

"My benefactor wants to meet you," the stranger went on. Sanjay was confused about what a benny facta was. He knew a Benjamin Foster in his class, but they'd already met, of course.

"He's going to take you, take us both, into the magnificent halls of his home. We'll play forever and have fun times together you and me. I can't wait!" The man's teeth snapped together on the 't'.

Sanjay felt a scream rising in his throat. Mummy had told him never to speak to strangers. But what if the stranger was standing in his bedroom?

The man stood there, a black shape in the room, silent now save for his wet breaths, bobbing side to side, his green eyes unblinking.

Sanjay looked towards his babyhood bear for comfort. When he was brave enough to look up once again, the giant was gone.

• • •

Lucy and Pig didn't need to contact Mr Waverly again because their teacher took the initiative.

A letter for Lucy arrived on Friday, hand-delivered and left on the front door mat. "Maybe you've got an admirer!" her mum said with a smile, spotting Lucy holding the letter in the kitchen. Deciding it was best opened in private, she shoved it in her bag and headed to St I's.

Behind the gym at morning break, Pig snacking on a bag of Twiglets (devil-food in Lucy's opinion), she opened the letter. "It's from Mr W!" she gasped. Having not seen him in school for several days, they'd assumed the teacher was away.

The letter had been typed and was quite formal in tone. Unbeknownst to them, Mary MacDonald had a significant influence in its drafting.

"Dear Korrey and Lucy," Lucy read aloud.

"Humph, putting the boy's name first," she huffed. Pig, reading over her shoulder, shushed her.

"I was rather rude the other day when we walked back from St. Isaac's. It was clear that you were trying to tell, or ask, me something, and I realise in hindsight that it was remiss of me to walk away from you.

"I was somewhat surprised when Korrey uttered that strange word, which I will not repeat here. As you may have surmised, it does hold some meaning to me for various reasons, but I do not wish to share these in a letter.

"I think perhaps it is best for us to meet face to face and talk things through. You can reach me on 07960 897787, call or text.

"DO NOT come to the orphanage. I am taking a few days away, so please telephone in advance, should you wish to meet with me. Any time is fine.

"With best wishes,

"Tim Waverly."

"Well," said Pig, crunching another Twiglet, "that's that. We may uncover the truth. Boom!"

"At the very least, what he knows," countered Lucy. "How odd he isn't staying in the orphanage, don't you think?"

Pig was agreeing as the bell tolled for the next period. Walking back to class, they decided Lucy would text Mr W that evening.

•   •   •

Tim, in his hotel room, found himself launched from a deep and sticky sleep, pinned to the bed in a state of paralysis.

Kresta hovered above him like a malevolent spider, face to face, as if suspended from wires attached to the ceiling.

A long-fingered hand clamped itself across Tim's mouth. "Shh!" Kresta said, "you don't need to make a sound, Timothy, not a peep." Tim, terrified and with Herculean effort, gave a tiny nod of his head.

"Good," Kresta went on, floating, speaking in a gentle whisper. "There's no need to be afraid. Here we are, just us.

"There's nothing to be afraid of. Nothing frightening, don't be scared," he soothed, flashing a yellow smile.

A line of greenish drool hung from Kresta's smiling mouth. The spittle wavered on a thin string, tiny maggot-like creatures twisting in its sickly warmth. The spit gave in to gravity, falling from Kresta's mouth and landing on Tim's lips, where he felt it *move*. Kresta made a small tutting sound and wiped it away with a flick of his fingers.

"Here's what's going to happen," the creature continued. "You're going to leave this place. Now. When you've left this place where you've been trying to hide, you're going to return to your home. It isn't haunted, Tim; you don't believe in all that nonsense.

"I have plans," he said. "Plans that don't concern you. But I sense interference, *meddling*. You will stop meddling. Tell the old woman and the naive children to look away. Do you understand?"

Tim swallowed, his throat dry and constricted. "Yes," he croaked.

"Oh, Tim!" Kresta frowning, his mouth in a sad droop, lowered himself. Their noses almost touching with sickening intimacy.

"I don't believe you. I don't believe you can stop your meddling. Obstructing me has consequences. Shall I tell you?" Tim gave a slight shake of his head. "It's quite simple, really."

Kresta suddenly shot upwards, pinning himself to the ceiling. "I WILL TEAR YOUR FRIENDS ASUNDER, LIMB FROM LIMB," he roared, his great voice booming around the room.

"I WILL RIP THEM OPEN, DRAIN THE BLOOD FROM THEIR VEINS AND DEVOUR THEM. I WILL CAUSE THEM PAIN LIKE NO OTHER. ALL OF THEM!" The voice was so loud it shook the room, Tim heard things crashing to the floor in the bathroom.

He closed his eyes, willing this nightmare to end.

Kresta's voice, quiet now, and carried on hot stinking breath, spoke directly into his ear. "And you, Tim, I will *enter*. I will *take* you, yes, and fuck your soul for the rest of your miserable, puny life. Then you will understand the true glory of Dr Kresta.

"Heed my advice, you and your friends. Look the other way."

Tim, petrified, and with hot tears running down the side of his face and into his hair, opened his eyes. Murky daylight poked through the thin curtains.

He was alone.

Unable to stop himself, he leaned over the side of the bed and retched, a stream of watery vomit spattering onto the brown polyester carpet tiles.

CHAPTER SEVENTEEN

"*He invited it in,*" Cecily had said.

In the end, all of Mary's preparation and considered thinking about meeting her sister proved pointless.

She'd looked for Cecily as she walked into the steaming air of the coffee shop. A few yards from Harrods, it was busy with Saturday shoppers laden with bags, preparing early for Christmas.

Cecily Bracken, her spinster sister, had been sitting towards the rear of the shop, dressed against the chill. A tweed overcoat was hanging on the back of the chair in which she sat, posture stiff, her grey hair perched on top of her head like a helmet. She had greeted Mary without warmth and gestured to the chair opposite. As she took her seat, Mary had hooked the handle of her walking stick on the tabletop.

Mary thought a subtle approach would help her learn about what happened during their childhoods and how it affected Tim.

Cecily ended up singing like a canary.

"You're here about Lionel." It was a statement, not a question.

"You were older than me, then he was sent away. I never really *knew* him, at least not well, even in the later years," Mary had said, remaining cautious.

"Were you at the funeral?" This, from Cecily, struck Mary as an odd question.

Mary sipped the awful tea, delivered to her by a sullen red-headed youth with a poor complexion. "Oh, yes. I was sorry you decided not to attend."

"I buried my twin long ago," Cecily had answered with a dismissive wave of her hand. "Many years before he died."

She had examined the look of confusion on Mary's face and mustered a smile which matched London's wintry weather. "I'll tell you," she'd said after a lengthy pause. "It doesn't matter now."

Mary had nodded and maintained a diplomatic silence.

"As a small child, Lionel was content. You know it wasn't the easiest time, what with ongoing rationing and everything else, but ours was a good, stable home. He resembled a pet to me, a small, adorable creature. He was always dashing around the place. I was more bookish, reserved, I suppose. Our mother doted on him. Father was less interested. I'm not sure he'd ever wanted a son."

Cecily had gestured at the spotty youth. He sloped over and she ordered another flat white. She gave a questioning glance at Mary's steel teapot. Mary shook her head.

"I don't know exactly when it started," Cecily had gone on, grey eyes staring into the past.

"I suppose Lionel would have been around twelve or thirteen. You must have been six, maybe seven. Like a lot of boys his age, I suspect, he became fascinated with uncanny things, the paranormal and suchlike. He'd always thrown himself into church with gusto, which Mother loved, of course, and I suppose this new interest might have been an extension of that, the notion of things beyond our understanding.

"He had a friend who lived along the street. His best friend, James…Bennett as I recall. The two of them were inseparable and used to spend hours reading about ghosts and spiritualism and playing with one of those silly…talking boards?"

"Ouija," Mary had said.

"Yes, that's it. They read everything they could lay their hands on about Victorian spiritualists and raising the spirits, all of that nonsense. I believe the local librarian expressed some concern to Mother about Lionel's choice of reading materials.

"After a few months, James Bennett's mother came calling. She was livid, claiming our brother told her terrified son he was consorting with otherworldly beings which had broken through the talking board, the ouija. She shouted at Mother, who was furious with Lionel, as you might expect, and the boys were forbidden from seeing one another.

"The tragedy came soon after."

"I hadn't heard about a tragedy?" Mary had asked.

"Oh yes, a terrible thing. James Bennett *went*. One night, his family assumed he'd retired to bed as usual. The next morning, no James. He vanished without a trace, and there was no indication that anyone had entered or left their house, as I gathered from overhearing conversations between our parents.

"In the end, it was thought he'd run away, and his poor, broken parents moved away a short while later. One would have expected Lionel to be distraught, but, to the best of my knowledge, he said nothing. He never mentioned the loss of his best friend, certainly not in my hearing.

"Around the same time, those terrible images started appearing. Fingers beckoning, eyes staring, ghastly smiles leering at us through the walls."

"Oh yes. Lionel reminded me all about them." Mary had chosen her words carefully.

"Not *all* about them, Mary, I'm sure. Of course, you know he was institutionalised?"

Seeing Mary's nod, she had gone on. "Lionel *changed*. We would hear him in his room, laughing. In the night he'd cry out nonsense words. I swear to God, I once heard many voices, *children's voices* coming from Lionel's room in the night. Perhaps I was simply dreaming."

She'd lowered her voice then, "Mary, he would stand at the front window, naked as the day he was born, shameless. He'd just stand there, laughing, screaming and *masturbate*."

Mary gasped with shock at this. Cecily had fixed her with a look before continuing. "For our parents, it all became too much, of course. Daddy resorted to beating Lionel, but he just laughed and spat, taunting him.

"Those dreadful images were all over the walls, the ceilings. That house became a claustrophobic, terrible place. You likely won't remember, but you started having horrifying nightmares. We all did.

"Lionel's departure, banishment, I suppose, brought both joy and sorrow. We just wanted our brother, my twin, back, the funny boy who warmed our hearts and who'd kicked a football around Oldfield Street with his best friend James.

"Later, Father informed me that images appeared on the institution's walls. I also learned later that he was a beast at the institution. He'd behave in a lascivious fashion, flaunting himself to the staff and the other boys. I couldn't say for sure, but I believe they *used* him. Or perhaps he used them."

Cecily had become upset at this point and Mary, careful to control her own feelings, had taken a clean tissue from her handbag and passed it over. "Thank you. I'm being a silly old woman. Lionel endured years in that awful place. Regrettably, as a family, we *chose* to forget about him. Not you, though, you always asked when he'd come back home.

"When he got out, he seemed improved. Not *well* exactly, but fine. He was quiet and reserved and kept himself to himself. Joining the forces seemed to suit him. I suppose he was institutionalised by that point and welcomed the structure.

"I used to think it was justified that he was disinherited. He caused such trouble, such grief. You won't believe me, but the way his life ended up saddened me."

Her eyes dry by then, Cecily had begun getting ready to leave, shrugging on her overcoat. "I have come to believe that our brother *had* been communicating with someone, some*thing*."

She'd paused for several moments. "No, I'm afraid it was more. *He invited it in.* Lionel, I believe, was still himself, somewhere. Yet, there seemed to be an indescribable darkness lingering within him, perhaps never truly departing.

"Perhaps it was there until the end. Maybe he'd learned to control it, to suppress it somehow. Or it was hiding away deep inside, waiting.

"For me, Lionel ceased to be my brother a long time ago. He was dead to me many years before he took his life. And now you know."

Cecily Bracken had picked up her bag and left. There were no hugs, no sisterly goodbyes. She didn't glance back on her way out.

Mary, against all her better judgement, stayed for another cup of the awful tea, feeling comforted by normalcy - the warmth, the burble of friendly chatter and the hissing of machines behind the counter. Cecily's story shocked her, and she experienced a twinge of guilt that she had thought so badly toward her sister who, she saw, carried a lot of pain and whom, she was certain, she would probably never see again.

Did Lionel's death trigger what was happening now? Did he invite evil, as Cecily claimed, evil that sought a new host? And there was the disappearance of Lionel's friend, James Bennett, to consider. Mary was certain of a connection.

She Googled the West London Holiday Inn and dialled the number. The receptionist surprised her when he said that Mr Waverly had checked out.

I do hope he hasn't gone back to that bloody place, she thought. She gathered her things, and stepped out into the cold London air - a small, anonymous old woman aided by a walking stick.

• • •

Sanjay tidied up his beloved Lego.

His parents had instilled in him the importance of putting things in their place and he was Good. He was also aware of what happens when a shoeless parent steps on a stray Lego brick, having once seen his Daddy reduced to tears of pain, which Sanjay had found very funny indeed.

He had about twenty minutes of his allocated playtime left before he and Mummy were due to leave. She was taking him to Ealing to see a film, and he was excited.

At present, his thoughts were occupied with matters unrelated to Lego. He placed each piece back in its allocated box, in order of colour, as was his preference. After having a quick check around the carpet, he took care when placing the lid back on the box and slid it into place in its space under his chest of drawers.

Glancing at his clock to check the time, Sanjay turned his full attention to the hole in the floor.

It appeared thirty minutes ago, but it took him a while to process what he saw. He had tried ignoring it in the hope that it would go away. It was still there.

It appeared to be perfectly square, a bit like the trapdoor they had on the stage in Sanjay's school hall. The children loved to speculate about where that trapdoor led, and Peter Eames had frightened everyone by making up a story about a dungeon filled with the bodies of children murdered by an evil monster.

Sanjay was scared.

He was certain the hole was super-Bad and debated calling for his Mummy, fearing her anger if she thought he'd damaged the floor.

He shuffled, on his belly, towards the edge of the hole, which ran parallel to the foot of the bed.

Peering down, he saw...blackness. Living in London, it was rare to see total darkness. Although Sanjay didn't have a torch, shining one into the hole wouldn't have mattered.

Darkness consumed the space, untouched by wintry light from his window. He was frightened and very confused. Was there something wrong with the flat?

Without realising it, Sanjay edged beyond the lip of the hole, his head now almost at its centre.

A sound emanated from the impossibly dark space. "*Aaarrcch-garghhh.*" It might have been breathing, made louder by the space, perhaps? Sanjay thought, madly, of Darth Vader, who was very scary.

A ripple of stale air came out of the hole, tickling his scalp. It was accompanied by a strange, sour smell which Sanjay could not place.

"*Aaarrcch-garghhh.*" A large hand shot out of the hole, roughly grabbing the front of Sanjay's shirt. Shocked into silence, the little boy didn't cry out, although tears sprang to his eyes.

"It's time for us to play," came a voice from the hole in the floor. The hand dragged the child down, down into the depths. Finally, somewhere, Sanjay started screaming, but nobody would hear it.

When Anita walked into the room fifteen minutes later to scold Sanjay for being tardy, the hole had gone.

A single, tiny Lego head smiled up from the carpet. It was the only visible sign her son had been in the room.

•   •   •

Mary watched the drama unfold while standing in her front garden, where she'd been clearing up the rest of the fallen leaves.

A police car roared up the usually quiet street, lights flashing, and screeched to a stop across the middle of the road, limiting traffic.

Uniformed officers rushed from the car, stopping outside Oldfield Court where they were admitted by a distraught-looking woman shouting and gesticulating into her flat. Mary couldn't be certain from her vantage-point, but thought it might be young Sanjay's mother, whom she had met after the poor boy had got into such a state a few weeks earlier.

Soon after that a second car, this one unmarked, pulled in behind the first, disgorging two plain-clothes detectives who also entered the block, admitted by one of the uniformed officers who was now posted outside the entrance to the building.

A few minutes later and Mr Mistry, Mary was certain, dashed up the street and into his home.

Despite detectives leaving hours ago, the panda car still sat parked against the pavement.

Various of the street's inhabitants, enticed by the drama like moths to a flame, were milling around in the road, gossiping. Mary observed Sean and Andrew handing around hot drinks, which she considered utterly inappropriate in the circumstances.

As she watched, worry soaked deep into her soul. She was concerned that something untoward had occurred, perhaps involving the Mistrys' polite little boy.

Having lately learnt from Cecily about the mysterious disappearance of her brother's childhood friend from this very street, Mary feared her concerns were justified.

Gardening done, she sat back on her sofa, fortified by tea, and re-read the text message she'd received from Tim Waverly and pondered on the implications.

It looked as though things at the Holiday Inn had gone awry, although he didn't elaborate, so he had briefly returned to that terrible place before heading off to a meeting he had arranged with Lucy Warwick and her friend.

Tim suggested Mary join the three of them at the orphanage, as he insisted on calling it, at 7 p.m. Mary had texted him back and counselled that it might be more conducive to have the meeting at her house, given the strange atmosphere at his home. His response was a thumbs-up emoji.

Concerned that things were accelerating, Mary typed out a new text outlining the activity at Oldfield Court.

Message sent, she glanced at her watch: 6:23 p.m. She shut her eyes for a few moments, bone tired after the busy day.

The others should be here soon. There was much to discuss, much to learn, and great danger ahead.

CHAPTER EIGHTEEN

"Fucking hell, sir, this is *LIT!*" Pig shouted in astonishment, heedless of his language, when Tim flicked the light switch at the entrance to his apartment.

Lucy stood, gaping open-mouthed, as her friend whipped his phone from the inside pocket of his jacket to take photographs.

"For God's sake Korrey, sorry, *Pig*, nothing is to go on social media," Tim cautioned.

There were many more images visible than before he'd decamped to the Holiday Inn. Sometimes, the definition was uncanny. Blue on blue eyes, surely Kresta's, stared out from several places and a chaotic swarm of rats appeared to be running along the top of the skirting boards, tails aloft, small, sharp teeth bared.

"Ugh, rats," Lucy sighed, looking away from the skirting. "Mr W, this is *amazing*! Frightening but amazing all the same." Tim heard a strange mix of fear and excitement in the girl's voice and was impressed by her fortitude.

He nodded, thinking that Mary had had the right instinct when she'd suggested the foursome meet at her home.

Pig jabbered on about the need to collect documentary evidence, and Tim zoned out.

It had been unlike any other day. After fleeing the hotel, experiencing a sense of terror as if Kresta was at his heels, Tim had returned to the orphanage. Once there, he had undertaken a quick check of the building before heading to the coffee shop, as arranged, to meet his students. He'd didn't know what, if anything, they knew, but he'd found their story fascinating.

Both he and Lucy were astonished to learn of their shared dream, which Tim now believed they had experienced in parallel to each other.

He was certain someone else was in the dream, just out of reach. He now suspected that this had been Lucy Warwick, unbelievable as it seemed.

Hearing about the strange figure the kids had seen at the rec., which disappeared when they gave chase, discomfited Tim.

Given his arrangement with Mary to meet this evening, Tim had decided not to share much with the pair at this stage. Meeting them for coffee was an opportunity for him to learn what *they* knew.

The clincher was Lucy's awareness of Kresta's appearance in his classroom. Although the thought disturbed him, he was pleased that he wasn't losing his mind.

Somehow these kids, Lucy in particular, had become caught up in these uncanny events and, although risky, he considered it important to invite them to the abandoned building, which seemed to be ground zero. Leaving the dim cafe on the A-road, which he'd chosen for its lack of patrons, they walked back to Oldfield Street.

The police were outside Oldfield Court, just as Mary had mentioned in her most recent message, and they were surprised by the presence of a news van, its satellite dish pointing towards the heavens, parked up in the street.

Some residents lingered outside, fishing for morsels of information, or wanting to feel caught up in the drama. The three of them slalomed around them, voicing brief greetings.

The initial excitement gone, Pig quietly surveyed the room for the last time.

He'd taken countless photographs and some video on his phone and handed it over to Tim to look at. The images themselves were almost photographic in places, particularly those which were more defined. The overall effect was eerie and unsettling.

Returning the phone to Pig, Tim looked around once more. There was no obvious pattern to the marks, which were of different sizes and overlapping in some places. The common factor was the impression they were coming from within the walls.

It seemed that, at any moment, the leering face or the grim rats along the skirting would burst through the plasterwork and into the room. Tim noticed his students were now holding hands and wondered if they even realised it.

"Time to go," he said. "Mary's expecting us, and I don't think that's a lady who we'd want to keep waiting!"

•   •   •

The last time teenagers were in Mary's home eluded her memory. Wracking her brain, she wasn't sure they ever had been.

She brewed a large pot of tea in readiness and wondered if she should have stocked up on fizzy drinks, which she had never kept in the house. She placed some French Fancies on the tray next to the teapot in the living room.

The doorbell rang just after 7 p.m.

Tim still looked haggard, dark circles framing his sunken eyes. Lucy Warwick, whom she knew in passing, was swathed in black, her long, dark (surely dyed?) hair pulled back with a purple scrunchy, and her eyes circled with kohl. The boy, who surprised her by introducing himself as Pig, was tall and lithe. He was also utterly beautiful, with his dark features and open smile.

The trio removed their shoes as she ushered them into the lounge, Pig falling on the French Fancies like a boy rescued from starvation.

The foursome took their seats, the teens on the sofa, Tim and Mary in armchairs opposite them. They sat in silence for a few moments, broken by Mary offering tea, and all of them partook.

Tim Waverly, on the verge of a breakdown, two teenagers torn between fear and excitement, and her, an elderly woman reliant on a stick due to a silly fall.

What could they achieve against this unknowable foe?

"I think it's best if we take it in turns to say what we've seen and how we feel about it," Mary began. "Let's wait until we've all spoken before assessing the next steps.

"I'll start, if I may, with the sad story of my brother, Lionel Bracken, which I suppose serves as the beginning. For me at least."

Mary, with great care, recounted the story of her relationship with her haunted, reclusive brother. She detailed how, over many years, she had drawn him out, persuading him to share some of his deepest secrets and fears.

For the benefit of the teenagers, she explained the perplexing letter she received before his death, serving as a warning.

She detailed her most recent activities, chief among them her meeting with Cecily. That it had only taken place that morning astonished her.

The others looked at her, rapt, as she set out the differences between Lionel and Cecily's accounts of Lionel's childhood and Cecily's revelation about another boy, Lionel's best friend, going missing from his home.

•   •   •

As Mary finished her tale, Lucy found herself almost fit to burst. "Pig and I used a ouija board, Mrs M!" she gasped, careful not to mention that the pair had broken into the orphanage in order to do it. "That's how I think it started for us and, it sounds like, for Lionel, too. He was only a bit younger than we are now."

Mary gestured for her to continue.

The story Mary had shared was a tragic one. Lucy, regularly interrupted by her friend, in contrast, threw herself into recounting their experiences with gusto.

They recounted their experiences with the ouija board, once with success and once without.

This perhaps triggered the appearance of the man they called, without embarrassment, the "horny ghost" inside Lucy's bedroom, followed by 'K is risen' graffitied outside her house, and her strange dreams one of which, at least, she'd shared with Mr Waverly.

When Lucy mentioned meeting Dr Kresta, Mary took a sharp intake of breath as if someone had placed a hand on her shoulder and glanced over at Tim.

Lucy and Pig recounted hunting down the staring man at the local rec. They talked over one another excitedly, Pig, with his white-socked feet propped up against Mary's coffee table, barely able to hide his enthusiasm.

• • •

Reaching the point at which they'd realised their teacher had also been experiencing uncanny events, Lucy and Pig completed their breathless account. Mary, satisfied but disturbed, gave a small nod. "The baby in the oven is a particularly fascinating, if ghoulish, development," she said.

"How so?" It was the first thing Tim had uttered in some while.

"Children, Tim," she said, fixing each of them with a look.

"It's the common denominator. My brother and his friend playing with dark forces as children, the baby cooking, Lucy and Pig experimenting with the ouija board," she heard a tutting sound from the sofa and smiled over at the youngsters "…forgive me but, to me, you are children, sorry but you *are*.

"Given the police activity over the way, I'm concerned the little Mistry boy might be caught up in this in some way. I encountered him and a neighbour, Michael Slade - a window cleaner - last week and sensed something was amiss. I brought the boy back to his mother and didn't dwell on it, given everything else going on."

The four of them considered this for a few moments before Tim relayed his own story, starting with the handprint on the wall in his apartment and concluding with the chilling warning he'd received at the hotel.

The temperature in the room seemed to fall as he detailed his experiences, and Lucy gave an involuntary shudder.

When he'd finished, there was a contemplative silence, which Mary broke. "There are images of rats, you say?"

Tim explained once again about the swarm of vermin pictured running around his apartment, as if looking for an escape.

"That's interesting," Mary said with a small nod. "Yes, very interesting indeed." Despite being bombarded with questions, she refused to be drawn further until she was sure.

•   •   •

"*Meddling?*" Pig asked later, thinking of Tim's account of the horror at the Holiday Inn. "Kresta said we're meddling?"

Seeing Tim's answering nod, Pig broke the grim mood and surprised them all by roaring with laughter, clapping his hands, and rocking back on the sofa. "We're meddling kids!" he said.

Lucy looked over towards Tim and Mary's blank faces. "It's like Scooby Doo," she said. Mary chuckled at this, realisation dawning on her.

Pig lifted his teacup into the air. "I propose a toast!" he cried, eyes ablaze, "to Mystery Incorporated!"

They all lifted their, mostly empty, teacups in return, Tim feeling rather silly, and Lucy gave the air a small punch.

It was Tim who spoke next, his voice serious.

"It's good, no, it's *important* that we keep each other's spirits up, but we need to understand that what's happening could be very dangerous. After all, we've been warned off, in frightening terms, and we now know that at least one child's gone missing, Lionel's best friend, James Bennett.

"We can only speculate, for now, about what's happening at Oldfield Court and why the police are there. I think Mary's right that there may be a connection to the events we've been experiencing."

The others murmured their assent; the mood becoming serious once more.

"I think we need a plan of action," Mary said. "Tomorrow's Sunday. Tim, are you able to spend some time and find out what's happened down the road?"

"Yes, there's a news van parked up outside Oldfield Court, so I suspect it might hit the airwaves shortly if it hasn't already."

"Lucy, do you have plans?" Mary asked.

Lucy shook her head. "I sometimes go to church with my mum. It keeps her happy, so I could do that," she shrugged.

"That's perfect," Mary went on, beaming. "Your task, I think, is to relieve the font at Bartholomew's of some holy water."

Seeing the look of confusion on Lucy's face, she added. "Better to be safe than sorry. We're going to need all the help we can get." She smiled at the girl, "After all, if there is a God, I'm sure he, she, or they would want to stop whatever's happening."

Finally, Mary turned to Pig. "Can you spend the day with me here? Bring a laptop or tablet if you can. I think it's time for some good, old-fashioned research."

"Roger that, Mrs M," Pig drawled, placing his hand to his forehead in a salute. "I'll bring my laptop, no worries. It'll be like the library scene in The Amityville Horror."

Despite their fear, the idea of taking action instead of passively waiting for more horror invigorated them.

Tim, however, remained concerned for the safety of his students. They were good, kind kids who didn't deserve to be put in harm's way and, given Kresta's warning early that morning, they were all in certain danger.

•　　•　　•

Sanjay regained consciousness in his room. He blinked blearily for several moments, remembering the strange dream he'd had about the hole in the floor.

"Hello, Master Mistry." The voice carried an air of importance, a little like a teacher.

Looking around more closely, he realised he wasn't in his room at all. He occupied a room *similar* to his own. The Transformers bedding his parents had given him last Christmas was on the bed and his Lego clock was next to it. Oscar the bear was nowhere to be seen. It was all wrong.

There was no window, and the room was illuminated by a single flickering bulb hanging from the ceiling. It made Sanjay think of sickness.

There were two other people with him.

In a dark corner, the giant swayed. A line of dribble was stringing its way from the corner of the giant's mouth towards the floor. Sanjay realised he was the man who'd rescued him from Peter Eames and maybe-Liam but couldn't remember his name.

In the chair (*not my chair,* Sanjay told himself) a second man was sitting. Sanjay thought he looked ancient and posh, with his thin, silvery hair and dark suit. The man smiled at him, yellow-ly, his blue eyes hypnotic.

"I am Dr Kresta. With a K," he said.

Sanjay sat up straighter in the bed, which was not his, his eyes wide.

The man's smile seemed impossible. It was too broad, and Sanjay was afraid it would split his cheeks. He was also very afraid of the man himself.

Doctors are supposed to be friendly, and besides, Sanjay wasn't feeling sick.

"I'm so pleased you have finally joined us. My companion," the doctor gestured at the swaying giant, "has been watching you for some time. You are a special boy, Sanjay, *very* special, and today is a momentous day. Do you know why?"

Sanjay stared and shook his head in response to the old man. The man, Dr Kresta, stretched his smile yet further, the flesh around his mouth beginning to tear, and stared back.

Sanjay felt trapped by the enduring gaze of those blue eyes.

"You are the first of my new Harvest boy, and that makes you extra special to me," the man said, his voice turning deeper. "Soon you will have hundreds of new playmates. Perhaps even thousands. Won't that be exciting?!"

"No!" Sanjay said, loud and defiant, his small hands bunched into fists.

Kresta's smile widened, the flesh splitting further to reveal more sharp yellow teeth.

"Yes. You'll like it, I promise. Sanjay, you will live for a loooong time. Your mummy and daddy will be dead, forgotten, food for the worms. Nevertheless, you will endure.

"I'm gifting you hundreds of years of life. Can you imagine?

"And in return for my gift, I will feed. I will feed and grow and you, first of the Harvest, will bear witness to my glory."

Sanjay began crying and, consumed by fear, dimly felt a hot wetness spreading between his legs.

Kresta stood and seemed to be taller than anybody Sanjay had ever seen. "REVENANT," he demanded, "clean that *thing* up!"

The giant looked up glassily as if roused from a deep sleep. "Look but don't touch," Kresta instructed, "story of your pitiful life."

Sanjay slipped back into the warm embrace of unconsciousness, which was a mercy.

CHAPTER NINETEEN

Sunday dawned, dank and dismal, yet the members of the newly christened Mystery Inc. awoke with a newfound sense of purpose.

By 10:30 a.m. Tim was standing in Shandrew's magazine-quality kitchen nursing a small cup of strong "artisanal" coffee, which Sean had lovingly prepared for him, having first stopped his dog, Molly, from her enthusiastic goosing of Tim's crotch.

Tim had watched the early morning news bulletin with a growing sense of dread. The information which had been released to the media was sketchy but centred on the disappearance of a young boy, publicly unnamed, thus far, who was living with his parents in a flat opposite Tim's temporary home.

Like Mary, he couldn't shake the feeling that the missing child was connected to their experiences.

Mary had been correct in suggesting Sean and Andrew might have more information. Tim's inbuilt reluctance to pay a visit to strangers, albeit neighbours, had proved unfounded.

Sean, working at home alone, was an inveterate talker and had welcomed him into the house with open arms, perhaps to show off both his home and his complicated coffee-brewing apparatus.

"As far as I can gather, Sanjay Mistry, a lovely little boy by the way, was playing in his room when poof! he was gone, just like that," Sean said.

"Anita, his mother, is distraught, as you can imagine. The police can't find any signs of entry or exit from the flat."

"That's dreadful," Tim said. "Those poor people. I'm sure the police are pulling out all the stops to find him. Which is something."

Sean placed his empty coffee cup on the vast island. "I gather forensics are going through the place with a fine tooth comb. It's like CSI round at their flat!"

He looked embarrassed. "Not to make light of things," he added. "Funny times," he said, looking thoughtful.

"How so?" Tim's curiosity was piqued.

"Well, I can't explain it, but I had a very strange experience walking Molly the other night." Sean placed a protective hand on his dog's soft head.

"I went to the rec. as I often do. She likes it and I was desperate for a cheeky smoke and," he flapped a hand in the air, "it's strange, but it felt like I was being watched. I saw a man, and, for some reason, was terrified, fearing for my life. It's as though I were in grave danger or something."

"That *is* scary."

"Silly more like. I'm a grown man. What could I be afraid of around here, aside from drugged-up muggers, and you get them *everywhere*? I put it down to the combination of fog and the nicotine hit. More coffee?"

• • •

While Sean shared gossip with Tim, Lucy Warwick attempted to acquire holy water from St. Barts' font.

Although she wasn't a believer, in God at least, Lucy enjoyed old churches.

Since she'd been a little girl, she'd enjoyed that unique otherness that seemed to emanate from places of worship. The way a person could walk off a busy London road, step into an old church and feel transported to an earlier age, with the sense of calm it brings, was appealing to her.

Saint Bartholomew's wasn't one of those churches. A low building, constructed from red brick in the 1970s and with a stubby bell tower jutting, like an afterthought, into the trees, it squatted at one corner of the rec. like a bloated toad.

The service had been grim, even by the standards of St Barts.

The vicar, Anthony ("call me Tony!") Stafford was straight out of central casting. He had a lanky frame, a tragic comb-over and thick glasses, which gave him a surprised, vaguely owlish appearance.

Revd Stafford had droned on at length, his words and the readings chosen to reflect the seriousness of the occasion, and the community's shock about the little boy who'd gone missing from his home in Oldfield Street. The sense of worry among the congregation, not least those with young children, was palpable.

The worship had been joyless.

It was outside, after the service, when inspiration came to her. Years later, she would wonder if it had been divine.

She was standing with her mother, who was chatting away with a group of her churchgoing cronies. Lucy was concerned she'd failed in her simple mission and was reluctant to tell Mary MacDonald, whom she found intimidating, that she hadn't been able to do this one simple thing.

"I'm just popping back inside," she announced, inspired.

Ellie looked at her, surprised. "Whatever for?" she asked. "It's good of you to come along, but the service is over!"

Lucy mustered what she hoped was a thoughtful expression. "I'm just going to sit by myself for a few minutes. Maybe light a candle for the missing boy."

"You are a kind girl under that gothic exterior," Ellie smiled, "good for you. If I'm not here, I'll be back at home, pondering lunch options."

Inside, St. Bart's was almost deserted, with just a couple of stragglers gossiping in the corner.

Lucy looked around the red brick interior, which was softened by pastel-hued wall hangings depicting various biblical scenes. She wondered, not for the first time, why a church had been built which was so ugly.

Glancing towards the font, which looked like something you might find in a carpark, Lucy saw her chance - no one.

She walked over trying to look casual, paused to light a candle, and surreptitiously removed an empty Coke bottle (liberated from the recycling bin at home) from her bag.

She checked around once again. No sign of anyone, least of all Revd Stafford. As she placed the bottle in the font, she offered a silent apology as insurance in case there was a god of some description. The bottle, filling up, started to glug, the noise loud in the empty brick space.

"Can I help you at all?" Lucy gave a start. *Shit the churchwarden!* She quickly removed her hand, which held the now half-full bottle from the font. Placing the bottle back in her bag, Lucy smiled at the warden and decided to style it out.

"Lovely service," she said quietly, "but so, so sad about that little boy." The churchwarden, a confused expression on his babyish face, nodded.

Not wanting to get into a conversation, or to be asked what she'd been putting in the font (or taking from it), Lucy smiled her goodbyes and beat feet, as Pig would say.

Outside, shouts from kids playing football on the rec. punctuated the wintry gloom, and a light drizzle was falling. Lucy, tightening the purple scarf around her neck, raised her eyes to the heavens and smiled. Mission accomplished.

•   •   •

At 11:00 a.m. Pig, fuelled by a late and large breakfast, biked fast to Mrs MacDonald's house, laptop secured in his side bag.

He felt invigorated. Who needed stories about a creepy old hotel when actual supernatural happenings were taking place right here, on your doorstep?

He thought this must the most exciting time of his life. Pig had found things a bit dull of late. He was stressed about exams, although working hard. He knew it was because his sister had got into a top university. His mum was proud of Sandra, although she'd never placed him under any pressure, he did that all by himself.

Freewheeling the bike into Oldfield Street, he secured it to the fence outside Mary's house. Removing his hated cycling helmet, he gave his hair a good shake-out and shouldered his laptop bag.

Mary was waiting at the open front door. She greeted Pig before ushering him into the kitchen-diner.

"Blimey, Mrs M, you've been busy," he said, impressed.

The artworks on the long side wall were replaced by Mary with large paper sheets. Post-its were stuck on many of the surfaces.

On the kitchen table, next to a steaming cup of tea, were a tablet computer and a leather notebook. She gestured Pig to the other side of the table where he set up his laptop, using the wi-fi password she provided. "It's like mission control for Mystery Inc.!" he exclaimed.

She smiled. "I tend to think that when something needs doing, it should be done properly," she said. "When the others come, we might have some understanding of what's been happening."

"We'll get there Mrs M," Pig replied.

"I rather wish I shared your confidence and spirit, young man. So, you make a start and I'll pop the kettle on. It's time to go down the Google rabbit hole."

•   •   •

It was 6:30 p.m. when the foursome gathered around Mary's kitchen table.

Over the course of the day, she and Pig had made use of the writing wall, which was now filled with an extensive collection of notes, queries, and speculations.

Pig had enjoyed Mary's hospitality, which involved a lot of sandwiches and biscuits, but he'd never drunk so much tea in his life and was feeling wired.

Lucy revealed the Coke-bottle holy water from her rucksack, like a magician pulling a rabbit from their hat. In hindsight, she enjoyed the subterfuge, but now a sombre mood fell over the group.

Mary, taking the bottle from her, decanted the contents into several smaller bottles, which Amazon had delivered earlier in the day. She handed one to each of them, saying she had a strong feeling it would be beneficial.

Tim shared the information he'd gleaned from Sean earlier that morning, the others listening grim-faced.

The account tallied with the news bulletins, which had been updated throughout the day, as well as providing more information on the lack of evidence. Sean had told him a press conference had been arranged for the following day, Monday. Anita and Chetan Mistry would appeal for information about the whereabouts of their little boy. "I just can't imagine what those poor people are going through," Tim added.

Mary, having brewed yet another pot of tea, stood up to present her thoughts based on the work she and Pig had done during the day. "A lot of what I'm about to say is speculation," she started. "Indeed, conjecture is all we have. Pig's support has been invaluable, and I am grateful he was here to help marshal my thoughts.

"Addressing fundamental questions is crucial - who, what, and why. Who, or perhaps what, is Kresta? What does he want and why is he here?"

Mary glanced at everyone, then pointed at the notes on the wall.

"Krampus, the Pied Piper, the Namahage. Stories designed simply to frighten naughty children? So I have always thought but now, I'm not so sure. It is my view that Kresta is closely related to these legends, indeed he may be the *source* of them.

"Hang on," Tim interrupted, "are you seriously suggesting Kresta and Krampus and the rest are one and the same?"

"I am merely saying they *may* be, Tim. It would be remiss to ignore the possibility.

"Consider the images in your lodgings. *Rats* running along the skirting boards. Children disappearing, puts me in mind of the mythical Piper. Regardless, I believe it's fair to consider Kresta in this way. Surely all legends, however terrible, have some basis in fact, in a history that's been lost to us?"

Once more, she gestured at the notes on the wall. "From our research, we have found countless accounts of entities, *demonic* entities, which take children from their homes, snatch them away. Why?"

Lucy, fascinated, gave an involuntary shiver. The room felt different, colder. It was as if something fundamental had changed since Mrs MacDonald had begun talking about the nature of the beast.

Mary went on. "Across the globe, centuries of belief hold that these foul beings feed on children. Many cultures and faiths view children as having a strong, vibrant energy, a precious lifeforce. This lifeforce is coveted by these foul predators."

Pig looked up. "From a number of the accounts we found today, this energy reduces over time. It burns brightest in new-borns and children who have yet to enter puberty," he said. "Once adulthood is reached, say around the age of seventeen or eighteen, it's become so dim it's of virtually no use to these beings."

"But why is it here?" Lucy asked.

"Lionel," Mary answered.

"Our sister told me he'd 'invited it in'. I think it's correct, but not in the way she imagines. That he did it for pleasure or to feed an unhealthy interest in the occult.

"Though he dabbled in unsuitable affairs, he's not the only one." Mary fixed Lucy and then Pig with a beady stare. "I believe Lionel acted out of the devastation caused by a terrible loss, the disappearance of his best friend, James Bennett.

"Perhaps Lionel and James had inadvertently contacted Kresta, and Lionel was aware the demon had taken James in order to feed off his essence. My brother, rightly, feared other children would be taken."

"He made some sort of deal?" Tim mused out loud.

"We can't be certain," Mary stated. "Perhaps he offered himself to Kresta on the basis that no other children would be taken. Perhaps Lionel's lifeforce had a particular appeal to the demon, or my brother found some way to trap the unspeakable creature, within his own soul, if you will.

"Cecily was of the view that Lionel was unmoved by James' disappearance. In this, I'm certain she was very wrong. In fact, it drove him to take drastic action.

"We've spent quite some time in discussion today and Pig and I concluded that Lionel may have *allowed* himself to be possessed by Kresta because he saw no other option. If this was the case, it could be argued he invited it.

"We asked ourselves: Did it work? The answer, like much else, is ambiguous."

Taking his cue, Pig spoke next. "We know that his parents sent Mr Bracken away to an institution, the place we tend to, wrongly, refer to as the 'orphanage'. He was around thirteen years old at the time. He was there for years. Doesn't bear thinking about, really."

He stood up and pointed towards a photograph, which he'd projected onto the wall from his laptop. A proud smile graced the face of a stern man standing in front of the abandoned building. "Henry Fraser, co-founder and principal of the Fraser-Ruck School for Boys, the place you now call home Mr W. We have learned the place was less a school and more of a prison.

"There's only sketchy info online because it was a privately owned facility which was forced to close in the late 1960s because of failure to comply with certain standards, from…"

Mary held up a hand and interrupted him with an apologetic smile. "I was involved in a campaign to close that terrible place.

"Most of us were, like me, those who'd loved ones had been incarcerated there. The place got a reputation for releasing young men in a desperate state, often far worse than whatever, often minor, troublemaking had got them sent there.

"It was battle. It even got raised in parliament, and I was delighted when the authorities finally decided enough was enough and it closed for good."

Pig, nodding, resumed. "From what little I've been able to find, it sounds like an awful regime which maintained what can only be described as a brutal, Victorian approach to dealing with these kids, many of whom were, probably, suffering from minor neurological disorders."

"Such as?" Lucy asked, hugging herself against the chill.

"It's hard to tell," Pig ran his fingers through his hair. "Maybe they were kids on the autism spectrum. I don't think it was a place where children were sent to heal. Anyway, this was where Mr Bracken spent his adolescence, and we can hardly imagine what his life would've been like.

"As Mrs M has said, there's the possibility that her brother was somehow possessed by Kresta before being incarcerated, and my research bears this out. Over several years, from the late 1950s, when he was first admitted, as many as ten young boys were alleged to have disappeared from Fraser-Ruck."

"Jesus," Tim said.

Thanking Pig, Mary stood once again. "Knowing the precise number is challenging, as records are scarce. It is certain that some children went missing from that terrible place according to news stories. Indeed, they were raised by our campaign, and there were lots of rumours flying around, as you can imagine. As for the lost boys, we can't give an exact count.

"We believe Lionel's death saw the demon released but, perhaps, its years of being hosted by, or joined with, a mortal had left it in a weakened state.

"Tim, you're the first person to live in that dreadful place since it was closed. If some trace, even a memory, of the demon remained imprinted there it might have been able to tap into your faded lifeforce and this, combined with Pig and Lucy's supernatural explorations, thinned the barrier between our world and his, helping him to gain in strength.

"We might also consider that Sanjay Mistry, himself only recently moved to the street, has certain spiritual attributes which attracted the demon's vile attentions. There may, of course, have been other triggers about which we aren't aware."

"And now you think he's taken that little boy," Lucy said.

Mary sighed, "We do. It's possible that Sanjay is the initial child selected in a new cycle. To reach full strength, the creature will need more. Many more."

As Mary retook her seat, the group discussed everything they'd learned. Pig thumbed an order for pizzas into an app on his phone.

The discussion had triggered a renewed sense of urgency, and all present shared a single, overriding concern - how to save Sanjay Mistry, assuming Kresta had taken him, while preventing other children from being used in such unspeakable ways.

Deep in thought, Lucy surveyed the table. "What about the other one? I'm certain the one we saw at the rec. wasn't Kresta."

Mary answered, pointing at various printed illustrations on the wall. "Some accounts suggest the presence of a factotum of some kind, more commonly known as a familiar, used by these creatures to support them in their foul deeds. Perhaps acting as some kind of bridge between their world and ours."

•   •   •

By 9:00 p.m. the pizzas were eaten, the meeting was done, and Lucy and Pig had said their goodbyes.

Before Tim returned to his dismal apartment, Mary touched him on the arm. He turned to look at her. "We require a leader, Tim. Not a teenager or an old woman," she declared. Tim, cornered, nodded, said nothing, and left.

Mary, alone once more with her thoughts, took a seat in her armchair and felt weariness deep in her ageing bones.

She was certain a fight was imminent.

What if they couldn't halt Kresta? How many children would the beast claim?

CHAPTER TWENTY

"You want to know? I'll show you. Meddling bitch."

Mary's eyes flew open, and she realised she must have nodded off in her armchair. It had been a long and challenging day.

She was in a bedroom, not hers, and experienced a momentary sense of dislocation as if she'd slipped outside herself.

The room appeared functional, sparsely furnished, and old-fashioned, the carpet threadbare underfoot. Model aircraft, Spitfires and other warplanes, were hanging from fishing line pinned to the ceiling. The light was dim and flickering, jerky, like looking through a zoetrope.

She remembered this room.

A boy of about twelve or thirteen, in faded paisley pajamas with thick black hair in disarray, was sitting up in the bed. The flickering light revealed his face, pale and frozen in fear, with tear streaks running down his cheeks.

Tears welled in Mary's eyes. Lionel.

Unaware of her, he stared without blinking into the room's corner. Mary followed his gaze.

Darkness shrouded the corner of the small bedroom. A figure could just be made out, seated on a chair. A thin man. Or perhaps something else. It kept changing. Now it looked like *something* else, something strange, grotesque, unknowable. The figure spoke:

"Thank you, boy, for your gift to me. The beginning of a new Harvest."

Lionel sniffed and roughly wiped at his eyes with his pajama sleeve. "I didn't give you anything. You took him."

He, now appearing as a man again, leaned forward in the chair. His eyes, two pinpricks, flashed red in the dark corner. "Oh no, Lionel. It was you who introduced me to James, a very *special* child, you with your primitive talking board. Now he resides in my palace and will enjoy a long life. A *very* long life. Soon you will join us, you and all your friends, Rupert, Mark, and little Sally."

"Please, no," Lionel, weeping again, said from his bed. "Tell me what to do to stop it. I'll do anything, anything at all. Please don't take my friends. They've done nothing to you."

Kresta, for it must be the monster, retreated to the shadows once more and fell silent. She heard Lionel's alarm clock ticking, like a heartbeat, and distant music carried by a faint wind. "A bargain," the creature said at last. 'Interesting boy, nobody ever seeks to bargain with Dr Kresta.'

Lionel's eyes held a glimmer of hope. *Here it comes*, Mary thought to herself.

"Yes, a bargain!" Lionel said, brighter now. "I'll do whatever you want. Just leave my friends alone. They haven't hurt anyone."

The pause went on for a long time, the ticking clock marking the minutes. Mary joined Lionel in staring into the dark space in the corner. She couldn't tell if the demon remained in the room.

After what felt like an eternity, the voice rang out once more. "Flesh," it said, "to breathe, taste the air, eat. To experience pleasure. And pain. Yes, is my answer to your bargain child."

"I, I don't understand?" Lionel stammered.

"I will become one with you, boy, and see the world through your eyes. I will live your life, both of us together in one body. I will remain with you until you die, which, for me, will be but the blink of an eye. I am endless. I am forever."

"You'll leave my friends alone?" Lionel asked. Mary wanted to cry out, to shake her beloved brother and warn him that he was about to destroy his life, but she knew it wouldn't work. She was a helpless onlooker at a decades-old abomination.

"I will leave your friends to live out their short, ordinary lives," Kresta answered. "More will be required for the Harvest, but being with you, Lionel, will suffice. For now."

Lionel looked towards the dark corner and made his decision, one which would send ripples through the decades. "Yes," he said, almost inaudible, "I'll do it." Mary uttered a cry.

Kresta stood and stepped into the light. "We're going to have such fun," he gave a terrible smile, wider than human, "Oh, I am going to enjoy this!"

As he loomed like a terrible, predatory, insect over the small boy in the bed, he paused, his piercing blue eyes locking onto Mary's. "Now you know," he said. "Stop with your meddling or I will destroy you all."

Mary awoke in her armchair as the grey morning light stole through the curtains.

•   •   •

In the living room at number fourteen Oldfield Street, the dark sludge on the floor no longer resembled anything human.

Fingernails lay scattered where they had fallen onto the bloodstained carpet, and in the dim light, the remains appeared to be moving. This motion was caused by multitudes of maggots squirming on the body's liquid surface.

Several neighbours complained about the stench, and one spoke with a police officer stationed at the front door of the Mistrys' apartment block. The officer advised her colleagues, who promised to take a look, but nothing had happened. Many of them were working overtime on the search for Sanjay Mistry, so they left reports of unpleasant smells down the priority list or didn't include them at all.

The heating continued to cycle every morning and every evening, hastening the decomposition of what remained.

• • •

Monday at St. Isaacs dragged for Mystery Inc.'s teenage members.

Lucy, tired after a sleepless night, almost lost her temper early in the day, snapping at some of the younger kids when she'd heard them engaged in ghoulish and giggling speculation about the fate of Sanjay Mistry.

At lunchtime, stationed outside the back of the gym and huddled together for warmth, she and Pig agreed that school, even their upcoming exams, didn't seem relevant given the ongoing danger posed by the demonic entity calling itself Dr Kresta.

As the afternoon wore on, Lucy struggled to stay awake, a discussion on the social codes contained within 'Pride and Prejudice' during her English lesson nearly sending her into a deep sleep. She pondered, as she had all Sunday night, about what could come next.

Although her deep interest in the supernatural still rang strong, she felt afraid. Aside from fear, Lucy was concerned that she and the others had no control over events.

How were they to stop an entity that, as seemed likely, enjoyed immortality? Where would they even find it? Whenever she asked herself this, she knew that Kresta would find them, which scared her more than anything.

As their teacher bored on about Mr D'Arcy's social standing as it pertained to marriage, Lucy fingered the small vial of holy water. Decanted by Mary last night, Lucy had attached it to a thong and roped it around her neck. The glass bottle hung like a talisman in the hollow of her throat, which she found reassuring.

Finally, the long day ended.

Meeting Pig amidst the crowd of parents buzzing around the school gates, ignorant of the impending danger to their children, they agreed to meet later at his for a sleepover. Lucy needed to check with her mum but was sure she wouldn't mind; she'd got serious brownie points from having attended church the day before and intended to use them.

"Safety in numbers, I reckon," Pig said darkly.

•   •   •

The police officer who dropped Anita and Chetan home remained silent on the drive back from the divisional station.

Whilst there, the Mistrys addressed a press conference in time to feature in the evening news bulletins. It was their first media interaction, carefully orchestrated by the force's press office. The police officer stationed at the front door of Oldfield Court had been turning opportunistic journalists away since their son's disappearance.

Anita sat through proceedings, medicated to dull her emotions. Fewer than ten journalists turned up to the conference, which wasn't the feeding frenzy she'd expected at all. But for the cameras present, it could have been a parish council meeting.

She felt confused. Why did only a few journalists think her son's disappearance newsworthy? Seated next to her husband behind a table placed on a low podium at the front of the room, she had choked back an anguished sob. After the event, her emotion broke through the medicinal barrier and she had lost her temper, screaming at the Senior Investigating Officer that a blonde, white child would have warranted greater attention from both the media and the police. The SIO's protestations to the contrary brought her no comfort.

•   •   •

Back at the flat, Chetan Mistry was absently toying with the television remote, about to turn on the news to see the results of their efforts.

He was desperate to *do* something, but the SIO had advised them to sit tight. The Family Liaison Officer who'd been assigned to the

Mistrys (he couldn't recall her name, didn't much care) placed a gentle, restraining hand on his arm, "Best let it play out, you were there and there's nothing to be gained from reliving it," she told him with an empathetic smile, as she removed the remote from his hand.

For this reason, the Mistrys never saw the fruits of their bitter labours, which was for the best. The conference, which had run on for thirty endless minutes, punctuated by the couple's tears, was reduced to less than half a minute by the television news editors, squeezed out by other reports deemed more relevant to their viewers.

Media interest was of minor concern to the police.

Unbeknown to the Mistrys, the press conference had served a dual purpose. First, to raise awareness of Sanjay's disappearance among disinterested members of the public, on the off chance someone might have seen the boy. Secondly, the police found it important to assess the parents' body language, which was being closely examined by an expert.

They were looking for any small markers that might suggest the Mistrys knew what had happened to their son. The father was under suspicion as a matter of routine.

The Family Liaison Officer made tea, Chetan stalked from the room, and Anita swallowed another tablet.

• • •

Michael Slade's revenant had had a strange day.

He'd been sent by The Other, Kresta, to the primary school latterly attended by Sanjay Mistry. He'd enjoyed his day among the children, unconstrained by the pointed metal fences which had kept him out in life, or by the suspicious stares of the staff.

Kresta had told him that he wanted to take some of the children for the next stage of the Harvest. He had a particular interest in those from Sanjay's friendship group.

According to The Other, Sanjay's essence was even more vivid than most young souls. It would provide sustenance for many years and the boy would unwittingly have spread it (like chickenpox, Michael had imagined) among his friends, their own lifeforces becoming stronger as a result.

During playtime, Michael had no trouble identifying them, or at least those children who appeared to have stronger essences. It was obvious when you knew what to look for - they were more clearly *defined* somehow. He imagined they could lead the happiest lives, or perhaps change the world.

He revelled in watching the children at play, running around, and screaming with laughter while wrapped up like small parcels in their coats and scarves. They were beautiful.

Although Michael no longer had any need to stand outside fences, he understood he could still be *seen* somehow. This was confusing to him. He watched as both the children and their teachers registered his presence, but they appeared unconcerned.

Slade didn't understand why, but some instinct told him it might be because he wasn't *touching* the children. He was a predator. Like the snake or the shark, he would only cause alarm when it was too late. Kresta's continued instruction to "look but do not touch" dismayed him, but he understood it was helping to keep him hidden from the full awareness of the living.

The revenant had listened, sitting on the ground at The Other's feet, as his master had outlined plans for his Harvest which, he'd pledged, would be the largest in centuries, perhaps ever.

While Kresta had enjoyed the early period of squatting in Lionel Bracken, he'd tired of it as Bracken had reached his later years and was now determined to regain both his power and his exalted position in what he referred to as The Endless Pantheon.

"The meddlers" continued to vex Michael's master, leading him to decide that they should be neutralised before the Harvest began in full. This had driven his refusal to allow Michael to take any of Sanjay's special little friends for the time being. Sanjay, Kresta said, would "do for now."

As for Michael, he had more pressing concerns; he worried he was running out of time.

He had at first believed that this revenant state would last forever, that Kresta had effectively shackled Michael to him. Now he wasn't sure. Michael had started to feel *dim*. It was as if he was losing his sense of himself for periods of time, and he wondered if he would become nothing more than an empty, mindless shell.

Michael feared he was about to die. Again.

•   •   •

That night, the members of Mystery Inc. shared the same dream. It was exact, down to the smallest detail.

Each stood alone in a corridor, bulbs flickering sickly in their sconces. Kresta walked towards them along the carpet with its ugly, twisted vines.

As he came closer, he seemed *younger*, the steel-grey hair thicker and flecked with brown, the lines around his eyes reduced, the blue stare even more vivid, depthless.

They were all afraid. Accompanying Kresta on his stroll came the sound of dim music, tuneless organs, and trilling pipes.

He stood in front of each of them, adjusted his tie, and smiled with that mad, wider-than-possible smile in greeting.

Kresta chuckled, and then, throwing his head back, screamed with laughter. As he laughed, a swarm of rats flooded from beneath the sleeves of his jacket, weaving around themselves on the floor, tumbling over one another, eyes and teeth flashing as they swarmed around the screaming dreamers' feet.

"I told you not to meddle," he said, his deep voice dripping with triumph.

CHAPTER TWENTY-ONE

Tim walked into his apartment, flicked the light on, and reflected on the day just gone.

That so few colleagues attended the dinner hadn't surprised him. Some attended for being 'lifers' like him. Others, no doubt, had come because they believed attending was expected of them because of their positions at St. Isaac's.

He was a fossil. The last teacher of a subject nobody cared about, a piece of the school's furniture. Hardly worth giving up an evening for.

As he removed his hat and overcoat, he felt the familiar pull towards the hallway mirror, which he had long resolved to remove but had done nothing about. At sixty-seven, officially retired as at the conclusion of tonight's dismal meal, Tim wondered, not for the first time, when he'd become an old man.

Of course, aging was a process that everybody went through, assuming they were fortunate enough to live a long life, but it had happened in the blink of an eye. Once he'd hated his tousled hair, now he longed for its return. And as for his eyebrows, he gave an audible 'humph', since when were they so long and wiry, his eyes so dull?

Cocoa made, Tim eased onto the sofa, knees cracking like small-arms fire, in his flat on Oldfield Street. Retirement would start busy, and he'd arranged for agents to get the flat onto the market. He palmed an anti-anxiety tablet into his mouth, noted its bitter taste, and took a sip of cocoa.

The flat, which he had purchased after living as a property guardian in the area for several years, had been a happy enough home. Bowing to convention, he had pushed out, which meant a larger kitchen and a generous bathroom. Being on the ground floor was a blessing for his knees, despite the noisy neighbours upstairs. His gossipy old neighbour Louise Sanglin, long gone after being forced to sell up following a messy divorce, had been a great help with architects and builders, so he'd avoided getting ripped off, unlike so many homeowners.

Now the time had come. The flat was convenient for St Isaac's, but he had no reason to go there anymore, and it needed someone, maybe a young family, to fill it with love and laughter.

Tim, a solitary man, deeply regretted never marrying as he grew older. Companionship would have been good, yet the idea of sharing his life with someone had always been unappealing. When he realised the mistake, he had little life left to share.

Looking around at his books and prints, many of which he'd decided to sell, Tim was struck by a sudden and surprising wave of sadness. He liked this flat. He'd looked after it and it had looked after him in turn. Sipping his cocoa, he wondered where next?

He had drawn up a shortlist of areas dotted around the south coast, where he might like to spend the winter of his life. Ideally, it needed to be a place without stairs, to save pressure on his knees, and within easy, level walking distance of the sea. Worthing, perhaps, or Bognor Regis, would fit the bill. He might enjoy a small garden to potter around in.

Maybe he'd take a train to the coast in the next day or two. He had time to fill.

He sighed. While he looked forward, albeit with trepidation, to the move, he would have to endure the sale and purchase process. He'd heard it said that moving proved second only to divorce when it came to stress. Although he'd never married, he could well believe it. Thankfully, he had no family or close friends to leave behind.

There were, he'd always been certain, benefits in a lack of ties.

A short while later, he eased his way along the narrow hall and readied himself for bed. Just as he was nodding off, he thought he heard someone calling his name. The sound was faint, as if carried on a gentle breeze. *Damn tinnitus*, he thought, drifting into sleep.

•　　•　　•

Mary wiped her hands on her apron when she heard Iain's key in the front door. She twisted the knob on the oven to select the temperature for the pie she'd assembled for their evening meal.

Iain stepped into the small, dark kitchen with his usual slightly befuddled expression and gave her a perfunctory kiss on the cheek. "How was your day, darling?" she asked him, as she always did.

"Good, all things considered. The Tube was a bit of a nightmare this morning though, and now they're talking about strikes," he tutted. "Oh, pie," he gave her a small smile, "lovely."

"I hope so. It's steak," Mary replied. "I thought about making a suet pudding but," she patted his stomach, "well, best not."

Her husband chuckled as he left her to her cooking. Mary's marriage was, in many respects, a deeply traditional one, Iain the breadwinner and she a housewife. When she had mentioned getting a job to relieve her deep sense of boredom, if nothing else, Iain's reaction had been one of horror. He sometimes asked her to entertain his work superiors and did not want them to find out that his wife had taken a job. "Imagine how it would look!" he'd said, firmly closing the door on the subject.

Things might have been easier if children were part of the equation. She had never considered herself the motherly type, but it would have given her some purpose. She sighed. At forty-five, she'd left it too late.

Later that evening Iain dozed, as usual, through the ten o'clock news. Mary, left to her own devices, brewed a cup of tea, and was finishing the Times crossword before returning to her Iris Murdoch novel. Looking around the small front room, she considered how opening up the space to the dining room would make it look lighter.

"Mrs M, where are you?" The voice, though faint, compelled her to lift her gaze from the crossword. Who was it and was she the Mrs M they were referring to?

She looked over at Iain, softly snoring in his chair, before glancing through the curtains to see if someone outside was trying to get her attention.

There was no one to be seen.

•   •   •

"Come on!" Jakub Szymański threw off his flip-flops and raced down the beach, bare soles flashing white against the wet sand, hollering a great "Hooo!" as he rushed towards the ocean, Pig running at his heels.

The beach was deserted this early in the morning, save for a solitary dog walker visible in the distance. Having joined Jakub and his family several times on holiday here over the years, Pig couldn't remember a time when it had been busy.

Hidden within a cove, the beach was invisible from the coastal path which ran along the cliff edge and didn't have any of the amenities expected by holidaymakers, even in this remote corner of the west country. The surf wasn't the best and ice cream sellers were non-existent.

The pair dropped bags, tore off their T-shirts and launched themselves into the blue water, the sound of the gentle waves mingling with the cries of the gulls which flew overhead. Jakub, laughing, placed his bronzed hand on top of Pig's head and shoved, pushing the other boy under the water. Pig emerged, laughing and spluttering, and grabbed the other boy by the waist, flipping him over.

Jakub had been his best mate for as long as Pig could remember.

He had met his friend on the first day of primary school, Jakub's family having recently moved to London for his dad's work. In the years since, Jakub grew from being a shy young immigrant boy, speaking in broken English and shunned by their peers, into the teenager he was today, captain of the rugby team and 5th-form prefect. A boy who, it was said by all, would 'go far'.

Lately, Pig's feelings towards his friend had changed, morphing into something deeper and more profound.

He believed it to be his first experience of love, and it was both beautiful and frightening. When he was alone, he found himself torn between longing and agonizing over whether he could ever reveal to Jakub the depth of his feelings.

Today, though, today was all about joy. The pair had wolfed down an early breakfast, Pig having an extra helping, lovingly prepared by Jakub's mum, Agata. They'd then slathered themselves in sunblock before roughhousing good-naturedly to the beach.

The boys spent what felt like a lifetime in the water. They roared, shouted, and laughed, dunking, flipping, and chasing each other through the foamy water.

Exhausted, they crawled back to the beach and flopped onto their backs in the sand. After getting his breath back for several minutes and basking in the warmth of the hot sun on his slender torso, Pig sat up and rummaged through the bag he had discarded before they'd entered the water. He emerged brandishing two, rather sticky and melted, Curly-Wurlys, one of which he handed to Jakub.

They sat for a time, enjoying their chocolate in companionable silence, and watching the gulls bobbing on the waves. They leaned forward with their shoulders, one skinny and the other broad, touching as they dug their toes into the wet sand.

Pig looked towards Jakub's golden-brown knees and contrasted them with his own, which had been burnished into deep mahogany from endless days spent in the summer sun.

Jakub, staring out to sea, broke the silence. "I know, Korrey," he said, his voice serious. Pig, surprised by the use of his actual name, looked straight ahead and fought not to react. Jakub went on, "I think I've always known really, you know, deep down. It's fine, it's all good."

Turning to his best friend, the person with whom he had the closest bond, Pig felt his soul sing as Jakub smiled at him. A smile filled with love and the promise of joyous days to come. "I didn't know how to tell you. I was afraid you'd hate me for it," Pig said.

Tentatively, the boys entwined their fingers deep in the warm sand, their hands fitting together like it was meant to be. "We should vow, today, right now, not to hurt one another, whatever happens," Jakub said, his voice merging with the sound of the waves. "Love should be a wonderful, happy thing."

These two boys, hands locked together, leaned into one another then and smiled. As they fell back into the sand, feelings out in the open at last, Pig closed his eyes and listened to the gulls flying overhead.

As their caws mingled with the sound of the waves at their feet, and the whisper of the sea breeze, Pig imagined, just for a moment, that they were calling out his name.

•   •   •

Tim Waverly sat in his armchair, a deep tide of loneliness washing over him.

His retirement from St. Isaac's, after years at the school, was a devastating loss. At seventy-six, he felt desolate and wondered what he had to live for.

He gazed around the small lounge in his bungalow, his books on the shelves and prints on the walls. Only these small things, worthless and uninteresting to others, remained as his legacy. Rain lashed against the window.

For some time, he had feared that he had nobody to mourn his passing. He supposed the school might send a representative to his funeral. It may well be someone Tim had never met, and they would probably find themselves the only person there.

Daily, he questioned why he had opted for such solitude. As an only child, he should have made more effort to connect with others, keep in touch with friends, and seek love.

Regret, like a thief in the night, had crept up on him over the years. It was a bitter pill.

Tim thought he had little time remaining. He had already experienced two mini-strokes, which the medics referred to as TIAs, and, from his experience of losing his father to a stroke, he knew the Big One might cut him down at any minute.

What a wasted *life*, he thought, fighting an uncontrollable sense of rage. No partner, no children, no friends to speak of. All he had were silent books, and medication which, these days, failed to lift his moods, and a handful of memories of happier times.

He checked the time: 8:30 p.m. Perhaps he should have an early night. Hope for happy dreams to take him away from this bloody place.

"Mr Waverly!" That voice again. He imagined it more and more these days, even as he made his slow, painful stroll to the local shop–often merely an excuse to speak to someone. It had come to something when a man's loneliness was so all-consuming that his mind was seeking to conjure up imaginary friends.

●　　●　　●

"Jack Daw!" Mary squealed with delight as a rat, black as night and as long as her arm, lumbered along the bottom of the garden fence.

She watched its progress as it made its way into a gap beneath the buddleia. "Jack Daw!" she cried again.

"I'm not sure it *was* a jackdaw, Mary," the carer said, her voice betraying distaste, as she tucked the old widow's blanket more snugly around her wheelchair. "I think it may have been a rodent."

"Jack Daw," she insisted. The dementia, which had driven probing, cutting fingers into Mary's mind a couple of years before, had worked with relentless efficiency. At eighty-three, she had very few lucid moments, let alone good days.

Today she was happy enough and had burbled along since she had been wheeled out into the garden of the residential home some forty minutes ago.

Despite her difficulties voicing them, Mary did have thoughts. These thoughts were no longer what could be described as linear. Had she been able to articulate it, she would have described her mind as short-circuiting.

Memories surfaced from time to time, in random order, often blending with other recollections. She could, for example, remember her wedding day but, to her, she had lost her husband, Iain, on the very same day. Their years of marriage were gone from her mind. She had no memory of her twin siblings.

She often had waking nightmares about demons and missing children, and these frightened her.

Mary didn't understand where she was. She had woken this morning in a strange bed before finding herself in this garden, which was not her garden.

She squinted up at the carer, with an uncharacteristic, shrewd look in her eyes. "Calling," she said as she heard the voices, "always calling, Mrs M, Mrs M! Who is that, anyway?"

"Piper," she added, her voice faint, searching along the base of the fence.

•   •   •

At thirty-three, Korrey Amari, his childhood nickname long since discarded, wore grief like armour. It shielded him from the world and forced others to maintain a wary distance.

He did not want to talk about his feelings.

It had been coming up for six months since he had lost Jakub in circumstances that were as banal as they were tragic. The police referred to his partner's death, with an astonishing lack of empathy, as "an opportunistic mugging gone wrong," five simple words which could not begin to convey the scale of Korrey's loss.

As far as anybody could make out, Jakub had chosen to walk across West London, his underground train having broken down en route between his office and their home. His walk, meant to be a pleasant springtime stroll through the park and Victorian streets, proved to be his last.

Someone had attempted to mug him, and Jakub, having maintained his rugby player's build, had resisted.

In the ensuing scuffle, Jakub had slipped, hitting his head on the edge of the curb, and this had cracked his skull like an egg. Still, his attackers managed to relieve the unbreathing tech entrepreneur of his wallet, watch and phone while his brains spilled onto the pavement. It was a fruitful day, at least for them.

The police investigation, such as it was, had petered out after several weeks with a kind of organisational shrug. Korrey received a letter explaining that the file would "remain open," and about which he had called bullshit.

Jakub had been his life. Best friend, lover and then husband. He had been there for so long that Korrey understood what it meant to be lost without someone.

Last week, returning to his marketing job in the city after a period of special leave, Korrey resigned from his position. His focus wasn't on work. The only thing he thought about, in his dreams, upon waking and during the interminable hours in between, was ending it all. Life after Jakub wasn't life.

Now he stood, wavering, a tall, beautiful figure balanced on the edge of the bridge.

Korrey had no interest in a dramatic exit, a leap into the Thames in full view of shocked onlookers, nothing more than a cry for help. This bridge, green, ugly, and surely the nesting place of a troll, spanned a bend of the river Fowey. It stood rusting just a few miles and a world away from where two happy, loved, and loving boys had run laughing under the summer sun all those years before.

Looking around, Korrey couldn't see another soul. Only the bridge provided proof of human passage.

On this bend, the river reflected the low clouds above and was running fast over unseen, treacherous rocks. The effect, a mesmerizing sound of churning pebbles, could have brought peace to Korrey in different circumstances.

He took a deep breath, centring himself, forcing thoughts of Jakub from his mind in order to do what must be done.

The water raced ever on, over its bed of rocks. "Pig, Pig, Pig," it seemed to say.

•   •   •

"I told you not to meddle."

Upon hearing Kresta's voice, Lucy found herself shaken from her nightmares and propelled into wakefulness. Surveying her surroundings, she instantly knew she wasn't at home.

She wondered if the others were also in the same place.

Clutching, for comfort, at the vial of holy water, which was hanging from its cord around her neck, Lucy stood, the rough-hewn floor hard beneath her feet. She called out to her friends.

CHAPTER TWENTY-TWO

Lucy looked down at herself. She was wearing the oversized Moose Blood T-shirt and thick thermal socks she had fallen asleep in. She began to walk.

Despite the chill, she was thankful it wasn't as cold as the snowy field she had been in before. The ground appeared to be stone. Large grey rocks were scattered about the place and there were occasional signs of stunted growth. The ground was littered with clumps of an unhealthy-looking purplish moss.

She reached a sheer drop, her stomach giving an involuntary lurch as she edged forward and tried to look down. A cliff? Perhaps. The light was dim, the ground only just visible far below. She thought it sensible to follow the cliff for a time. Tearing off a small strip of fabric from her top, she secured it under a heavy stone to mark her location.

After walking for hours, her socked feet blistering, Lucy realised she had awoken on some kind of stone tower or pinnacle. There was no obvious way down, no steps hewn into the rock.

At one point, she spied what looked like a palace or citadel, *Kresta's lair*, she surmised with a shudder.

It was impossible to determine the scale of the structure; the conditions made it hard to judge distances. The citadel emitted an odd, flickering light, making it hard to maintain focus for more than a few seconds. It stood monstrous in the semi-darkness and exuded a terrible sense of foreboding. Just glimpsing the building brought tears to Lucy's eyes, and she felt a deep sense of loss. It was as if the structure itself was drawing any happiness from this awful place.

Some while later, she came across the scrap she had torn from the hem of her T-shirt. She was right. This was a pinnacle, pointing skywards, like a dying plant searching in vain for a source of light, and her walk had taken in a wide circle around its perimeter.

Fear penetrated Lucy's core, distracting her from exploring the perimeter. What if she could not escape this place? She might die in this desolate land, lost and forgotten, punished for her meddling.

She sat for some time, her fingers worrying at the scrap of cloth torn from the old T-shirt. Not moving, her awareness focussed on other elements of this strange place (which might be her tomb, her thoughts intruded).

The light was of a sickly, milky quality, not dissimilar to moonlight on a cloudy night, although of the moon there was no sign.

There were noises that sounded like birds crying in the darkness, wheeling unseen overhead. At ground level, occasional scrabbling noises gave the impression of small animals, rats, or some other vermin.

It was impossible to see the centre of the pinnacle, so it was hard to work out how long it might take to reach the other side. Wanting to keep busy, despite her tiredness, and wishing she had a torch to light her way, Lucy decided to explore further and move away from the edge of the structure.

Picking her way into the depths of the interior, her socks sticking to the burst blisters on her feet, she did her best to ignore the discomfort. Stubby trees, ugly, poisonous things stood about the place, clinging to life in this inhospitable environment. Mysterious creatures darted through tree roots, always too fast to identify.

As she explored, Lucy slowed down. She was thirsty and had seen no source of water, not that she would have wanted to try it even if it had been available to her. The air was cold, and she experienced a raw sense of complete terror. Lucy pictured herself starving to death, wracked with pain and alone at the end.

The icy breeze carried a baby's cries.

The crying was joined by laughter. Kresta, she was sure of it, and then the sounds of ancient machines, clanking, and hissing. These dimmed after a time, lost to the winds of this desolate place.

It was like she had been walking for days, yet there had been no daylight. The circumference of the pinnacle had not seemed *that* wide. She was certain she should have reached the far edge by now. She stood and listened for a moment. Again, the cawing of the birds, the rustle of small, quick animals. Without thinking, Lucy gripped the small vial of holy water in her fist.

Later on, if anyone had been there to witness it, they would have seen a young woman, exhausted and hunched, shuffling painfully across a bleak and seemingly endless landscape.

This witness would sense that the girl had been walking, unshod and without nourishment, for many days. They would see blood smeared by injured feet on the ground in her wake, and that her lips are cracked.

In her hands, the girl was clutching a piece of black cloth and a small glass vial bounced against her throat, winking slightly in the dim light, where no sun would ever shine or provide warmth. This girl, to the witness, would look as if she were running out of time. They would fear for her life. She seemed close to the end.

But there was nobody to bear witness. At least nobody human.

Lucy walked. Her feet and legs were on fire. She stumbled occasionally, each time finding it harder to resume her journey.

The stony wasteland went on. Her legs giving way, Lucy fell with a small scream, throwing her hands in front of her to break the fall. As her palms connected with the solid ground, shockwaves travelled along her arms and deep into her shoulders. Gingerly, she sat back, folded her legs, and cried, hot silent tears falling to the desolate earth.

It was pointless. She found herself trapped here alone, either for eternity or until death claimed her. Whichever it was, she resigned herself to her fate.

Lucy sat for so long she that feared she must have turned to stone. Had she melded with the inhospitable environment and become a feature of this terrible place, just another rock?

Over time, Lucy reached a near-meditative state. Her field of vision shrinking, perhaps in response to the lack of sustenance. She focussed for great lengths of time on tiny features, a pebble, or a small piece of the sickly purple-grey moss.

Wincing but resolute, she got back on her feet and started walking again, concerned about retracing her steps. She thought she heard the dreadful laughter again, but it might have been the wind.

Mirage, she thought, as a small mound appeared ahead. No details were discernible. Perhaps it was just some kind of plant growth, but it was a feature she hadn't seen before and was therefore worthy of closer inspection.

As she drew close to it, Lucy gave a small gasp of mingled horror and joy. Pig, Mary MacDonald and Tim Waverly were laying prone on the cold ground.

Their bodies were barely visible. Covering the three of them was a thick blanket of semi-translucent web - in the strange light, it appeared to be yellowish in colour and it moved with slow undulations as if it were pulsating with life.

Lucy walked closer and slowly eased herself onto her haunches. Thousands, many thousands, of fat white maggoty creatures were causing the web to rise and fall. These insects tumbled wetly over one another, and the prone bodies of her friends, in blind and ceaseless movement, emanating a foul smell like spoiled meat.

As she watched this seething mass of grotesquery and with the smell of offal catching in her throat, Lucy felt her gorge rise. Unable to stop herself, she turned her head to one side and vomited a thin line of watery bile.

Lucy's fury rose uncontrollably as she wiped her mouth. She would not allow this obscenity to continue. Without hesitation, she took a deep breath and angrily plunged her hands into the seething mass. She ignored the maggots wriggling against the flesh of her exposed arms as she started to tear at the vile, surprisingly strong web they had spun.

She destroyed all but a few sticky, straggly remnants of web. Exhausted and kept going only by a surge of adrenaline, she swept maggot-things off her arms and, heedless of the pain, began stamping on the disgusting creatures as they sought to escape from the web's remains. They exploded beneath her bloody feet, leaving smears of thin, yellow pus.

Like Lucy, the others were wearing the clothes they had fallen asleep in. She stifled a bark of hysterical laughter as she noticed with relief that none of them had slept naked. Mrs MacDonald was still fully clothed, and Lucy surmised she must have fallen asleep in her chair.

Examining each of them, she was relieved that they were still breathing.

Brushing away a few of the remaining maggots, Lucy sat and pondered her situation.

Assuming her friends were not somehow existing separately in this place, there must have been a reason she had escaped being cocooned in the disgusting web.

Her hand strayed to the holy water, the vial still hanging around her neck. That must be it!

Lucy offered a silent apology to her best friend and frisked Pig who was wearing only a pair of baggy Stranger Things pyjama shorts.

She was right, no holy water.

Feeling awkward about searching the others, Lucy thought it safe to assume they had also fallen asleep without their vials, which she recalled Mrs M describing as "insurance."

The holy water, regardless of the existence of God (something to ponder later, perhaps), was the differentiator. It had to be. Despite its failure to prevent Lucy's arrival, it possibly spared her from the maggots' web and near certain death.

Perhaps she had been *placed* in a position where she could save the others?

Heart racing, Lucy decided.

Her fingers trembling, she removed the vial from around her neck and teased out the tiny cork stopper. She bent down and placed a small amount of water on the sleepers' lips.

From somewhere unseen there exploded a roar of anger, or perhaps dismay.

Task complete, Lucy sat back and closed her eyes.

She waited.

CHAPTER TWENTY-THREE

Many times in her life, Anita Mistry had experienced hate and anger, but she had never known this. Despair.

The search for her little boy had stalled. It never truly began. A detailed forensic examination of Sanjay's room, followed by the rest of the apartment and the apartment block's communal areas, turned up nothing. Not an unexpected fingerprint, not a stranger's hair.

The agonising televised press conference and desultory subsequent newspaper coverage also drew a blank (Anita was unaware of the police incident desk being flooded with calls from people claiming some disliked neighbour or another was a predatory paedophile. Enquiries went nowhere). Anita remained bitterly convinced that a missing white child would garner front-page headlines.

There was no indication that Sanjay was snatched from the flat. Nor was there any suggestion that he had left his room and run away, which was beyond him. When she managed to sleep, her mind was filled with terrible, unspeakable dreams about her little boy.

The police had spoken with Sanjay's primary school teachers and his friends, including sweet, devastated Jacquie. They had canvassed the other occupants of Oldfield Court, and their responses to events varied. Some residents were afraid, others confused, and others disinterested. The result of all these conversations? A big fat nothing.

Anita popped another pill, unconvinced they were having much effect, but afraid to test this theory.

She sat in the small living room. The curtains were closed because rubberneckers seemed to think it was acceptable to stare in from the street at their pain, as if they had a degree of ownership over it.

For her part, Anita tried not to engage with the FLO, whose presence, comforting in the early stages, had become an irritation. The dispensing of endless cups of tea, biscuits and kind, empathetic smiles pissed her off.

The Event, as she thought of it, her mind seeking to separate what came before from the unspeakable thing that had occurred, couldn't unite Anita with her husband. Instead, they were like two repelling magnets, circling one another around the home she hated, both locked away with their private fears, accompanied by their own personal demons.

She yearned for Chetan's embrace, for comfort and reassurance, but he was never at home.

Her husband had left at first light to meet a group of well-wishers (*do-gooders*, she thought) searching the canal, a search which the Mistrys both thought fruitless, but which gave him *something* to do, while enabling him to avoid his wife's stormy orbit.

During a rare moment of interaction, Anita had insisted to Chetan that they ask the SIO to remove the Family Liaison Officer from their home, her job to support them through the initial shock of The Event having been done.

Chetan, who always bent over backwards to accommodate his wife's wishes, asserted himself in his resistance to this idea. He pointed out, in reasonable tones which Anita hated, that the FLO served as a useful gatekeeper, not least for answering phone calls and diverting what little media attention remained on their son's disappearance.

Anita knew of cases, albeit afforded a much higher profile, where children went missing and never returned.

Before The Event she had often sat with Chetan to watch the television, feeling false safety in their cosy little bubble as true-crime documentaries revisited these mysteries years later.

Reporters would speak in hushed tones with prematurely aged parents (often separated by this point, presumably because of the pressure wrought by their loss) as they dabbed soggy tissues to their faded eyes and begged for knowledge about the whereabouts of their child. Even if it meant they could 'lay them to rest'.

Now, feeling like a ghost in her own home, Anita directed a thin smile towards the FLO as she shuffled through to her bedroom, fingering the blister pack of sedatives in the pocket of her old cardigan.

She had propped Sanjay's favourite teddy, Oscar, on their bed shortly after The Event. Now, sitting on the bed, she held the bear, nails digging into its patchy fur, and took a deep breath, believing she might still detect the unique smell of the baby she had cherished eight years before.

Her tears soaked its thin fur.

●   ●   ●

The denizens of Oldfield Street carried on with life, but with a constant unease, fearing another destabilising shock.

The residents were acutely conscious of the ongoing police presence, and, in the manner of most law-abiding citizens, they all felt a momentary, misplaced, guilt when they walked past someone wearing the uniform of London's Metropolitan Police, afraid they were going to be collared for some wrongdoing or other about which they had been unaware.

Sean and Andrew, great fans of Anita and her son, did everything they could to support her at this terrible time. They had searched the rec. and other local parks, an excited Molly in tow, and prepared various foodstuffs for the family, which they suspected went uneaten.

Sean, who spent most of his time working from home, even had flyers printed bearing Sanjay's school photograph and the number of the police incident room. These he had delivered, carried in a rucksack, to the surrounding streets, attaching them to lampposts and trees in the immediate vicinity and handing them to passers-by.

The residents of numbers sixteen and eighteen Oldfield Street continued to bombard the police with complaints about the horrendous smell emanating from number fourteen to no avail. None of them had seen any sign of Michael Slade for several weeks. Although this was hardly unusual, he was a very private man.

•　　•　　•

Louise Sanglin, as founder and administrator of the street WhatsApp group (Oldfield Family), saw herself as having a key role to play in the unfolding drama. Despite posting daily updates to the group, she was largely ignored by its members, since she had no real idea of what was happening.

Her proximity to the crisis was a boon to Louise, and she had set up camp in her front room to witness the various comings and goings. Despite all this, and her many offers of support, she could not help but feel *rebuffed*.

She had gained access to Oldfield Court just once since Sanjay's disappearance, taking with her an expensive bunch of blooms. Unfortunately, the FLO, polite but firm, headed her off at the front door of the Mistrys' flat, saying that the couple did not want visitors (something she knew to be incorrect as she had witnessed Shandrew heading in more than once, laden with casserole dishes, that bloody dog in tow).

After that failed attempt to get to the heart of the operation, Louise had latterly found herself stopped at Oldfield Court's main doors by a succession of uniformed police officers, prevented even from making her concern known to that poor family.

One result, which pleased her, was the phone call with a journalist writing for a national tabloid.

While insisting on remaining anonymous (she wasn't stupid), Louise had used all the knowledge she could muster as a "close neighbour" of the tragic Mistrys to give the journalist a sense of events in the street.

She painted a vivid picture of a tight-knit community which, she told them while pacing back and forth across her living room, was "up in arms" about the "abject failure" of the police to provide any significant updates, or reassurance, to either the poor Mistrys or parents of other young children living in the area.

During her conversation with the journalist, remembering the rumours about the abandoned building at the street's entrance, now home to the handsome but standoffish Tim Waverly, Louise alluded to "dark, unexplained forces" in the road. They left her disappointed when they didn't include this insight in the article, either online or in print.

•   •   •

Other parents living in the area had mixed feelings about what was happening.

Those who knew the Mistrys, many of whom had children at Sanjay's primary school, experienced a sense of horror. In the darkest hours, they pondered how a child could simply vanish.

Others experienced a guilty sense of relief that the tragedy had happened to somebody else.

Only a few children grasped the implications of the situation. Some were troubled by the anxiety they picked up from their parents, many of whom insisted on always keeping them within their field of vision until the culprit was safely behind bars. Some children had to share a bedroom with their parents, as their parents held them close.

The headlines generated by the shocking events at the local maternity ward, which were to push the Mistrys further down the news agenda, would trigger a fresh wave of fear.

CHAPTER TWENTY-FOUR

The alarm erupted at 7.30 a.m. like a scream in the night.

Pig, shooting up in bed, killed the intrusive noise and looked around at his surroundings, disorientated.

He was no longer standing at the edge of a rusted bridge, gazing at the gloomy river. Nor was he in his own home, the beautiful apartment close to the Thames that he and his husband had scrimped and saved for, and about which they had enjoyed a sense of pride.

He was in his childhood bed. Stormzy glowered from the poster on the wall, intense as if he were looking down the barrel of a gun. A haphazard pile of old Fortean Times magazines stood in the corner, gathering dust.

Slowly, so slowly, Pig came back to himself.

He wasn't a man. An adult weighed down by a career and life-altering, tragic loss. He was just a skinny fifteen-year-old boy, on the cusp of exams, and living with his mum; his older sister having flown away to university.

The pain when it hit seemed almost physical as it surfaced from deep within himself. "Jakub," he said, "Jakub." How had this happened?

Pig remembered his love and his joy; he remembered how Jakub completed his life. Life had been wonderful. All those years, years in which he and his partner built a wonderful life together, laughed and loved with such genuine feeling.

He recalled the terrible news of Jakub's senseless, lonely death ("an opportunistic mugging gone wrong") and his desperation as he laid his husband to rest. He vividly remembered feeling desolate as he and Jakub's mum, Agata, clung to one another, both rudderless and lost in their bottomless grief.

It hadn't been real.

Jakub hadn't been real.

None of it had been real.

Sitting in his narrow childhood bed, wintery light encroaching through the blinds, Pig struggled. He struggled to accept that the depth of his love and the joy derived from sharing his life with Jakub, all his memories of their time together, were gone. Had never existed.

He realised that final awful loss, the worst experience of his life, amounted to nothing. It had been nothing more than a cheap parlour trick, smoke and mirrors manipulated by someone, some*thing* acting out of hate, not love.

Pig, drowning in grief, put his face in his hands and wept. Howling waves of grief and rage wracked his thin body.

"Jakub," he sobbed, fighting for breath, "I have nothing."

•   •   •

In his apartment, an exhausted Tim Waverly barked a laugh of relief when he saw the image in the small bathroom mirror, touching his stubbled face to confirm what was reflected there.

Happiness overwhelmed him as he recognised himself once again. A young man, hair, which needed cutting, sticking up from sleep. He no longer resembled the old, lonely person he had been for years.

His joy soon turned into anger, and anger into an all-consuming rage, stronger than any he'd ever known before. *Kresta*, he thought, *I will not rest until your terrible deeds are ended.*

He understood he had a mission to fulfil, a purpose, whether or not he wanted it.

Tim knew, with pin-sharp clarity, that the demon's dark work would never, *could* never, cease. This creature would move through the world like a shark through the depths of the ocean, always taking, its needs never sated. And, like the shark, it was the nature of the beast.

How could he make it stop?

Ignoring the images which surrounded him with their hateful insanity, Tim prayed. A silent prayer, it emerged unbidden from deep within the recesses of his consciousness. He prayed for answers, to find a way to stop Kresta while protecting his new friends. He also prayed that his life would not take the course conjured by the demon.

Not for him, the years spent alone, his only company a sense of regret. Not for him a slow, pitiable journey towards death, unloved, in some sad place surrounded by old books and dusty memories.

If he experienced victory in the battle ahead, he would allow other people into his life. He would seek out shared experiences, embracing love and companionship if given the opportunity to do so.

He fully understood the irony that the demon's punishment for his "meddling" might hold the key to escaping the ditch he had been digging for himself throughout his life.

Tim took his phone and thumbed a message to the other members of Mystery Inc.

Given the wasted years he had just endured, he wanted to know whether they had faced similar horrors. He also wanted them to understand a confrontation was coming. They had to take a stand.

●   ●   ●

Jackdaw.

The word careered through Mary's mind as she awakened, disorientated, in her living room. She was alarmed to have slept in her chair through the night once again. Standing, she winced from the resulting aches.

As she headed up the stairs, she clutched the banister, feeling the weight of her years. Although she had always been of the mind that hell would freeze over before she got a stairlift, her recent tumble made navigating the stairs more challenging than before.

Given the years she had just experienced, she felt gratitude her body looked to be wearing out faster than her mind, a fate which her own mother could not escape.

She had been through hell. She could recall the point at which the dementia had hooked itself into her, her thoughts becoming jumbled and an inability to place things where they belonged. Amidst her years-long night, a memory surfaced - the struggle to boil the kettle.

She remembered standing there looking at this *thing*, understanding its purpose, but being unable to make it fulfil its simple task. She remembered, too, the day, much later, when the carer she had employed to help around the house said to her in soft tones that it was "time."

She remembered also the final, confusing journey away from the home she had loved, this home, about which there had been precious few fragmented memories left.

Mary wanted to luxuriate and started running a foamy bath. She pondered the mechanics of the night's events.

She thought back to Kresta's invasion of her dreams, his stark warning. She could only surmise he had made good on his threat to stop them from meddling. But why hadn't it worked?

No doubt what she'd been through, and perhaps the others as well, had been a terrible ordeal, but here she was, back in her own life. Or that's how it appeared. Had something happened to stop the demon's influence? She needed to find out.

In her heart, Mary was certain that the culmination of last night should have led to their demise. How had it been prevented?

Her phone pinged a notification from the bedroom. Turning off the taps, she walked through and felt a deep sense of relief at seeing the message from Tim Waverly. She agreed with his points and responded to the group chat.

So, Mystery Inc. lived to fight another day. And they would have to fight. The demon would not take kindly to their continued existence.

· · ·

Three pairs of socks paired with a pack of blister-plasters and her most comfy trainers, about which she'd be reprimanded at school, were just about enough for Lucy to make her slow way to St. Isaac's.

Having spent the night on her endless exploration of the pinnacle, her exhaustion was almost total. It consumed her. The weariness in her bones was tempered somewhat by her sense of elation about having been able to save her friends from a fate she thought worse than death.

Sitting, for the longest time, Lucy had watched with alarm as the others slowly faded from view. Initially, it was a slow and hardly noticeable process. It felt like they were becoming one with the fabric of this place. The process quickened until only shreds of webs remained as evidence that the others were once there.

In the end, she had come back to herself, her bedroom appearing slowly at the edges of her vision, imprinting itself over the dark view of Kresta's realm like the changing of theatrical flats. Soon her bed appeared, and Lucy found herself in it, feet bloody and legs on fire.

She made a long, painful journey to the bathroom, gathering ointments and painkillers from the cabinet to lessen her wounds.

Later that morning, Ellie had done motherly worry as Lucy made her way into the kitchen for a quick breakfast. Thinking on her pained feet, she elaborated a story about turning her ankle in PE. Getting a note from her mum to excuse her from enforced school exercise had seemed both a positive and necessary result.

Tim's text, followed by the response from Mrs M, filled Lucy's heart with joy. They were alive! Somehow, the holy water worked, despite her low expectations. She had waited for a response from Pig, but nothing came. Nor had he returned any of her direct messages.

As she walked to school, she worried about her best friend.

As the day dragged on, her worry grew. Pig wasn't at school and, by lunchtime, Lucy, her messages unanswered, was frantic.

She broke the rules by leaving the campus, and made her way painfully to his house, but there was nobody there. Or nobody answering the door at least.

She couldn't shake the impression someone was inside, watching her and waiting for her to leave. Finally, she quit, praying Pig had escaped alive, just like the rest. She was unsure she could cope with the alternative.

• • •

In another place, far away and alone, Sanjay Mistry slept.

CHAPTER TWENTY-FIVE

Less than two miles from Oldfield Street, just off the A-road, sat the Princess Royal Hospital.

A rag-tag collection of buildings, old and new, made up the hospital's large footprint. They had grown and developed over a century, littering the grounds like discarded waste.

Day or night, visitors and patients would wander, confused and lost among the illogical maze of corridors and outbuildings.

The maternity unit at the Princess, like most other departments, was suffering from years of underinvestment. Its dedicated staff struggled to cope with the volume of women and babies from the local area who relied on it to keep them safe from harm.

By 9:30 p.m., only a few doctors and midwives remained in the unit. Those who were working were harried, kept busy by an emergency caesarean and a young couple who needed close support after learning their baby would be stillborn.

Senior Midwife Sue Prodger, strong coffee in hand, sat back in the staff room, exhausted, and eased off her white-soled sneakers. Today's shift, like many, had been filled with a heady mix of joy and tragedy, new life versus none.

She had to take a breather.

Sipping her coffee, she felt pleased to have been able to spend much of her shift with Dr Ayoub. His kind smile and punctilious nature were always reassuring to overwhelmed new parents and his colleagues.

She *needed* coffee right then. She *wanted* a large glass of wine.

• • •

On that night, the nursery unit accommodated twenty babies, including the newly named Emily Porter, who had recently been freed from incubators.

The soundtrack to the space was like nowhere else at the Princess Royal. Earlier crying was now replaced by soft happy gurgles, the babies having been fed a short time before and lulled by dim, pinkish lighting. An occasional hiccup could be heard.

Emily had been born four weeks premature to first-time mum Ania. The first few days of her baby's life triggered in Ania a level of anxiety unlike any she had experienced. That she planned to raise Emily alone, having been unsure which, from a choice of men, might be the father, only increased her concern.

Ania spent the first few days after the birth reading up on the internet about myriad risks posed to premature babies, worrying that Emily would be suffering, perhaps from a defective heart or sepsis. She feared that the life of this tiny person, which she hadn't even been certain she wanted and now loved more than her own life, might end after just a few days.

Sensing her fear, Sue Prodger had taken Ania into a quiet room, sat her on a wipe-clean sofa, handing her a plastic cup of tea, and told her to "quit Dr Google". Nurse Prodger assured her that the Princess' maternity team was experienced in caring for premature babies. She advised Ania to prioritize her mental well-being for the sake of the new arrival.

Now, laying in her plastic crib, swaddled by soft blankets and oblivious to her mother's fears, Emily was just a couple of days from being able to go to her new home. A quiet, interested baby who warmed even the most jaded hearts in the maternity unit. The kind of baby Dr Ayoub liked to describe as "watchful."

The change in the room was first noticed by Emily.

•   •   •

The revenant which was once Michael Slade (to his confused mind, a long time ago), entered the ward from a portal he had placed in a dark corner. Although Kresta had not afforded him many advantages in death, he had taught Michael the simple mechanism which allowed him to travel wherever Kresta required him to be.

It was by generating a portal that he had taken Sanjay Mistry from his bedroom, and he was now required to remove Emily at Kresta's request, the demon having identified her as a *special* child, ripe for the Harvest.

Slade, growing dimmer with time, was grateful to be tasked with leaving The Other's house. Kresta had been a terrifying, raging force, thwarted as he had been by the "puny, meddling cunts" whom he sought to vanquish.

Kresta couldn't comprehend how these powerless people had eluded him. His volcanic reaction left Michael cowering in fear at his feet.

The baby he was instructed to take was unmistakable. Like Sanjay and, to a lesser extent, his school friends, Emily seemed different to the other children. Michael thought it odd, she didn't glow, as such, but he sensed an *otherness* which distinguished her.

He passed across the maternity unit, his rattling breaths loud in the relative quiet of the room. He pondered why he still drew breath, given his remains were rotting in his old home. Perhaps it was just habit, some residual muscle memory of life.

Reaching Emily's crib, Michael looked down and felt sad. Once, in life, he would have done anything to be in such proximity to a child, and a baby, no less! Now he was dim, and his appetites extinguished. He existed to fetch and carry for his master, and nothing more.

The baby boggled up at him, the soft pink light she was familiar with now blocked by an unfamiliar presence.

Even in her new mind, she sensed a threat, for she was indeed a special baby. She stared unblinking at Michael for several long moments and gurgled.

As he reached in to take her from the crib, Emily sucked air into her tiny lungs and started screaming.

•   •   •

Sue Prodger was thinking of wine when her shift ended. After a long workday, she looked forward to a brief respite and a good night's sleep before returning to work.

The screams from the maternity unit sliced through her head like a lance. In her many years as a midwife, Sue had become accustomed to babies' cries, so much so that she barely registered them. This was different.

The sound of all the babies in the nursery wailing together was completely new to her. The cries weren't from hunger, she was sure. Although entirely irrational, she was convinced that these screams were borne out of fear.

Besides the awful nursery noise, there was an indefinable *something else*. A new atmosphere enveloped the maternity unit. The lights seemed dimmer, the air thicker somehow.

Heading towards the nursery at a near-run, Sue stole a glance at the nurses' station: deserted. She had the strange impression that she was the only adult left in the unit. Just her and a room filled with babies screaming in primal fear.

Sue's plimsoles squeaked against the linoleum as she dashed along the length of the corridor, petrified about what might await her when she got to the nursery. For Sue Prodger, at that moment, there was nothing else in her life more important than helping the crying babies. Nothing more important than stopping them from being afraid.

Sue threw open the doors to the nursery and added her voice to those of the children.

•   •   •

Emily's scream seemed almost to shake the room.

Michael's revenant, who had been leaning over her, ready to scoop her small, defenceless form into his gigantic arms, shot back, confused. He waved his hands about in a pointless attempt to soothe the child.

It was too late. As the air left her small lungs, which had taken seconds at most, the other children in the nursery howled. The noise was intense, and he clapped his hands over his ears to try to block it out, resisting the urge to scream himself.

The cries of the babies were filled with a sense of outrage. It was as if they had knowledge of his instructions to remove Emily and take her as part of his master's Harvest. He became convinced that they were trying to stop him.

Just like in life, Michael felt deep guilt for his mere existence.

As he backed away from the crib, he was confused. His instructions were explicit, to bring the child to Kresta, who would feed off its special lifeforce. Despite this, Michael couldn't bring himself to try again to pick up the child. He worried people would come now that the babies had sounded the alarm.

He had to complete his mission. He did not want to think about the consequences of failure. He *must* take the child.

He made his way back to Emily. Still, she screamed, her face scarlet from her efforts. As he loomed, the baby looked knowingly at him.

Michael closed his eyes; he didn't want to look at the baby. "Come on, you little *fucker*," he hissed, ignoring the cries, and scooping the wriggling child into his arms.

Yes! Michael, clutching the baby, lifted his arms into the air in triumph.

The doors flew open, and a woman's screams joined with those of the babies. Michael realised, too late, that holding the baby made him fully visible.

•   •   •

Sue Prodger couldn't stop herself from voicing a scream, her first since she had given birth to her own child some seventeen years before.

A man, who shouldn't be here, stood in the room's centre, holding a baby up like an offering to the heavens. *Predator,* she thought, her scream dying.

She was a being of instinct now. A midwife and a mother. This man was not taking a baby, not from her ward. Not today, not ever.

Sue ran for the man just as the doors to the unit were pushed open once again, this time by Dr Fayad Ayoub, who had been trying to get some sleep in his office midway through a challenging shift.

•   •   •

Still only half-awake, Dr Ayoub looked on in astonishment as the senior midwife launched herself at a strange man who appeared to be holding one of their charges.

•   •   •

A battle cry erupted from the midwife, while Dr Ayoub swiftly struck his palm on the panic button near the doors to summon the hospital's security team. A button Sue had forgotten about in her shock and anger.

As she reached the man, not knowing quite what she was going to do, Sue launched a kick at his knees. Although she was wearing soft shoes and the man didn't go down, she heard a satisfying grunt from his lips.

•   •   •

Michael was momentarily stunned. Given that he was dead, he didn't understand how he felt pain and this woman's kick (her *attack*, he thought, indignant) had hurt.

Furious and confused, Michael gently placed Emily on the floor. He couldn't risk harm coming to the baby. Kresta would be furious.

•   •   •

Sue observed the man placing the baby on the floor and suddenly felt fear for herself. He seemed to become harder for her to focus on, and she became confused as his image flickered before her. Taking advantage of her confusion, the man lunged and grabbed her on either side of the head, hands clamped like a vice.

Michael twisted his hands.

Dr Ayoub heard a crack which he could feel in his bones.

Sue Prodger's lifeless body dropped.

•   •   •

Michael was reaching to the floor, where the squirming, screaming baby lay next to the dead woman. Just as he was about to lift her, a commotion distracted him. Security guards, three of them running into the nursery. He heard the doctor shout something about the police.

He had no choice. Michael abandoned the task. There would be more, many more, children to harvest. The Other would have to understand.

Ignoring the security guards' shouted instructions to stop, and knowing they couldn't quite *see* him, he made his way as fast as he could to the darkest corner of the room, slipped through the portal, and sealed it behind him.

In the maternity unit, Emily and the other babies fell silent.

CHAPTER TWENTY-SIX

As investigations at the Princess Royal Hospital got underway, the founding members of Mystery Inc. met at Mary MacDonald's home for what was to be the last time.

Lucy, having not received any responses from Pig since her long walk, arrived stressed. Her worry for her best friend grew, especially since he didn't come to school and it was unlike him to be out of touch.

Exhausted from living through the rest of his life, or some facsimile of it, Tim Waverly took a seat at the kitchen table and asked Mary for a strong coffee rather than tea.

At last, Pig arrived, grim-faced. Lucy fought down a gasp of surprise.

His beautiful hair, loved by Pig and coveted by Lucy, was gone. With his head shaved, Lucy thought him *harder*, somehow, less like a kid. It saddened her in ways she could not understand. Assuming the others noticed this change, they were pretending not to.

She greeted her friend, and he responded with a thin smile which didn't reach his eyes and took a seat.

Once they were all seated, coffee steaming, Tim looked at each of them, serious. "We must address what occurred last night. For my part, it was unspeakable, but we need to understand how we got away.

"I believe Kresta wanted to remove us from the board, to take us out of the 'game', so to speak."

Lucy, mindful of his status as her teacher, raised her hand. Tim smiled and motioned for her to go on, which she did.

She shared what she saw in Kresta's realm during the long walk, including the citadel at the demon's dark kingdom's heart. As she recalled the events of that unspeakable night, her blood shivered, as if chilled on its journey through her veins. Finally, she explained how she had used the holy water to free them.

"It seems the holy water has apotropaic qualities," Tim mused. "In other words, it has the power to stop evil. Whether that's evidence of God's existence, I wouldn't like to speculate, but it seems to give us an advantage."

"Well, we should certainly be thankful that Lucy had the good sense to wear her holy water on her person." Mary added. "It's a lesson for us all to be vigilant and defend ourselves. I'll fetch some string."

Mary rummaged through a drawer and found a ball of thick string. Tim, Mary, and Pig threaded a length of this around their vials, which they then hung from their necks.

The conversation went on for some time. Lucy felt distressed when she learned about Mary and Tim, having to endure years of misery and strife.

When it got to Pig, he gave them a sad smile, shook his shaven head, and declined to add anything. "I'm sorry," he said, eyes shining. "I can't, I'm not...I'm not ready.

"I'm not sure I'll ever be ready."

Lucy's devastation grew as she realised that her friend had experienced something that affected him in ways she couldn't understand. He wasn't the boy she knew, the one who had been there since she was a child. The best friend who lifted her up when she was feeling low, who was always there with a smile and a laugh. With tears welling up, she tightly grasped his hand for a fleeting moment. Tim and Mary, realising the importance of this gesture, placed their own hands on top of hers.

Pig, locking eyes with Lucy, smiled, and she was glad of it.

The sound of many sirens roaring up the A-road, heading toward the Princess Royal Hospital, broke the moment.

•   •   •

Michael Slade was nothing more than pain.

The revenant lay on the stone floor, a broken thing, a soggy mass of flesh and blood. These mirrored his earthly remains, still spilled across the floor of his old home. Michael hoped he was dying again, and for good this time. He prayed in desperation for the end, which he feared would never come, despite the dimming.

Kresta's fury at his failure to retrieve the baby from the hospital had consumed the demon. He railed and roared. Michael, cowering on the floor, had watched in horror as The Other grew, stretching himself to a preternatural height. His hair became fire, and he stared at Michael with gigantic eyes, now the darkest blue, the blue of a forest at midnight.

The demon had *plucked* Michael from the floor as if he were a troublesome insect he intended to crush, and *squeezed* him in the palm of his terrible, vast hand. Michael had lost consciousness then or lost whatever passed for consciousness in his current state of being.

He awoke to a sense of much time having passed.

Michael had come to in a series of increments, noticing various sounds, hissing pipes, squeaking wheels and what sounded like the bleating of a thousand sheep, the noise cutting into his ears like agonised screams.

He had been restrained. Above him hung a dirty, old-fashioned halogen strip light that flickered on and off at random. The effect of this made him feel sick.

Michael was strapped, naked, to a cold, hard surface, some kind of narrow gurney, his sides spilling over its edges. He was afraid.

Hearing a sound on the far side of the room, a place he had never been before, he turned his head. Kresta, now of human size and wearing a white lab coat, was standing over a trolley of some kind. It wasn't the kind of trolley that Michael had seen in hospitals. Although similar, this appeared to be hewn from some type of dark stone.

Kresta's attention was on the trolley's contents. There were many instruments: blackened pliers, a dark metal contraption resembling a hand drill, a rusted chisel. Michael felt hot tears falling from his eyes, wetting his filthy hair as they fell to the gurney.

Kresta looked over, seeing Michael was awake. He flashed a broad yellow smile, his fury dissipated. Straightening up, Kresta wheeled the trolley towards the gurney. The wheels squealed like drowning rats and the instruments, those bringers of torture, rattled as his master continued his passage across the room.

"Hello revenant," Kresta smiled down at him. "No need to be alarmed. The doctor is in."

•   •   •

Mystery Inc. broke off their meeting when the sirens were joined by yet more sirens. "Something's happening!" Tim exclaimed.

Mary went to the front garden and looked towards the A-road. Blue pulses strobed through the dark, bouncing against the brick of the buildings. Further evidence of some kind of emergency response. *Accident*, she thought, *emergency services heading to the Princess Royal.*

Walking back into her house, she found the others crowded around Pig's laptop. "Someone tried to kidnap a kid from the hospital, a baby!" Lucy said, shock in her voice.

Tim stood up and paced the length of the kitchen-diner, thinking. "It *has to* be Kresta," he said, running his fingers through his hair. "We knew the Mistry boy was just the beginning. Fuck!"

Pig, still monitoring the rolling news, turned round. "If it was the demon, it looks like he failed. According to the BBC, the baby is safe, but a staff member is believed to have died."

All were relieved to find out the baby was doing fine but saddened to learn of the casualty. To distract herself, Mary brewed more coffee. She thought they were all too wired to drink it.

Lucy and Pig watched the news for further updates.

Tim, clearly exhausted, but made edgy by the caffeine, continued to pace the room, oblivious to how irritating Mary was finding this. She flicked on a television news channel to supplement the updates Pig was viewing online.

From outside, the thud-thud-whump of a police helicopter which was circling above drowned out the sound of the sirens.

"Oh shit, it's the man from the rec!" Upon hearing Lucy's cry, the others turned to the television. The police had just released an image by a specialist sketch artist which, according to the ticker at the bottom of the screen, represented a person they wanted to speak with, "in connection with their enquiries."

According to the report, the sketch artist had been working from a description provided to them by a Dr Fayad Ayoub, an eyewitness.

The image, charcoal, showed a person standing in shadow. It was clear from the drawing that it depicted a man of broad stature. No neck was visible, instead a roll of flesh at the base of the chin seemed almost to melt into a pair of muscular shoulders. The depiction used shading to highlight the man's tiny, frightened eyes and thin lips.

"It looks like him," Pig said, frowning. "I haven't seen him that close, but I think that is the man I chased at the recreation ground."

"It is him, Pig. I'm sure of it," Lucy agreed. "That's the creep."

• • •

Coffee made, Mary peered at the screen, experiencing a jolt of familiarity. She knew this man; she was sure of it. Her brain, fogged by exhaustion, failed to come up with a name to match the picture.

Tim resumed his seat at the table, and Mary was grateful he'd stopped his infernal pacing. "So," he said, "we had it right. A connection exists between this man and Kresta. Mary, I think you said he might be a factotum, a familiar?"

"I did. It seems like the logical explanation. If any of this madness can be called logical."

"But he's failed to kidnap the baby," Lucy reminded them.

"I hate to think that someone has died, and we still can't know the whereabouts of Sanjay Mistry, but," Tim continued, "we know Kresta is fallible. We escaped from his punishment, which he won't have expected. And now he's failed to take a baby from the hospital."

'So, what next?' Mary asked, looking at Tim and willing him to lead.

"We have no choice," he said. "We need to act. *I* will act, but if anybody wants to back out, then they should. No one should risk themselves further. There's a strong chance we won't win against this monster. I truly believe it could be the death of us, and that terrifies me more than I can say."

"Especially you children," Mary added, ignoring Lucy's flash of irritation. "You have your whole lives to look forward to and mustn't underestimate the peril we are facing."

"I'm in," said Pig, running a hand across his stubbled head, "I have nothing else to lose." Looking at her friend, Lucy nodded in silent assent.

A text chiming from Mary's phone stopped the conversation. "Hang on," she said with an apologetic shrug. "Oh, good heavens."

"What is it?" Tim asked.

Mary showed them the glowing screen. "A text from the Sanglin woman. She thinks the man in the sketch is Michael Slade, from number fourteen. She's called the police."

• • •

Kresta had begun with Michael's right hand. "Your best friend," he said. The demon referred to it as "degloving".

Ignoring his familiar's tearful and desperate pleas for mercy, Kresta had taken a large scalpel from his trolley and, first, slit the flesh open all the way around Michael's right forearm. Michael, strapped to the hideous gurney, looked away, almost blinded by the pain.

"You probably wonder how you can feel pain, yes?" Kresta had asked, his voice was conversational. "You are a revenant, not a ghost, which would've been terribly dull for both of us. The simple reason you can experience your punishment is that I *choose* for you to feel it."

Thick blood dripped from Michael's arm and pooled onto the gurney. "Nor can you die, although you will certainly beg to after my work here is done," Kresta had added, smiling, "I choose for you to live with your agonies."

Then, far, far worse than the cutting, Kresta had hooked his long fingers under the skin he had sliced through. Michael, weeping and moaning through clenched teeth, bucked on the gurney, fighting against the thick straps as the demon's fingernails scraped and caught against his nerve endings.

With a roar, Kresta stood back and *pulled.*

Michael's flesh was no match for the beast. The pain was the most intense agonising experience of his miserable life. He was consumed by it. It was also slow. The process of degloving his right hand felt like it took many hours, although it might just have taken a few minutes. Inch by painful inch, the flesh was rent from its moorings. Wet, red, agony.

The ends of Michael's fingers were stripped of the last remnant of skin, causing him agonies and forcing an unholy scream from his dead lungs. His flesh being removed sounded like someone peeling off a wetsuit.

Kresta walked around the gurney and dangled the skin-glove above Michael's face. "Hurts, doesn't it?" he said, before throwing it across his shoulder.

Michael struggled to think through the wall of pain. It was impossible to remember a life before this utter anguish. He prayed it was over. It was not.

Kresta walked back to the instrument trolley, humming to himself, and straightened out his bloody lab coat. After spending several minutes in contemplation, he selected a tool for the next job and brought it into Michael's eyeline.

A pair of copper secateurs. Kresta held them up to the light. They were old, with green veins of verdigris spreading across the dull metal like cancer.

"So," Kresta said, "I think it's time to deal with the root of *all* your problems. Testicles off, I think."

Michael's screams travelled across the citadel and far beyond its thick stone walls.

•   •   •

Later, much later, Michael was a being made of pain and hate. He had nothing else.

The Other had laughed with joy as he performed the castration, secateurs flashing in the blinking overhead light. Once finished, he had popped Michael's balls one by one into his mouth and brought his sharp yellow teeth down upon them, tearing, chewing, grinning all the while.

Task complete, Kresta had abandoned Michael after unstrapping him from the gurney, from which he, barely conscious, had fallen wetly to the gore-drenched floor below.

Through his curtain of pain came the realisation that he was dimming once again, losing his sense of himself to this half-life.

His hate, like the pain, was total.

He thought he was dying again, but Kresta had told him he wouldn't die, that his hurt would last forever. Prone on the floor, Michael let out an anguished cry.

He knew what he had to do, even if it took all his strength.

He fought against the unconsciousness that was determined to take him, and with great care, consumed by his agonies, he conjured a portal.

CHAPTER TWENTY-SEVEN

Louise Sanglin was livid. Having fulfilled what she considered her civic duty, by alerting the police to the startling resemblance between the sketch they'd issued on the news and her near neighbour, she was being ignored.

She'd called the incident room three times by 08.30 the following morning, seeking confirmation that she'd been correct in her assumption that the window cleaner, Michael Slade, whom she had always found weird, was the man from the hospital.

Each time she'd called, the police had stonewalled, polite but firm. By the third call, the police had become firmer and instructed her not to call again unless she had specific, relevant information.

Furious, Louise tapped out a message to the street WhatsApp alerting them about Slade, deleting it when she realised (*thank goodness*, she thought) it might not be prudent to risk attacks on a neighbour based on a hunch, however sure she might be. She had rather hoped that Mrs MacDonald could confirm her suspicions, as Louise had seen the woman speaking to Slade in the street some days before, but Mary hadn't responded to her text from the previous evening.

Now, frustrated, and a bit redundant, Louise went back to her post at the front window. Unbeknown to her, the police, alerted to the window cleaner's identity by other callers (many of whom were parents of children on his round), had made Mr Slade a primary person of interest in their investigation.

·   ·   ·

Anita Mistry had scored a hollow victory–she'd lost her temper, and the FLO was gone.

As the days without news about her son's disappearance merged into an unending nightmare, Anita found she was retreating into herself. She no longer washed or changed out of her dressing gown, because she had no reason to.

All she was, all she might ever be, was the mother of a missing child. Perhaps she would, like others before her, be branded with the taint of suspicion, forever speculated about by faceless internet trolls and investigative journalists as somehow responsible for what had happened.

Her life was over.

·   ·   ·

The members of Mystery Inc. had experienced a troubled night.

Tim dreamed of old age, a lonely experience, friendless and with no family. Once more, he suffered a minor stroke, aware of the impending end.

Lucy journeyed on blistered feet. Her long walk would never end. There was to be no relief.

Mary found herself staring at the kettle, wanting to make tea. What was this contraption? *Jackdaw?*

Pig sat at the front of the crematorium, Jakub's coffin on its lonely platform in front of him, like a taunt. He and Jakub's mother leaned into one another and wept, consumed by the grief they shared.

·   ·   ·

Tim, exhausted, slept until 10:00 a.m. He dragged himself from the bed, feeling like the old man he had become in his dreams.

It wasn't until he'd fortified himself with a strong cup of coffee that he registered the lack of images. The walls were clear, unsullied. He made his way around the rest of the building, having neglected his duties as guardian for days. There were no rats, faces, or fingers in sight.

He wondered what this signified. Perhaps Kresta had no use for him now that he'd reached the strength he required to take the innocent? Perhaps it was over?

As he reached the threshold of his living room, he pulled up short.

No images appeared on the walls. But there was a hole.

About half a metre in diameter, it sat, a black trapdoor on the floor in front of the chair.

On closer inspection the darkness in the hole, itself more an absence of floor, was complete. An icy breeze entered the room through the void, accompanied by the sound of distant machinery and, perhaps, the cries of animals. Tim pulled back, coughing as the stench of rotten flesh assailed him.

Tim fetched a torch from the kitchen and, squatting at the edge, shined it into the hole. He couldn't make out any features. The torchlight had no effect. Its beam did not penetrate the blackness within.

He rocked back on his heels for several minutes, thinking. Then he messaged the others.

•   •   •

The police had roused no response from Michael Slade's Oldfield Street home, following numerous tip-offs to the incident line that he was the person depicted in the sketch issued to the media after the incident at the Princess Royal Hospital.

Two uniformed officers were stationed outside the house. They were waiting for officers from the Tactical Firearms Unit. The SIO, concerned for his people's safety, believed it was right for the TFU to force entry into the house. After all, at least one person had lost their life.

The officers could not fail to notice the smell. Fetid, it was hanging in the air outside the building like fog so strong it was almost solid. They were sure their firearms colleagues would make a very unpleasant discovery.

• • •

Tim greeted the others as they arrived. Like him, Mary came to a dead stop when she first saw the hole. Leaning on her stick, she removed her hat and looked back at him with a raised eyebrow.

The others arrived minutes after. Tim was concerned about them.

As their teacher (albeit on a leave of absence), he had a duty of care and felt conflicted at seeing them now. He held a deep sense of worry for Pig in particular. The lad, who had been enthusiastic and excited, seemed *lost* somehow. It was as if he'd endured something from which he would never recover. Perhaps he had.

The four of them crowded into the apartment, made even smaller by the hole in the floor.

"I think it's an entrance of some kind," Tim began.

"Or an exit," countered Mary.

Thus began the debate. About the meaning of the hole, or what to do with it, there was no consensus. Mary speculated it served as some kind of route for Kresta, Lucy countering that he and his familiar appeared able to come and go and, besides, why would the demon create an obvious exit in the place of his enemies?

• • •

Pig remained silent.

Despite giving it its name, he no longer felt part of Mystery Inc. The once enthusiastic teenager, brimming with curiosity and optimism, had vanished.

Although he was still a boy, he felt like a man. His heart had been shattered and life no longer held meaning or hope.

As the debate went on around him, Pig remained detached. Yes, he was fond of these people. He even loved them in a way, but it wasn't enough. Not anymore.

• • •

It was Lucy who saw it happen. As the discussion became more heated, her attention drifted away. Mr W and Mrs M could not reach a view about what action to take and, despite all the drama, she found herself bored by their circular conversation.

"Pig!" She cried out as her friend jumped, not making a sound, into the hole. The others stopped speaking, Tim's mouth hanging open.

"What the fuck did he just do?" he asked, throwing his hands into the air.

"Perhaps he…fell?" Mary said, peering down into the hole.

Lucy shook her head. "He…he *jumped*," she insisted, "but *why*?" Shocked, she had begun to cry.

Mary led Lucy to the kitchenette and turned on the kettle. Lucy, through her tears, thought she heard the woman say "jackdaw" as it boiled, and decided she'd misheard.

"I'm going to follow him. I've no choice," Tim announced.

Mary glanced up. "I'll come too. I won't pretend I'm not afraid because I am. I'm petrified. But I will come."

Lucy, drying her tears and barely listening, said she would also enter the hole in the floor. She listened to the others' protests and held up a hand. "Pig's my best friend. He's been my best friend since I was five years old, and I love him.

"I know he'd do the same for me. I know this because that's what our friendship means to us. I'm going in there and, I'm sorry, you can't stop me."

Tim smiled at her. "Okaaaay, I hear you. We both do. But let's do this properly. Stout walking shoes and water - of both the drinking and holy kind. Let's go get our friend and slay the demon.

"Let's pack torches as well," he added. "Lucy, I have one I think might belong to you. I found it in an old bathroom recently." He winked at her.

•   •   •

Sean, standing in his living room after getting back with the dog, watched the firearms unit arrive.

Two large grey vans, liveried with the Met Police shield, roared into the street, lights flashing. The vans disgorged half a dozen officers, armed and dressed like paramilitaries, with their faces covered.

Two of these officers used a battering ram on the door of number fourteen, splitting it like paper in order for the others to run in with a battle cry: "ARMED POLICE, ARMED POLICE!"

One by one, they emerged from the house, empty-handed. One officer pulled his mask down, revealing a handsome face. Turning to one side, he vomited in the front garden.

Another officer put tape across the space where the door had stood until a few moments before.

This entire series of events started and finished in seconds.

•   •   •

Tim attached a length of rope to one of the window bars, testing it before carefully lowering himself into the hole. He was carrying a backpack filled with provisions.

The moment he put his legs through the aperture, they disappeared from view. The effect was disconcerting but, if he wiggled his toes, he could still feel them in his boots. "*Geronimo,*" he called as he gave himself to the darkness.

Mary, next, said a small prayer and fingered the holy water at her neck. She was afraid she'd never escape from this, whatever it was. But she was determined to play her part in trying to destroy the demon and saving Sanjay and thousands like him from harm. As she slipped into the hole, helped by Lucy, she heard the call of pipes, sharp in her ears.

Lucy took one last look around the room, now clear of those vile images and, not pausing like the others, went for it, giving herself to the door in the floor. She was going to find Pig and bring him back alive.

The room, empty of people, stood dim in the winter daylight. The hole was gone.

• • •

Kresta, in the citadel, cracked open his eyes. He knew what was taking place and cursed the revenant.

They were here now, and he would enjoy playing with them before resuming the Harvest.

He smiled wider than a human smile. Where to start? Of course, with the lovelorn boy. First in, first out.

"Come on then. Let's be having you," he chuckled.

CHAPTER TWENTY-EIGHT

It was cold.

His breath misting, rubbing at his arms for warmth, Pig looked at his surroundings with a heady mixture of trepidation and awe.

The dimensions put him in mind of a cathedral, but any cathedral he'd seen would pale in comparison. A vaulted ceiling soared high above, while unseen birds screamed shrill cries to one another as they flew between its dark beams.

Or, perhaps, they weren't birds, just very large bats.

The far end of the room, which was lit by a source Pig couldn't discern, was impossible to make out. Ornate windows of stained glass were randomly placed around, but they did not admit any light from outside. Gigantic stone pews stretched across the vast, echoing width of the space.

Pig felt small, a little boy lost, afraid and insignificant. He glanced at his phone, which proved pointless. Its screen, dark and lifeless, taunted him.

As he began exploring his new surroundings, a roar went up. It sounded like a giant train, or a great mechanical insect passing by the space. Or passing through, somehow unseen. Pig, yelling, placed his hands over his ears in a futile attempt to block out the terrible din.

The noise was so violent, so all-consuming it was like a physical violation. His legs shook, his scrotum tightened, and his scalp tingled.

Eardrums popping and throbbing, Pig fell to his knees, bruising them on the blood-red flagstones.

The auditory assault seemed to take hours. Pig experienced an intense sense of release when the sound passed, heading off into some unknowable distance. He sucked in a deep breath, choking on the cold air.

Feeling an unfamiliar warmth, he touched the side of his neck with a shaking finger and brought it up to his face. Blood was running from his ears. Gritting his teeth against the pain, Pig stood up from the dirt-strewn floor and gripped the freezing back of a pew, needing a few moments to regain his balance.

As he walked once more, he pondered everything that had happened. His naivety appalled him. His determination to rush in to investigating the weird and the supernatural, without ever thinking about what might be unleashed.

All the books, the horror films, revelling in the fear they caused, laughing with Lucy about scaring themselves. The documentaries and internet forums, reading breathless accounts of people's experiences with the 'other side'. The late-night conversations with Lucy, trying to frighten one another, and playing stupid games with the ouija board. His desire to see, to know, was foolhardy.

What a pathetic, childish fascination it had been.

The supernatural wasn't fun. It was an obscenity, an abomination. It was terror, shame, and loss. He should have found other interests. It had robbed him of all his joy and enthusiasm, leaving him a mere shadow of the boy he had once been. It felt like an amputation over which he'd had no choice. Pig didn't think he would ever find that person again. He was torn between the schoolboy and the shattered, suicidal widower.

He walked on.

After many hours, he saw a wall, the endless room finally ending. Only a few details were visible in the flickering light, but at least he had a destination to aim for.

He was thankful there had been no repeat of the assault on his ears, which still rang, but could still hear occasional sounds, which chilled his soul. Sometimes, the terrified bleating of many sheep. Occasionally, music and mechanical sounds emerged, carried on cold air as if from a dreadful forge.

An altar-like structure stood at the far end of the space. This altar, unlike one in a church, appeared rough-hewn, as though carved by giants from solid rock. On top of its surface burned candles, many thousands of them, their wax black and misshapen, giving off a stinking, smoky yellow light.

Behind the alter, loomed a vast window, its glass cracked and dulled by the ages. It admitted only darkness.

Standing next to the altar was a large object carved from blackened wood:

X

The X looked to be crafted for a specific purpose rather than for any aesthetic quality. It stood about ten feet from top to bottom, its 'arms' pointing to the vaulted roof far above, as if in an offering. Or in supplication.

A loud creaking and groaning interrupted Pig's examination. It sounded as if the sky was collapsing, and he brought his hands to his throbbing, bloodied ears. Looking behind, in the direction he'd walked from, a shaft of yellow light appeared - giant, arched doors opening far off in the distance.

Minutes passed, yet Pig remained fixated on the distant light, reflecting on his past trials and the demon's deceitful lies. He heard a new sound, *tap, tap, tap*, footsteps on red stone. He squinted and barely discerned a figure. Its walk along the nave was relaxed, unhurried.

A tickle, almost a burn, pricked his chest.

"It is so kind of you to visit my citadel, child." The voice sounded as if the speaker was right next to his ear, but Pig understood it was the man (demon) walking towards him. He did not reply.

"I told you not to meddle, but meddle you did. Dear oh dear, what am I to do with you?" Kresta's suit was the black of the deep ocean, his eyes the blue of a midwinter frost.

"Little Pig, little Pig. Oh! All those old stories. So many of them are about me.

"Parents warning their children, for thousands of years, 'Be good or the Lamia will find you!' Even today, 'Behave child, or you'll be snatched by the Namahage.'"

"So much beautiful fear to feed off. So much *innocence*."

The tickle at Pig's chest had become more defined, pinching. Unthinking, he scratched at it.

At long last, Kresta reached a stop in front of Pig. He appeared no more than fifty years old.

"And you thought you might *thwart* me, Sow? That you could stop the Harvest, save the children, starve the beast." Kresta tutted, "Silly. Silly *little boy*."

Kresta raised his arms. Pig, stomach roiling, found himself lifted, gasping, into the air. As Kresta moved his hands, Pig's body, over which he had no control, was spun around, and pushed back through the cold air. It came to a painful stop when his spine slammed into the centre of the wooden X.

Kresta removed his jacket and adjusted his black tie, its ram's head pin glinting in the torchlight. Pig's body lowered until his feet rested on two wooden pegs protruding from the X.

Singing tunelessly to himself, the demon walked over to the bruised boy and, with strange tenderness, removed Pig's trainers. He set these to one side before peeling the socks from his feet.

Kresta winked and clicked his fingers.

Pig could not resist, as his arms were pulled upwards. Thick ropes snaked around his thin wrists, tying each arm to one branch of the X.

More ropes coiled tight around his ankles, shackling his legs to the apparatus.

The burning against his chest was unbearable, causing him to cry out. Frowning, Kresta loomed before him, growing in height to match the scale of the X.

"Ah, give the boy a round of applause." The demon, smiling, wrapped huge fingers around the string hanging from Pig's neck and yanked until it snapped. As the vial was removed, the burning became nothing more than a faint sting, a memory of pain.

Kresta peered at the vial of holy water with a moue of distaste before flinging it into the dark shadows beyond. "That won't work. Your soul is broken," he said.

Now, human height once more, he glanced up at Pig's immovable body.

"Crucifixion," he mused. "Quite an iconic way to go, don't you think?"

Pig, shivering from cold and shock, cried. His nose and eyes streamed as he coughed out some words.

"Oh, I didn't catch that?"

"I want Mum," he stuttered. "Please, I just want to see my mother."

The demon smiled.

It began as a faint wrinkle at the edges of Kresta's lips. They turned up at the sides and stretched. Wider and wider they went until the skin at the edges tore. Ichor, almost black, ran down the sides of the manic grinning face, covering the sharp yellow teeth and pattering onto his shirt.

Kresta, saying nothing, turned away and walked towards the shaft of light from whence he had come. He clicked his fingers once more.

Four blackened iron nails shot into view, hurtling along the dark nave. About eight inches in length, they came to a dead stop in front of Pig's hands and above his feet.

They began to turn and twist in the air and, with agonising slowness, started to drill into Pig's extremities.

The boy screamed as he had never screamed before. His screams came back to him as echoes while the nails pierced his tender flesh, their twisting, pushing motion grinding against delicate nerve endings and crushing bone.

By the time the nails came to a stop, penetrating the thick wood behind his hands and under his feet, the pain was all-consuming.

"IT HURTS. OH GOD STOP, PLEASE. MUM, HELP ME!" the boy cried out.

From far away he heard laughter, "You won't find God here Piggy-wig. You're in *my* house now."

Hours passed as Pig drifted in and out of consciousness. Sometimes he dreamed of his life with Jakub, weeping lonely tears when he remembered it had been a pretence. Blood oozed from the stigmata, pooling on the floor. The shaft of light reduced, thinning to a sliver before the doors came to a booming close.

Kresta was gone.

At one point Pig, a fearful sweat pouring into his eyes, heard harsh cawing, and glanced up, his vision blurred. Great birds of prey swooped and circled overhead. He knew their unquenchable hunger for carrion would soon be sated.

From time to time, his thin body slumped as his hands ripped further apart, unable to carry his weight on the nails. He burned with fever and his heart stuttered in his ribcage.

He wept. He screamed until he had no strength with which to voice his agony.

As he neared the end, he thought of his Mum. Dorothy, a good person, raised two children alone. She had taken good care of them, sacrificing so much.

His heart beating faster than he knew possible, he murmured a whispered prayer for Tim, for Mary and for Lucy, who he loved.

As Pig's ruined heart beat its last, he pictured Jakub, and his body allowed him one final tear.

CHAPTER TWENTY-NINE

Louise Sanglin liked to think of herself as one of life's tenacious people. Once she had the bit between her teeth, she would not let it go.

People who knew her would label Louise as "persistent," but it was not meant as a compliment.

The police sketch *was* of that awful Michael Slade, the window cleaner. She knew it and she was not prepared to be fobbed off. After multiple calls, the people at the end of the police incident line had morphed from firm to downright rude. Even so, she'd employed her *tenacity* to get results.

The outcome, when it came, surprised her. Eventually, someone connected her to a higher-ranking officer involved in the case (or at least that's what they claimed).

Louise was informed that Mr Slade had been "eliminated from their enquiries" before the line was cut. This couldn't be right. It had to have been him, it *was* him, she told herself, outraged.

Nevertheless, stepping out into the street, she spied an officer standing by the front of Slade's house. What was all that about?

Despite her earlier reservations, she thumbed a message to the Oldfield WhatsApp group. If the Met would not do their job, she'd do it for them.

Aiming for subtlety, she asked if the neighbours had seen the suspect sketch from the "hospital drama" and, if so, was the person familiar?

Nobody replied.

• • •

At number nineteen, Sean glanced at the message from Mrs Sanglin and chucked his phone back onto the sofa.

She wasn't wrong, he suspected, but he wouldn't give her the satisfaction of being validated. *Gossipy cow*, he thought.

Sean had seen the police sketch later than Louise; he'd only scanned the reports after the drama with the armed police earlier in the afternoon.

He hardly ever saw the man who lived across the street. From time-to-time Sean had spied the window cleaner making his way along the pavement, eyes facing down as he walked to his van but, in the normal course of events, the main signs of life were a succession of takeaways arriving via moped and supermarket delivery vehicles.

Seeing the sketch made the skin on the back of Sean's neck crawl. Not only did it resemble his elusive neighbour, but it also looked like the strange man he'd seen at the rec., frightening the life out of him.

It hadn't occurred to him until he saw the drawing that his neighbour and the man in the park might be the same person. The police activity over the road offered compelling, if circumstantial, evidence that the man had been linked with the awful events at the hospital.

Sean glanced out of the window. A uniformed officer still stood outside number fourteen and police tape fluttered across the empty doorway. *They must be waiting for someone to come home*, he thought.

• • •

PC Aaron Woollard was cold and hungry. After seeing what was inside the house, he doubted he would ever eat again.

From his vantage point at the front of number fourteen, he gazed along the street. He could make out a colleague whom he didn't recognise, posted outside the door at Oldfield Court. The investigation into the disappearance of that little boy was ongoing. And going nowhere, so he'd been told.

Despite all the strange events of recent days, PC Woollard observed that some of the residents had already put up Christmas decorations. He considered this to be both early and rather thoughtless, given the ongoing agonies of that boy's parents.

Or perhaps people were just trying to hold back the darkness.

He glanced at his watch and sniffed. PC Woollard hoped the clean-up crew wouldn't take long to arrive. He was cold and bored and could still smell the rot.

CHAPTER THIRTY

Lucy sensed she was in the wrong place, but couldn't remember where she should be. An organ droned, its pipes tuneless. She sneaked a look at her phone. Dead, it must be out of charge.

Revd Anthony ("Call me Tony!") Stafford was boring on as per from the pale wooden pulpit.

"Leave them," he intoned. "They are blind guides. If the blind lead the blind, both will fall into the pit."

Revd Stafford's eyes found hers and locked on, owlish behind thick lenses. *Odd*, she thought, *I thought call-me-Tony's eyes were brown, not blue.*

Tearing her own eyes away from the vicar's stare, she looked around at the familiar surroundings of St Bartholomew's. As ever, she thought it looked grim.

Cloth hangings, which depicted various family-friendly scenes from scripture, failed in their attempts to hide the bare brick walls and did nothing to lift the atmosphere. In the corner stood a box of second-hand toys which were designed to distract small children who lost it during services. Many were given to her as a child. Lucy smiled at the memory.

St Bart's was never full. Few churches were these days, even at Christmas. Today's congregation comprised elderly people and the odd shiny-faced couple in their twenties, perhaps hoping attendance would ease their wedding plans or help get their kids into the right school.

Lucy sat on her own in the pew. This was odd. She never came to church unless coerced by her mother, who wasn't anywhere to be seen. She shifted attention to the font, vaguely remembering stealing water from it. Why the hell would she do that?

Scratching her chest through her thick black sweater (*bloody gnats*, she thought), Lucy recognised with alarm that nobody was moving.

In her experience, congregations fidgeted. They squirmed in their seats, coughed, and peered at their watches when bored. Sometimes people even played with their phones during the service.

Nobody moved. At all.

She scratched at herself again. Maybe this thick jumper was irritating her? She peered around once more, paying closer attention this time.

The eyes of the congregation stared straight ahead, unblinking. Hands rested on knees. None of them moved a muscle.

Ignoring Tony's ongoing sermon, Lucy stood up and walked over to a young woman sitting closer to the front, next to a good-looking guy, the woman's partner, Lucy imagined. She waved a hand in front of the woman's face. Nothing. Then she clicked her fingers. No response.

Lucy looked at the man. A thin line of pale dribble leaked from the side of his mouth.

She was frightened. *What the hell is going on?*

Revd Stafford broke her thoughts by clapping his hands together twice, the sound echoing off the brick walls.

"COMMUNION TIME!" he called, giving her a wave.

Lucy never took communion. She scratched herself, wincing.

"Lucy," Tony called to her, "time for the host."

Her legs moved as if compelled. Lucy gave a small cry. She had no control over her legs. *What the actual fuck?* Looking around, she saw that the young couple, and the rest of the congregants, were gone. She was alone in the church, save for the vicar.

Revd Stafford stood in front of the pale oaken altar. The silver crucifix, always proudly displayed, was missing.

He clicked his long fingers and Lucy fell to her knees in front of him.

The vicar's voice darkened as he said, "This is my body, given for you." He removed a small arm from his cassock. The arm of a little child, tiny, lifeless fingers curling into the palm. Lucy watched in horror as he took a huge bite, his lips stretched beyond their limits, chewing it with a shiver of pleasure. Swallowing, he looked at her. "Nom, nom," he said with a wink.

Placing the tiny, broken limb on the altar, Tony (*Kresta*, her mind insisted madly) lifted a goblet carved from dark stone.

"This is my blood. Shed for you." Lifting the giant cup, the vicar drank. His throat moved in deep gulps, dark blood spilling down the sides of his great mouth.

The itch against her chest was burning, snagging her mind away from the unspeakable terror that threatened to consume her.

"Your turn," the vicar smiled down at her. He opened his cassock, and Lucy began shaking uncontrollably, tears falling from her eyes.

"This is my body," he intoned, his erect member twitching in front of her face, "given for you."

Lucy found herself unable to look away. Her eyes were pinned to the horror, as if by force. Thick veins ran along the length of the vicar's penis. Moisture dribbled from the engorged tip.

He chuckled. "Take this and think of me."

With a herculean effort, Lucy screamed and pawed at her burning chest. Something was hanging there. Of course!

She thrust her hands down the front of her thick sweater and found the vial of holy water, crying out as it burned the skin of her palm.

She saw the vicar's smile falter as the horrific scene dissolved.

• • •

"Do you understand what I'm explaining to you, Mary? Hmm?"

The doctor gazed over at her, his disinterested eyes blue on blue. *I didn't say he could call me Mary,* she thought, irritated.

A card lay before her. On this was scrawled a random collection of shapes, letters, and numbers. These spread across its surface as if scattered from a great height.

"I asked if you would draw me a clock face, remember? That," he gestured at the card, "is your creation."

Can't they turn the heating up in this place?

Mary had a strange sensation. Something akin to déjà vu, but not quite the same somehow. She had experienced this scenario before, or she had in some other life.

The doctor, she couldn't recall his name, was still speaking. She hissed as a sharp itch bloomed across her chest.

"...stop it, but we can delay the later stages, assuming we can find a mix of medication that works best for you. Am I saying this in a way that's helpful, Mary?"

Why was she listening to this patronising young man? She had somewhere else to be, didn't she?

"Earth to Mary! I know you've got dementia, but you still have a tongue in your head."

The doctor, Dr Kresta she remembered now, such a silly name, waggled his fingers at her.

"Thank you, doctor, yes I understand you perfectly well," making her tone arch enough to convey her annoyance.

"Yes, well, jolly good," he gave her a too-wide smile. "As I was saying, we can't stop it. The train has left the tunnel, choo-choo!"

"You're going to lose your marbles, Mary. Give it a few years and you won't know yourself, let alone anybody else. You'll just sit in your own effluent, praying for the end. I assure you, death will not come soon. You'll remain alive for the longest time."

Mary, shocked and afraid, questioned the doctor's audacity.

"Just who do you think you are, Dr Kresta, speaking to me like this? I might be old and my mind a little softer than I'd like, but I'm nobody's fool." She scratched at herself.

"Ooh, feisty, I like it!" the doctor said, standing up behind his desk. Walking over to a dark cabinet carved from black stone, he pulled open a drawer and removed a large, rusted surgical instrument.

"Bone saw," he said, holding it up to the light. "I'm going to offer you a choice."

Mary chose not to answer and waited for him to go on.

"Slow dementia or quick death. I know which I would go for.

"A simple procedure. I cut, here and here," he ran a long finger across and along Mary's head, the nail catching in her hair, and she gave an involuntary shudder.

"The cutting done, I will use this instrument to saw through the top of your skull. Imagine opening a tin of sardines and you'll have the idea."

Mary felt the itch burn a little, annoyance becoming discomfort.

"Sawing complete, I peel your face down just like the skin of a banana. But red.

"Then I can really get my hands down into the cavity and *scoop* out your rotting brain. I'll just throw it away; you'll be dead by then, and I have no use for such a worn-out, useless, organ."

Mary was paying him scant attention now. The burn was focusing her mind, as was the realisation that everything about this was wrong. She shouldn't have been here, hearing the man's lunatic ravings.

"So, what do you say? I can start cutting straight away. It will hurt, I'm afraid. I won't be bothering with anaesthetic."

"I say you can rot, you bastard," she said. A large grey rat ran along the skirting board and squeezed behind the cupboard.

Mary knew there were things she had to do. She placed her hand through the buttons on her blouse and wrapped her fingers around the vial she had remembered was hanging there.

It burned, and she welcomed the pain.

•   •   •

Tim tried not to squirm in the hard wooden chair, thinking it would be inappropriate.

He hated these events and was pleased he had a seat a few rows from the front. Not difficult, as there was nobody else in attendance. Sad. The room was plain, with magnolia walls and dark red drapes setting the mood.

The coffin stood at the front, held up by two fragile A-frames. Next to it was a lectern hewn from dark stone, and a bunch of pale lilies which looked artificial.

Organ pipes, tuneless, began to play. Unable to make out the source of the awful music, he assumed it was coming from hidden speakers.

Tim stood as the celebrant walked in. A tall man in a black suit, his dark hair swept back from the temples, and his eyes the blue of deep space. The celebrant gestured for him to retake his seat and, when he did so, a broad smile tinged yellow was his reward.

The man clicked his fingers. The sound echoed through the room, and the grim music stopped.

"We," he looked around and cleared his throat. "*You* are here today to commemorate the life of a man. A teacher, one who brought little joy to his students."

Bit harsh, Tim thought.

"A man who was shattered by the loss of his mother when he was just a small boy. He locked his feelings deep inside his heart and threw away the key.

"In this box, the man lies withered and rotting. A husk.

"His life lacked commendable attributes. He had few friends, and those he did have, he drifted away from," another yellow smile. "Emotions were pushed deep inside. Medicated.

"He died as he lived. *Alone*."

Tim was finding the service very odd. He was trying hard not to squirm, the lack of comfort to the wooden seat compounded by a ticklish itch just below his throat. He pretended to adjust his too-tight tie in order to hide a scratch.

"Sometimes," the celebrant went on, "the deceased liked to *meddle*.

"He became involved in situations which need not have been of any concern to him, his *minor* role having reached its natural conclusion.

"But, sadly, he meddled. In the end, he had to pay the price. Pity.

"If you would be so kind as to stand." The celebrant pressed a red button on the side of his lectern as Tim got to his feet, and the coffin slid off its moorings on metal rollers. "We commit the body of Timothy Andrew Waverly to endless agonising flames."

Tim, alarmed, looked around and absently scratched at his chest. Was this some kind of joke?

His stomach lurched and, eyes watering, he could smell smoke. He found himself lying down, his movements restricted. He coughed as the smoke tickled his airway.

Terror hit him. He was in the coffin.

Desperate, he squirmed about and got his hands onto the inside of the lid. He gritted his teeth and let out a scream as he pressed his palms against the blond wood, determined to escape.

Nothing happened. The lid wasn't going anywhere. He coughed again, eyes stinging.

Through his fear came a voice. It sounded like the celebrant was in the coffin with him.

"...simple process. The heat, all of which you will experience, I'm afraid, will be intense. You will never have known pain like it.

"Your eyes will burst, your flesh will vaporise, and your bones will turn to ash.

"And here's my gift to you, meddler. You will feel it all and, when you are but a pile of dust, the process will begin once more. In fact, it will never end. Imagine that, burning forever."

The pain, the burning. Eyes streaming as smoke consumed the tiny space and small flames danced around his feet. The pain was worse, far worse around Tim's chest, although he could see no fire there yet.

He managed, causing himself great pain, to manoeuvre a hand to his chest where something hard and boiling hot vibrated wasp-like under his shirt. Tim, coughing, tore open the top of his shirt and placed his hand on the fiery object.

His vision turned black.

CHAPTER THIRTY-ONE

Sanjay Mistry slept.

In his dream, he sits in his bedroom, which isn't his bedroom. Sometimes Dr Kresta comes to visit.

When he does, the doctor says nothing, but he *takes* from Sanjay. He doesn't know exactly what it is the doctor takes, but it makes him feel so tired, even though he's already sleeping, or thinks he must be. His thoughts became confused, and he was sure that, with each visit, the doctor somehow looked younger.

Dr Kresta is Bad.

The giant has not been to this place since Sanjay was first taken from his real bedroom and, for that, he's grateful. The giant is frightening, and Sanjay never wants to see him again.

Sometimes Sanjay thinks his Mummy is nearby. He knows she is very sad and spends a lot of her time in bed. He finds this strange because his mother never lies in, even on Sundays. She always says it's a sign of laziness and he and Daddy aren't supposed to spend weekends watching TV in their PJs, even though they both want to.

Sanjay is afraid.

He is afraid of Dr Kresta and the giant and this room and afraid for his Mummy, who he thinks is crying a lot, even if this is a dream.

The child slept on.

CHAPTER THIRTY-TWO

Tim, terrified by the flames, patted himself down with frantic hands. He screamed in desperation.

"Mr W!" Lucy's voice, "you're okay. You're *okay*. We're at the citadel, remember, the one I saw on my walk."

Disorientated and relieved, he took in his surroundings.

Before him there stood a huge building formed of black stone. It appeared organic, as if it had grown out of the rock, rather than being built from it. The ground was the same hard material.

The citadel soared high into the firmament. No stars hung in the sky, but it emitted a sickly pale red light. Birds circled high above, screaming and, from somewhere, came the sounds of machinery and farm animals.

Tim felt an uncontrollable wave of despair. The building seemed to drain his soul's hope for the future. His eyes teared up, but he brushed them away, resolving to remain strong. He had to resist negative thoughts.

He was relieved to see Lucy and Mary, who looked at him with a raised eyebrow.

"More trials for you too?" he asked.

"Oh yes, Mr Waverly, for all of us," Mary answered.

"And no sign of Pig," Lucy added, her eyes red.

"Shit," Tim sighed. "Well, he came to this place some hours before we did. He could be anywhere. We'll find him, I'm sure. Are you physically alright?"

Lucy nodded and Mary gave him an exhausted smile, adding, "As alright as I'll ever be, I'm too old and too tired for this caper, much as I don't like to admit it."

Tim placed an experimental hand on the wall. The black stone was cold, so cold it seemed to leach the warmth from his entire body and soul. *This place feels like...grief,* he said to himself.

Removing his hand, he looked back at the others. "I hate to say this, but I think we need to find a way to get inside."

• • •

In his place, the demon raged.

Once again, these puny beings thwarted him and he was furious. He needed to build his strength in order to deliver the final, crushing blow.

Damn them. If he had only got the Harvest properly underway and if the useless revenant had fulfilled his simple task and brought that baby to the citadel.

Ah! That baby, so filled with lifeforce. A ripe fruit, waiting to be plucked.

Nor can he take any more energy from the Mistry boy. That young soul needs time to rest and recover itself, otherwise it will simply become useless.

Kresta's plans had been great. He would join others from the Pantheon, restored to their rightful place as destroyers, revelling in their handiwork.

In his rage, fires burst into life and the black stone shook.

"MEDDLERS!" the demon roared.

• • •

The walk took its toll on each of them. Mary, in particular, was struggling, and the others watched on, concerned, seeing her concentrate on every step. Sometimes she took a sharp intake of breath and squeezed her eyes closed for a few moments.

Lucy tried hard to contain her discomfort. She didn't want to burden anyone, especially Mary, who was clearly struggling, but she still hadn't fully recovered from the Long Walk. The sharp tearing of half-healed blisters punctuated her every step.

"Let's take a breather," Tim said, to the relief of his companions.

Together, they sat on the hard ground in the dismal shadow cast by the citadel, thankful they had packed provisions. Lucy was tortured by gnawing anxiety about Pig as she sipped her water.

Tim surprised them with a small laugh as Mary revealed a thermos of tea from her small carryall. She returned his smile. "I might be petrified, but I'm an old-fashioned Englishwoman and nothing keeps me from my tea."

He raised his bottle of water. "To tea. And to you Mary, you Lucy and Pig, wherever he might be. I'm privileged to know you, to have you as my…friends." They tipped their drinks together in acknowledgement.

Lucy's mood lifted a little as they rested in a companionable silence, broken only by the strange sounds of their environment.

That this was a place built from terror and grief wasn't in doubt. But the presence of Mary MacDonald (and her tea) as well as the teacher gave Lucy a sense of safety, even though she knew it was misplaced. Since they'd found themselves at the citadel, she had fought with everything she had against the waves of despair and sorrow emanating from the place, drawing away all energy and hope. She resisted, fearing that surrendering meant losing herself.

It was Mary who broke into their thoughts - "Rats."

"They seem to be a familiar theme," Tim responded. "I've always hated the bloody things."

"You misunderstand me, Tim, look," Mary pointed an arthritic finger.

Ahead of them, a long line of rats made its way towards the citadel. Lucy's flesh crawled in silent protest.

In the dim, reddish light, the rats looked to be a single seething creature, undulating like a giant snake along the ground. Their procession was almost silent, which added to the eerie quality of the scene.

"Come on, let's follow them," Tim said, standing as he lifted his pack.

"Er, hello?!" Lucy said, as she stood. "Why exactly?"

She helped Mary to her feet. "Because," Tim said, "I suspect they know a way in."

•   •   •

Awake and deep below in his room (tomb), Sanjay leaped from his bed/not his bed, where he had been sitting thinking about Mummy and Daddy.

He didn't understand it, but he knew there were others here. Others who had come to this awful place, so very far from home, but who wished him no harm.

For the first time since the giant had brought him to this scary place, Sanjay sensed Good.

•   •   •

The running of the rats was something to behold. It was impossible to gauge their number.

Some were small, runty creatures which were trampled by larger specimens as they skittered around the citadel.

The rats had no obvious leader. They bowled over one another, their sharp teeth biting at the tails of their swarm-mates in their eagerness to reach their destination. It was this that interested Tim the most - despite the chaotic run, there must be a destination.

Sometimes, a struggling rat could not continue. These were swarmed by their pack mates in a frenzy of sharp teeth and grappling claws, feeding until there was little of the creature left where it had fallen.

· · ·

Mary was struggling. Even though she had entered this godforsaken place with her walking stick hooked to her bag, it had remained in the doctor's 'consulting room'.

Lucy, despite her obvious pain, insisted she take Mary's arm, which proved more of a comfort than a help. One she was happy to accept. Like the others, she experienced waves of distress from being in such proximity to the citadel, and she was determined to resist its evil.

At last, as they rounded an ill-defined corner, the line of vermin shrank. The effect was strange. It seemed like rats were pouring into the ground.

Tim held up a hand. "We'd better wait, I think, for the swarm to pass."

Much later, a final rat, a small creature with seemingly three legs, limped to its goal. It looked back at them, dark eyes forlorn, and hissed before tumbling out of sight.

· · ·

Motioning for the others to stay put (Mary looked fit to drop), Tim went to examine the gap the vermin had entered.

The hole, surrounded by stinking rat droppings, tunnelled into the stony ground and, he gave a silent prayer of thanks, looked large enough for a human to squeeze into. He wondered if the hole served a purpose, providing ventilation for the citadel perhaps, but the most important thing was that it existed at all.

He shined his torch into the space. The beam struggled to penetrate far into the darkness, but he was pleased to see an incline rather than a precipitous drop.

Tim walked back to his companions, and they debated for a while. He was concerned about Mary's ability to carry on, but she would not hear of splitting up. "I will walk until I drop," she said, "and, if that happens, I will very probably die. So be it. But I am not finished yet."

Sensing the finality of her words, they made their way into the tunnel.

CHAPTER THIRTY-THREE

Sanjay, in his waking/sleeping state, fought to remain aware.

"Come on, Good people," he said in a small voice. "I want to go home."

•   •   •

The tunnel was dark, narrow, and claustrophobic. Their progress was slow.

Although the decline was not steep, it remained constant. It seemed they were going to enter the building in a space far below ground level.

With no room to walk other than in single file, Mary brought up the rear, resting her hands on Lucy's shoulders for support. She was in a lot of pain. Her advanced years and the recent tumble meant she was going to struggle. She was determined to plough on.

She listened, interested, to the sounds of the place. There were noises which sounded mechanical in nature. It was as if giant machines, perhaps many miles beneath them, were fuelling Kresta's realm.

Since they had entered the tunnel, she had also experienced something else. A benign presence, almost. The effect, in this dismal place, was akin to catching something beautiful from the corner of one's eye. It was elusive, a hopeful, warm feeling of some kind. She wondered if the others felt it, too.

Tim's determination impressed her. As they walked, he assured them they were going to get through this. He told them he wanted, more than anything, to find Pig, rescue Sanjay, and start living a life of his own. Really live, open himself up to others, because he had suffered a plausible alternative.

Mary looked at Lucy. Even from behind, the set of the girl's shoulders showed that her anxiety had reached fever pitch, her body was tense and, on the few occasions that she spoke, her voice was quiet and carried a tremor. Little wonder, she must be terrified for her friend.

The ending of the tunnel was abrupt. One moment, they were walking through a space so tight they would never have been able to turn around. If it had been a dead-end, they would have starved, tunnel become tomb.

The next moment, they emerged into a great cavern. Pulsating yellow light gave illumination to a floor-space so wide it was impossible to make out the other side. A barrelled ceiling soared far above, and in the nearest corner, a set of wide stone steps had been carved into the wall.

"More walking," Tim said, shrugging his shoulders with a resigned smile.

• • •

Kresta roared. He ranted and raged, rending his clothes. He sought communion with the Pantheon, but the calls went unheeded.

He pulled the heads from his beloved rats and, tipping the carcasses over his lips, drank from their open necks as their lifeless bodies twitched on between his long fingers.

Where were they? He would find them and trap them, devour the meddlers like the rats they were.

• • •

Lucy gasped, and Mary clasped at the vial, still hanging from its cord around her neck.

A huge passageway branched out of the curved wall of the cavern. Its vaulted ceiling was hanging high above, lost in the darkness.

The passage appeared to be some kind of tomb, reaching into the distance. Along each long wall were a series of open crypts, carved into the rock. Many of the crypts were occupied.

Tim switched his torch on and directed its light along one row of crypts, revealing their contents.

Children, their bodies in various states of decay. As they made their way through the crypt, they were overwhelmed with sadness at what lay before them.

In some crypts, there was just a tiny bundle. *Babies*, Lucy realised, her heart crying out to them. Compelled to look closer, she saw small, delicate bones, almost birdlike. In one crypt, a tiny, skeletonised fist was held in the air, and she turned away, unable to cope with the tragedy.

As the companions looked through the tomb, they drifted away from one another, each using a torch and lost in their own thoughts, their attention snagged on particular details.

•   •   •

The range of clothing on display, much of which was rotted, fascinated Mary. By the light from her torch, she saw that some of these poor children were clad in ancient robes. The demon must have taken them countless centuries before.

"Mr W! Mrs M!" Lucy's urgent shout, echoing around the space, pulled Mary away from her thoughts. Torchlight waved up ahead as the girl signalled them.

She, in pain, and Tim made their way over to Lucy, who pointed her torch into one of the crypts. "I think she's alive," she said.

It was a girl of around ten or twelve, clad in a faded dress. Although she was pale and thin, she looked peaceful. Tim searched for a pulse.

He frowned. "It's faint, but I think you're right, Lucy. I don't know how it can be, but she's alive."

"I suspect she still has some sustenance, some lifeforce which, however dim, Kresta can continue to use," Mary speculated.

Tim and Mary realised Lucy had left them. She was a short distance away, looking along the row of crypts.

"There are others!" Lucy called out with excitement in her voice.

•　　•　　•

Sanjay was not prone to great emotions. He was a restrained type of child.

But now he experienced an overwhelming sense of joy. He leaped onto the bed, which was not his bed, and bounced, knowing full well that his Mummy would take a dim view of such behaviour. He started laughing.

An unfamiliar sensation washed over him, a wave of Good which overpowered the Bad that had surrounded him since the giant had brought him here.

This was love.

•　　•　　•

Among the countless dead, the existence of living children among those taken by Kresta over untold generations was nothing less than a miracle.

Mary agreed to rest, sitting on the floor with her tea while Tim and Lucy dashed among the rows, seeking the living and Sanjay Mistry in particular. When she heard Tim's shout, joy filled her heart.

His torchlight shined faint in the distance. Standing, she began the slow walk to the source of the light.

"He's here, and he's alive!" Tim called out when Mary was close enough to hear. Lucy stood by with a smile on her face. Arriving at the crypt, Mary saw the little boy who lived across the street, the one she had saved from the dreadful Michael Slade. A small smile graced the child's face. He seemed lost in a happy dream rather than drowning in an endless nightmare.

Mary looked at her companions. "Tim, Lucy showed us the way, but, if she is agreeable, I think you should do the honours."

Lucy nodded. With shaking fingers, Tim released the small glass vial from around his neck and removed the stopper. He bent down to Sanjay's slight form and placed a small drop of holy water between the boy's pale lips.

•   •   •

Kresta had slept, or at least switched off as demons do, determined to escape his rage.

His eyes snapped open. "No," he said, voice dripping with venom.

•   •   •

Time stood still. As the boy's eyelids fluttered, Tim took a series of shaky breaths and said a silent prayer.

After a while, Sanjay slowly sat up. He wavered a little, as if from lack of sustenance. Ironic, Tim thought, given the child had been used to sustain the demon.

"Shh, shh, I've got you." Tim lifted the boy (so light!) from his bed of rough-hewn stone and gently placed him on the floor, propped up on an empty crypt below. He retrieved the water bottle from his rucksack and offered it to Sanjay, cautioning him not to gulp it down.

The tired and bedraggled boy took a small sip. "I know you," he said, his voice a whisper, "you're good. You're love."

The others laughed, letting go of their anxiety for a moment, as the tension broke. Tim placed Sanjay a hand on the boy's shoulder. "I don't know about that, son, but I know we need to get out of here."

"What about Pig?" Lucy asked, "and all the others. The living ones?"

•   •   •

It was Tim that noticed it first. Vibrations thrummed through his boots, like great machines awakening deep below his feet.

He and Lucy worked hard to revive the surviving children. A dozen or so confused kids, including Sanjay, stood in the chamber, under Mary's care.

It wasn't enough. Their supplies of holy water were low, and the cavern so vast they could never know how many mausoleums might lie off its central core.

The ground shook and a little girl, who Tim was leading to the central chamber, gave a small cry and pulled tighter to him.

•   •   •

The tremor was short but intense. At one point Lucy, racing towards a crypt, put her arms out, fearful she might lose her balance. She wondered if there was a connection between the revival of the children and the tremor. Whatever the cause, it alarmed her and added to her anxiety about Pig. Where was he?

•   •   •

Mary wasn't suited to childcare and, blinded by exhaustion, was struggling. The children, many of whom didn't speak English, were confused and terrified. In her own fretful state, she could do little to help. The shivering ground added to the children's terror, and they clung to one another like desperate survivors on a life raft.

She was relieved when Tim returned with a small Asian girl whom he deposited, showing real gentleness with the others.

"There's so many dead, but even still, we'll never be able to locate and rescue all those who live," he gasped. "I think time's running out." As if to punctuate his thinking, a more powerful tremor erupted through the cavern.

Mary looked at him. "We can't save all of them, Tim," she told him. "We don't even know if we can find a way out and rescue those we have found."

Lucy called out as she reached them. She was carrying a small child of about four.

"I'm not sure I can…" the words stopped in her throat.

The cavern rocked like a snow globe, shaken by an angry god. Tim grabbed at Mary to support her. He lowered them both to the ground and Lucy, with her small burden, followed suit.

A short distance away, a huge chunk of stone dropped from the ceiling. It hit the ground like a bomb, shrapnel flying. The sound, deafening, was like standing in thunder.

All present covered their eyes out of instinct, as sharp chunks of black stone flew through the space like bullets. More masonry collapsed as the ground shook beneath them.

·   ·   ·

The cavern settled. From the distance came more thunderous noises, booming as the citadel's structure continued its inexorable collapse.

"NO!" Hearing Lucy's shocked cry, punctuated by desperate screams from the children, Tim motioned at Mary to remain seated, lest the violence should begin anew.

He carefully stepped over chunks of stone, heavy and sharp, across to Lucy who, covered in dust, looked like the survivor of an earthquake. Wordlessly, with tears washing the dirt from her face, she pointed to the floor.

It was a little boy. He couldn't have been more than ten years old. A jagged piece of black stone had entered his temple, pierced the delicate skin and become lodged there, a senseless violent obscenity. Tim removed his jacket and covered the still body. "There was nothing anyone could do," he said.

After a few moments of silence, they made their way back to Mary, the remaining children so traumatised that they stayed where they were. "I don't think we can risk going back to the crypts," he told them. "Shit, I feel so impotent."

They looked up as another tremor hit, milder this time, Lucy and Mary holding onto one another.

There was a small tug at his sleeve. He ignored it and it came again. He looked down to see Sanjay, an intense expression on his face. "Hello Sanjay, what can I do for you?" he said. Determined to hide his own fear for the sake of the child, he mustered a tight smile.

Sanjay gazed up at him, eyes large and serious. "Stop," he said simply, his voice small in the vast space.

Tim sighed. "I think we're going to have to. We should leave. It's too dangerous."

Sanjay shook his head and gestured to the other children. "We can find our own way home," he said. "You *can* save the others, but you need to go somewhere else for it to work."

"Go where?" Tim asked.

Sanjay thrust a small finger into the air.

•　•　•

Reluctant to leave the children in a dangerous place, they were surprised by Sanjay's assertiveness, considering his age. He *insisted* that he and the other children would find their way home and that the grown-ups' destinies lay elsewhere.

The stairs were a challenge. Hewn into the black rock of the citadel, there were few handholds, and the ascent would be arduous. Tim and Lucy were aware that Mary might not make the climb, although she would never admit to such a thing.

Tim suggested Mary remain with the children. Mary and Sanjay both resisted, with Sanjay gesturing to the ceiling once more. In the end, Tim was forced to relent.

Mary, sandwiched between the others and wishing for her walking stick, said she was unsure she would make the climb but would not remain behind. Tim listened in awe of her determination to try. "We must do everything possible to save the children," she said.

•   •   •

Lucy, desperate to take her mind off Pig, had tried counting the steps but soon gave up. Their irregular shape, some wide, some narrow, some deep, others shallow, made it impossible to think about anything other than the climb itself.

The ascent was arduous. Some steps were slippery underfoot, which, combined with their mix of dimensions, meant they had to keep their wits about them. Progress was slow. At one point, Tim cried out as his calf muscles cramped, and they stopped for a moment. He massaged his legs, saying, "I wish I'd made more use of my gym membership." Lucy was barely listening, concerned whether Mary would make it up the stairs? And where *was* Pig?

As they carried on, the air seemed to thin. At one stage, a colony of bats, large, screeching, and black as midnight, burst from a hole concealed in the nearby rock. Lucy shrieked as she almost lost her balance.

She couldn't make out the children, lost as they were to distance and the dust hanging in the air caused by tremors in the stone. From time to time, she heard Mary coughing and wheezing as they ascended the stairs.

"Get down!" Her thoughts scattered like dreams in the daylight as Tim sat down on one of the stone steps, arms covering his head as if braced in a falling aircraft. She and Mary did as he'd instructed.

"It's coming!" he shouted. The air itself shuddered with the force of movement and Lucy's ears popped from the change in pressure. The space roared with the ferocity of the quake; its ancient stone torn asunder with a sound like the end of time.

Vast chunks of debris were flung around, and the stairs shook like they were nothing but a cheap stepladder. Lucy, clutching her head in her hands, could not stop the scream which burst from her mouth. The booming violence of destruction drowned out her scream.

• • •

As the world slowly settled once more, Tim stole a glance ahead, sure he could hear screams from the children far below. Looking above, he could make out the top of the stairs at last. His watch didn't work in this terrible place, but he estimated the climb lasted more than an hour.

An urgent shout from Lucy snagged his attention. Mary lay prone a few steps below his position. He was worried about Pig and determined not to lose any more of his friends.

Easing past Lucy required great care, the stairs having narrowed as they reached their apex. He placed one hand on either side of the girl, flashing an apologetic smile, and carefully stepped down.

For several heart-stopping moments, his foot failed to find purchase and hung in mid-air, his stomach twisting and nervous sweat stinging eyes. It was a few agonising moments before his boot connected with step. Taking the utmost care, he made his way down and examined Mary, perched on the edge of the steps where she lay. Alive, but unconscious. Exhaustion and shock finally having caught up with her.

He lifted her in his arms. Despite her low weight, he gave a grunt as his body protested about the additional burden. "You go on," he told Lucy.

They went on, Tim's heart thudding and his arms shuddering from his burden. Minutes passed before they reached the top of the stairs, the distant ground lost in the dusty air beneath them.

Finally, they made it.

CHAPTER THIRTY-FOUR

The children were terrified by the violent ferocity of the quake. Miraculously, they sustained only minor injuries, cuts and scrapes caused by tumbles, or from being hit by fragments of stone broken away from the citadel's structure.

Throughout the furious destruction, they stole occasional glances at the small body on the floor, covered by Tim's discarded coat. The fabric showed blood seeping through where the child's head had been destroyed. Some cried and others prayed in a myriad of languages, ancient and modern. All were confused.

Sanjay worked hard to grasp the implications of events. He believed he was the most recent child taken in the group, and his conversations with some of the English-speaking children supported this.

One girl, several years older than him, had seemed very uncertain when she told him about her last memory, something she had called "Armistiz Day." She wanted to know if the war had restarted and reached England. Sanjay tried hard to answer her questions, explaining that he wasn't aware of any fighting where he lived.

As he worked with some of the older kids to try to calm everybody down, he thought about his *feelings*. He was sure the best way to save those children who hadn't yet perished, and he'd done his best not to see the many small skeletons, had to be the death of Dr Kresta.

For this reason, he had asked the adults to go *up*. He felt guilty about this. Killing a person was very Bad, the worst of all things. Worse, even, than smoking or using rude words. Despite this, he knew there was no choice.

Dr Kresta was a Bad man. He took children. And he took *from* them. He had to die.

Sanjay coughed from the thick dust clogging his throat and lungs. He'd told the man from across the street that the children would find their own way home. This was another of his *feelings*. He sensed a different journey was necessary for the grownups' return.

Sanjay gazed towards the stairs. Amidst the dim light and swirling dust, it was impossible to see if they were still travelling or had reached the top.

He gave a small shudder and closed his eyes.

CHAPTER THIRTY-FIVE

The stairs ended at an arch, the point of which soared high above. Dark clouds floated through the space.

"Tim, I'm mortified."

"Don't be Mary. We've made a hell of a journey on top of everything else." She flapped her hands in the air as he let her slip from her arms, Lucy helping her to remain upright.

He felt relieved to see his friend with some colour in her cheeks. "I'm not sure even my husband carried me over the threshold, so thank you," she said, maintaining a brave face despite the circumstances.

"Can you walk?" he asked her.

She gave a thin smile. "I'm not dead yet. Yes, I can walk, but it won't be fast, I'm afraid."

Together, Lucy supporting Mary once again despite her protestations, they went through the arch.

It was as if they stepped into a cathedral meant for the damned.

The space stood vast and somehow *obscene*. Far above, great oaken trusses supported a vaulted ceiling which thrust towards an unseen sky. Shadows danced there, birds screeching as they flew among the rafters. From the distance came a dim, flickering source of light.

To the sides there were great pews, carved from the familiar black stone. These pews appeared to have been built for giants. Had any congregation had ever sat upon them, and, if they had, what hellish deity had they worshipped?

• • •

The tempest came from nowhere. It started as little more than a faint whisper, growing in power as it roared down the aisle.

"Hold on!" Tim shouted. Mary and Lucy hunkered down between the stone pews.

It sucked the breath from their lungs and Tim thought, for a horrible moment, that he might vomit or lose consciousness. The wind carried the scent of rot and corruption, the smells of the charnel house. They tried their best to reduce the impact by covering their noses and mouths with their elbows.

With the cloying smells of decay came music. The relentless wind carried the sound of pipes on its back. Discordant it came, as if forced from some ancient organ, played against its will by the fingers of insane beings.

As the blast left the travellers behind it, the birds screamed overhead.

• • •

Mary's struggle made the already long journey even longer.

She asked them to leave her in a pew to rest, but Tim refused, telling her he would do everything in his power to keep them safe. Separating would not be an option.

Their footsteps echoed around the vast hall, punctuated by the cries of the birds circling high above, and occasional sounds of machinery, great engines and grinding gears, which set teeth on edge and rammed painfully against delicate eardrums.

From time-to-time great rumbles shook the floor, dust raining from the rafters.

Ahead was the source of the light. Countless candles, their dim, stinking flames guttering. Distorted shadows bounced on the dark walls. The candles covered every visible surface, dripping fat blobs of wax onto the sills of great windows, which let in no light. Others hovered, suspended in the air. These had been fashioned from dark wax, black or blood red.

At the front, a stone altar loomed, emerging from the flickering light like a boat lost on a stormy sea.

Something lay on the altar, barely visible until they drew closer.

"Don't look," Tim implored. Too late.

Mary turned away and uttered a silent prayer.

Lucy's scream of anguish almost destroyed Tim. His spirit broke and his tears fell. That poor, kind boy.

Lucy's cries echoed. It was as if thousands of others had joined her, united in grief and outrage, creating a cacophony of mourning and despair. She ran to the altar and climbed the dais on which it stood.

"No, no, no, no, NO!" she cried. "Pig, what did he do to you?" Her friend's body lay broken on the cold stone slab. Desecration was wrought on his beautiful hands and feet, shredded by evil metal nails, one of which still hung limp from a ruined palm, surrounded by dried blood.

His kind eyes were gone, pecked away by the birds, leaving only ragged holes filled with blood.

Tim gave her a few moments' space before joining her. Mary, shattered, took a seat in one of the pews.

He opened his arms, and Lucy stepped into them. As he held her, the sobs wracked her body. This physical manifestation of her pain and grief shattered her heart anew as she stole another glance at what remained of her closest friend.

They stood like that for a long time.

·   ·   ·

Mary wept bitter tears. In the short time she'd known him, she had recognised Pig as one of life's decent people. She thought back to the day they had spent researching at her home, the enthusiasm, humour, and simple common sense he had brought to the task.

What had happened to him during that unspeakable night in which Kresta had manipulated their lives? The change in the boy had been obvious. He had seemed older, somehow, and had worn his sadness like a cowl.

She couldn't bear to look upon his ruined body. It was unbearable for her, and her heart went out to the girl who loved him so deeply.

• • •

"Poor Piglet. So sad to die like that, and such a slow, lonely death. He called out for his mother, of all things. Pathetic." The voice drifted from the darkest reaches of this obscene cathedral.

Lucy, pulled out of her shock, screamed into the darkness. "Show yourself, you bastard! How could you do this? Beast!"

Kresta emerged from the shadows, his spine bent, an old man once again. More ancient than they had ever seen him.

The demon stooped as he walked towards them, a few strands of hair barely covering the darkly mottled scalp.

"You couldn't stop with your *meddling*," he said. He fixed each of them with a gaze, his eyes the faded blue of a late November sky.

"This, then," he gestured at the altar, "is the result. This is what you wrought. As you have taken from me, I have taken from you in return. My sustenance, my Harvests, gone. The Pantheon is silent to me. Because of YOU!"

Kresta, once so terrifying, stood wavering before them, pitiful, though none of them experienced pity.

Tim's reactions were too slow as Lucy rushed towards the demon. "Lucy, stop!" he yelled, attempting to grab the back of her hooded top.

"Bastard! Killer! Abuser!" she roared, the tears drying on her face and spittle flying from her lips. Kresta, boredom on his features, held up a hand.

It was like being hit by a tidal wave. The breath slamming out of her lungs, Lucy flew back, the pain when she hit the altar intense. She felt sickened that she had landed on the remains of her friend, his precious blood seeping into her clothes.

Kresta let out a laugh as dry as parchment. "You threaten *me*, child. Worthless worm. Even in my weakened state, I will suck the marrow from your bones, bitch."

"And you!" He turned to Mary where she slumped, exhausted, on the pew. "An old crone who will not stop poking her nose into the business of others. 'Lionel, Lionel, Lionel'. All those memories of your *insane* brother.

"I was with him, part of him. Watching your foolish attempts to help, to get him to communicate, to lead some semblance of human life.

"The joy of being inside him all those years. The pleasure, all that *fucking*." He licked his lips, drool falling from his mouth and dripping from his chin. "And the pain, oh yes, the beatings and burnings.

"I loved it all, and you knew *nothing*."

Mary sniffed in disgust as she thought of what the demon had done to and with her brother. *Unspeakable animal*, she thought with contempt.

•　　•　　•

As Lucy fought to escape the dark altar and Kresta traded verbal blows with Mary MacDonald, Tim pulled the vial of holy water from where it hung around his neck. Despite the creature's bravado, he could see that, robbed of sustenance, he was failing.

He had an idea which had to be a longshot, but he could think of nothing else to try. His mind had picked through the clues contained in Lionel's random final letter. Being an RE teacher, Tim didn't consider himself an expert in scripture, but he knew more than most. He was certain that Lionel had a specific intention, possibly influenced by his long possession by the demon.

Seizing the opportunity provided by Kresta's distraction, Tim wracked his mind and spoke, haltingly at first. The sound of his voice snagged the attention of the demon, which turned its terrible gaze upon him.

"Whoever dwells in the shelter of the Most High will rest in the shadow of the Almighty," Tim said, praying that he was getting the words right. Kresta, turning to him, let out a mocking laugh.

Tim, undeterred, continued, "I will say of the Lord, He is my refuge and my fortress, my God." He paused for a moment, trying to remember before exclaiming, desperate, "in whom I TRUST!"

His shout bounced off hard stone, his own voice becoming one of a multitude. "Surely he will save you from the fowler's snare and from the *deadly pestilence*," he roared, pointing a shaking finger at the demon.

As Lucy limped her way from the altar and its terrible cargo, Kresta let out a great roar, "MEDDLARS!" he cried out, "I WILL DESTROY YOU ALL!"

The demon raised his hands in the air and, as he brought them down, he threw the remaining members of Mystery Inc. hard onto their knees. Each felt crushed by a great weight.

Tim heard a querulous cry as Mary was thrown from the pew in which she had sought refuge.

Through gritted teeth, his kneecaps grinding onto the stone floor, Tim ploughed on through the pain.

"I will not fear the terror of night, nor the arrow that flies by day," he yelled as stinking winds whipped around them.

"Nor the pestilence that stalks in the darkness, nor the plague that destroys at," he struggled to take a breath, almost overcome by the tempest, "MIDDAY!"

Kresta placed his hands against the side of his head and screamed, the sound lost to the great winds. Tim, spotting the chance afforded to him by the creature's distraction, fought his way to his feet and, shielding his eyes from the tempest, made his painful way to the demon.

"Tim, no!" Lucy cried, but he did not heed her plea.

Tim knew this was his only chance. He grabbed the frail old man, pulling his head back by thin strands of hair and, with the other hand, pushed the vial with its few remaining drops of precious water into the demon's mouth.

With both hands, he forced the jaws closed and could feel the glass crunch between those awful, yellow teeth.

The silence was deafening. The blood roared in Tim's ears as it replaced the scream of those terrible winds, which had now stilled.

Kresta broke the silence. "No," he said in a quiet voice. "No."

Tim stood back and witnessed what lay behind the visage. A great serpent-like creature stood before him. A long, thick tail covered in wet, green scales whipped around the monster and thrashed against the ground. Globules of some viscous liquid dripped from its pendulous breasts and fell steaming to the stone. The creature grimaced, its sharp yellow teeth flashing in the candlelight.

•   •   •

Mary, from her position on the cold floor, witnessed something different. For just a few moments, she observed a small boy, black-hearted and filled with evil, gazing upon her. The child, her own brother, licked his lips and smiled, winking at her. The smile widened, stretching the skin to an impossible breadth, cheeks splitting, ichor dripping from its jaws.

The smile went on until there was nothing left of Lionel's face other than an endless maw of gnashing yellow teeth.

•   •   •

Lucy watched in disgust, confronted with what lay beneath Kresta's surface. Before her stood a many-armed creature. A thin layer of pulsating, milky flesh covered its spidery body, revealing a network of veins and arteries through which Lucy could see black ichor pumping from its dying heart.

Between its legs swung a monstrous barbed penis, its hooked tip generating sparks as it scraped against the stone floor.

•　　•　　•

"No," the demon sighed one last time. And then they saw it no more.

•　　•　　•

The earthquake was as sudden as it was violent. A wrenching, creaking roar was followed by one of the great ceiling trusses falling from far above, smashing onto the stone pews with a thunderous roar and an explosion of debris.

As they came together in a protective huddle, Mary shouted above the noise, "What on earth were you saying to him?" she cried.

"Psalm ninety-one!" Tim shouted back. "Lionel tried to warn you in the letter he sent, but we couldn't understand it. I always knew RE was good for something!"

Despite his levity, Tim knew they had reached the end. The demon, perhaps, vanquished, but there was no way out of this unearthly place. Their lives would end with the collapse of Kresta's lair. He clung to the others, pleased to have human contact as this world shook itself to destruction.

•　　•　　•

Lucy cried out as her best friend's remains tumbled from their place on the altar. Looking back, she shouted, desperate to get the attention of her friends through all the chaos.

They didn't hear her. She pulled away from them and frantically pointed.

At last, they looked up and witnessed what she had seen.

Mary called out, "Michael Slade!" Or what remained of him. That the man even stood confirmed their suspicions, that, somehow, he was beyond death. A familiar used by Kresta to enable the demon's dark deeds.

What stood swaying before them was barely recognisable. It was a shadow of the man who had been an all-too-human monster. The broad figure stood there, swaying before them, wearing nothing but a thin pair of torn and filthy underpants. He was shrouded with blood, and bodily fluids splattered on the surrounding ground. Tears had driven their way in rivulets through the bleeding crust of his face.

Next to Slade there stood a hole, very much like the one which had appeared in Tim's apartment at the institution. It was placed upright like a doorway, black and unknowable, impervious to light.

What remained of Kresta's revenant shook on his thick legs. He licked his cracked, bloody lips as he gazed upon them.

"Go," he said, falling to his knees. They didn't need to be asked more than once.

CHAPTER THIRTY-SIX

Her husband was gone. Whether to search or to drink, Anita didn't much care about.

Her sole concern was sleep. How long could she escape the nightmare The Event had brought to her waking hours?

Curling up in the bed, she clutched Oscar closer, seeking solace from the polyester bear. The world moved on, leaving Anita to her agonies.

The media had found fresh stories and had lost interest in what it had dubbed the 'Mistry Mystery'. The police had new investigations. No officer was stationed at the entrance of Oldfield Court anymore. Her child had been forgotten; they had been forgotten. She choked back tears. Her Sanjay, her beloved, kind boy.

Looking up at the light filtered by the always-closed curtains, she watched through blurry eyes as her son, in filthy clothes, clambered onto the bed. Grinning, he prised Oscar from her and kissed its head. She gave a faint smile at this vision of her boy, wondering if she had ever shown him enough of the love that filled her heart.

Setting Oscar aside, dream-Sanjay held Anita's hand, and she enjoyed the touch of his small fingers and warm palm. The darkness in her soul was washed away by wave after wave of warmth and light.

"Mummy," he said, "can we not have tofu anymore? It tastes like poo."

Then, realising she was witness to a miracle, Anita wrapped her arms around her little boy and laughed with disbelief.

• • •

None of the surviving members of Mystery Inc. saw the private ambulance arrive at number fourteen Oldfield Street, although Sean, from his vantage point opposite, did. He watched as the young, uniformed woman dashed back out of the house to throw up in the front garden, followed by her older colleague, pale-faced and indulging in a hit of nicotine.

In the end, the operatives emerged from the house with a body-bag strapped to a gurney. This they hoisted, without delicacy, into the back of the van, closing the doors with a slam that sounded like an ending.

Sean turned away from the window. He was going to take Molly for a long walk.

• • •

Tim, Mary, and Lucy were propelled from Slade's portal and back into Tim's spartan living quarters at the abandoned Fraser-Ruck School for Boys. Despite the wintry conditions, bright sun was streaming through the windows mounted high in its walls.

Checking her phone, Lucy told them in a choked voice that less than an hour had passed from the point at which they had entered the demon's realm.

Their celebrations, while heartfelt, were muted. Losing Pig had affected them all beyond words.

• • •

Their work continued and decisions were made in the coming days and weeks.

They agreed Tim would give notice on the place he'd never thought of as home. The place which had never been an orphanage. His time as property guardian was at an end. He moved into Mary's spare room, and he decided to embark on a period of travel.

This was not to be a holiday. They had heard about the mysterious return of Sanjay Mistry (who would himself become a member of Mystery Inc. one day, many years hence), and were concerned about the whereabouts of the other children of Kresta. Tim announced his plan to seek them out and offer them any support he could.

The police investigation had concluded. They were satisfied with the Mistry boy's description of his abductor, which clearly identified the late Michael Slade, the human monster who had lived in the community unnoticed. That Sanjay could not say where he had been held was dismissed in their eagerness to close the file. Investigators told themselves that Slade's death had saved the boy from far worse horrors. They swept loose ends, like Sanjay's mysterious escape, under the carpet. Slade had taken the boy and, perhaps remorseful, taken his own life.

Case closed.

Between them, Mary and Sanjay expended a *lot* of effort persuading the Mistrys to allow Mary to babysit the boy as they recovered from their trauma. Mary urged them to leave their cramped flat and strive for a normal life. After a while, Anita (without consulting her husband) conceded defeat, mindful of Sanjay's desperation to get out of Oldfield Court.

Sanjay's presence at Mary's house proved invaluable. He had insight into the other children and could predict their return accurately. If Sanjay was right, survivors would return, like him, to the place they were taken, or as close as possible.

Mary believed Sanjay had likely returned first, as the most recent child snatched away from his home.

For his part, Tim announced he would use his impending travels as a driver for personal growth. He was up for meeting someone and hoped to find love and companionship. Finding someone to spend life with and potentially start a family. Of course, she needed to be open-minded about the esoteric.

Mystery Inc. had no knowledge that various governmental agencies had decided upon an international approach to suppress media stories, as confused children, some of whom had been missing for countless years, started to knock on the doors of places they'd once called home or appear close to where they had gone missing. Many of the children had confused stories about being held by a man. Some described him as young, others old, all claimed that he had impossibly blue eyes.

In the end, media suppressed, it was left to Pig's beloved Fortean Times to chronicle the strange case of the returning children, stories which were ignored by all but the most credulous.

·   ·   ·

Lucy spent many days walking the streets on blistered feet, placing posters on lampposts, and in the windows of small shops, fruitlessly asking for information about the whereabouts of Korrey 'Pig' Amari. Her heart would break over and over as she saw the smiling face of her friend, laughing out of flyers which would fade to nothing over the turn of seasons.

She would never tell Pig's mum, Dorothy, the truth about her brave and brilliant son, and it would take many years for Lucy's heart to mend.

·   ·   ·

"TIM!"

Hearing Mary's call, he thundered down from her spare room, which had become both his home and a centre of operations, and nearly slipped on the narrow stairs. He had plotted a course, starting in Hamelin, based on Sanjay's intel and various online rumours about the appearance of once lost and unaged children all over the world.

Arriving at the bottom of the stairs, he saw Mary at the front door, where a young boy was standing. The boy, shoeless in holey grey shorts paired with ancient socks, which were rolled down to his ankles, looked nervous and was twisting a grubby school cap between anxious fingers.

"Tim, I want you to meet James Bennett," Mary said with a sad smile as she stood aside. "He's come looking for his friend, Lionel."

"Hello James," Tim smiled, prising the boy's dirty fingers away from the rotted cap and shaking him by the hand. "Lionel's not at home. We have a lot we need to talk with you about. Why don't you come in?"

"I'll pop the kettle on," Mary added.

•   •   •

As she walked through to the kitchen-diner, the happy heart of her home, Mary gave a wry smile.

She'd never wanted a child, never known what she would do with one.

She had a feeling she'd just become a mother at the age of seventy-three.

EPILOGUE

The beach was deserted, save for the teenager who sat on a rock. Far ahead, in the distance, someone was walking their dog.

Had anyone been there, they would have found it a strange image. The boy, who was skinny, wore rags. His hair, perhaps blonde, lay down to his shoulders. Blackened with dirt and unkempt, it moved a little in the gentle sea breeze.

The boy felt disorientated. He thought for some time and then, *Jakub*, he remembered, *I am Jakub!*

As he listened to the calling of the gulls which circled above in the cloudless sky, he remembered other things. He had been taken from this place. Stolen, a long time ago, he was sure. Taken by someone, a creature of pure evil and hate.

But...

He shook his head. In another life, he hadn't been taken, and he couldn't grasp what this meant. He had spent time in this place with another boy, a boy he loved.

A brief smile transformed his tired face. *I loved Pig*, he remembered. The smile faded from his lips. This boy, Jakub, was confused. He had been taken from here but, somehow, he had not. He'd experienced life with another, one who wasn't here with him now, and this made him sad.

Rubbing his damp eyes with filthy fists, he stared at the world before him.

Then he smiled. He would mourn for Pig in time, but today he would honour the memory of their love. Today was to be about joy.

Jakub Szymański raced down the beach, bare soles flashing white against the wet sand, hollering a great "Hooo!" as he rushed towards the ocean.

THE END

ABOUT THE AUTHOR

Alex Hunter was the first child in his school year to be given an adult library card. He borrowed *The Rats* by James Herbert which began a love of the frightening and strange. As a teenager, Alex was asked to model clothes in a catalogue. Despite his excitement, this did not result in a jet-setting international career.

As an adult, he has enjoyed a career as a corporate communications specialist with experience leading award-winning teams around the world. Alex lives in London with his husband, Ben, and willful pug, Bertie. He is a member of the Horror Writers Association. *The Harvest* is his first novel, and he's currently working on his second.

NOTE FROM ALEX HUNTER

Word-of-mouth is crucial for any author to succeed. If you enjoyed *The Harvest*, please leave a review online—anywhere you are able. Even if it's just a sentence or two. It would make all the difference and would be very much appreciated.

Thanks!
Alex Hunter

We hope you enjoyed reading this title from:

www.blackrosewriting.com

Subscribe to our mailing list – *The Rosevine* – and receive **FREE** books, daily
deals, and stay current with news about upcoming
releases and our hottest authors.
Scan the QR code below to sign up.

Already a subscriber? Please accept a sincere thank you for being a fan of
Black Rose Writing authors.

View other Black Rose Writing titles at
www.blackrosewriting.com/books and use promo code
PRINT to receive a **20% discount** when purchasing.